A Gangster's Grip

The Riverhill Trilogy: Book 2

by

Heather Burnside

A Gangster's Grip

The Riverhill Trilogy: Book 2

by

Heather Burnside

DM Publishing

Also by Heather Burnside:

Slur – The Riverhill Trilogy: Book 1

Crime Conflict & Consequences – Short Story Collection

***

Introduction

'A Gangster's Grip' is set in Manchester in 1991 during a period of escalating gun crime. This was mainly attributable to inter-gang rivalry. Since the 1990s the levels of gang-related crime in Manchester have decreased substantially as a result of ground-breaking measures that the city has adopted.

Because 'A Gangster's Grip' is based on violent gang warfare, this is evident in the book's content. Likewise, the bad language and slang used throughout the book reflects the way the characters in the novel would have spoken. I apologise if readers find the language offensive but I have chosen to include it because I want to give an accurate portrayal.

Although my previous novel 'Slur' had a glossary, I have chosen not to include one this time, as feedback from readers (including those overseas) indicated that they could understand most of the words from the context. However, if you want to check out any of the meanings, you can find a good online dictionary of slang words and phrases at: http://www.peevish.co.uk/slang/.

***

Chapter 1

Rita couldn't wait to get to her parents' house, and had been discussing it with her husband, Yansis, during the taxi ride from the airport. It had been so long since she'd been back from Greece, and she had missed everyone, despite their shortcomings. She got out of the cab, and waited for the driver to take their cases out of the boot.

Once the cases were on the pavement, Yansis carried them to the front door while Rita settled the cab fare. She had no sooner taken her purse out of her handbag than she spotted something in her peripheral vision, causing her to look up.

Too late!

Before she knew what was happening, a youth swung by on a bike. Maintaining his speed while riding one-handed, he snatched her purse and zoomed past.

She gave chase, yelling and screaming. Yansis joined her when he realised she had been robbed. But it was no use. They couldn't keep up with a bike, especially Rita in her high heels, and the youth was soon out of sight.

"Fine bloody start that is!" she cursed. Walking back to the taxi driver, she continued her rant, "And a lot of help you were."

"Don't blame me, love. If you think I'm leaving my cab round here, you've got another think coming."

"Oh, come off it! Just because my purse has been snatched, doesn't mean your cab's gonna be robbed."

"Doesn't it? You don't know what it's like! How long is it since you've been back, love?"

"A few years. Why?"

"I think you'll find it's changed, and not for the better either."

Rita shrugged off his comments, anxious to get inside the house, while Yansis paid the cab fare.

Her mother, Joan, answered the door. "Hiya love, how are you? Where's that lovely husband of yours?" she asked, hugging Rita.

"I've just been robbed, Mam. Some bugger's just whipped my purse out of my hands while I was trying to pay for the taxi."

"You're joking! The bloody swines! What happened? Where are they?" her mother replied and, within seconds, her parents were both outside, searching up and down the street.

"You're too late; he'll be long gone. There was only one of them; some kid on a bike. He was off like lighting."

"Well, what did he look like?" asked Joan. "We might be able to find out who he is."

"I don't know. I only saw the back of him. Young, a teenager, I think. He had a dark hoody on, navy or black, and jeans. That's about all I saw. It all happened so fast."

"Oh, I'm sorry Reet. That's all you need when you've only just got here!"

"I know," Rita replied, her voice shaking. "It's gonna be loads of hassle … I'll have to cancel all my cards … I'll need to find out the bank's phone number ..."

"Can't trust no-one these days," interrupted her father, Ged, who was hovering behind her mother looking shifty. That wasn't unusual for him, but he looked even more shifty than usual. Rita released her mother and gave him a tentative hug while her mother greeted Yansis.

When they had spent a few minutes in the hallway discussing the theft, Joan said to Rita and Yansis, "Come on you two, I'll make you a cuppa; I bet you could do with one after that. Let's get in and have a sit down."

Although tiny at 5ft 1, Rita had a big presence. Her towering heels increased her height, and her liberal application of make-up enhanced her moderately attractive features. She had dark brown hair, which she wore in a fashionable textured bob, and was dressed casual but smart.

Leaving their cases in the hallway, they headed towards the living room. Rita was the first to step into the room and stopped short at the sight of a large, mean-looking black man sprawled across the sofa. Spliff in one hand, can of lager in the other, he was resting against some cushions with his legs stretched out across the coffee table. As Rita entered the room, he took a long hard drag on the spliff as though challenging her. Then he slowly exhaled the smoke, his face forming a sneer, as he examined her in minute detail.

Rita noted the scar that cut across his forehead, the primed muscles and the abundance of tattoos. She saw the letters H-A-T-E tattooed across the fingers of his right hand. '*Why did these self-professed hard men always have to make a statement with this LOVE and HATE tattoo thing? It was so corny and pathetic,*' she thought.

When he lifted his can of lager, she glimpsed the tattoo spread across the fingers of his other hand, expecting to see the letters L-O-V-E. However, disconcertingly, that also bore the letters H-A-T-E.

There was a break in the tension as Rita's father dashed to her side, "This is Leroy, Jenny's boyfriend," he gushed.

Rita already knew that her sister, Jenny, had a boyfriend, but she didn't know much about him. Despite her automatic reservations, she tried to appear friendly as she said, "Hello, Leroy, pleased to meet you."

Leroy briefly nodded his head in response then continued to take drags of his spliff while Rita's mother, Joan, and Yansis entered the room. When Joan introduced Yansis, he received the same cool appraisal. During this time Leroy remained seated and didn't attempt to converse with them.

Rita suspected that her parents were equally aware of the uncomfortable atmosphere created by Leroy. This was borne out by her mother's waffling, "Rita and Yansis have got a restaurant in Greece but they've come back to stay for a while, haven't you love? It's alright though; Yansis has got a big family so there's plenty of people to look after the place for them while they're over here. You're looking well our Rita. You've got a lovely tan and I love that leather jacket. Was the flight alright? You two must be shattered. Let me make you that cup of tea ..."

"Where's Jenny?" asked Rita.

3

"She's just nipped to the loo. She'll be down in a minute," said Joan. "Oh, here she is now."

Rita turned round and rushed towards her sister, but stopped when she noticed Jenny's swollen stomach, "Jesus, when did that happen? You might have bloody well told me!"

"How about congratulations?" said Jenny.

"Sorry, it's just … it's a lot to take in. There's been a lot of changes since I was home. Yeah, congratulations. I'm pleased for you; you look well."

Rita gave Jenny's arm a gentle squeeze, attempting to hide her mounting levels of unease, and surreptitiously flashing Yansis a concerned look. Apart from the pregnancy, Jenny had changed in other ways in the few years since Rita had last seen her.

Like Rita, she was tiny, although taller than Rita at 5ft 2, but there was now a maturity about her. She was an attractive girl and pregnancy suited her, bringing with it a radiant glow.

"I'm sorry, Reet," said Joan. "We were going to tell you, but it didn't sound right in a letter and I never seemed to find time on the phone. You know how it is phoning there. It costs a bloody fortune, and I've no sooner said hiya than the pips are going. Anyway, I knew you'd be coming home soon so I thought I'd tell you face to face."

"Soon! She's about five bloody months gone."

"Twenty two weeks actually," verified Jenny.

"What's the big deal?" asked Leroy.

Rita turned to see a look of undisguised aggression cross Leroy's face, and decided not to pursue the matter.

"Anyway, are we having that cuppa, Mam, or what?" she asked.

While Joan went to make the drinks, everybody else sat down on the three piece suite. Her father, Ged, took an armchair and Jenny settled herself next to Leroy. Rita felt uncomfortable sitting next to them, so she sat on the remaining armchair and invited Yansis to sit on the arm. They told Jenny about the theft of Rita's purse, and she seemed concerned, but Leroy showed no emotion.

Apart from the discomfort of sharing her parents' living room with the hostile Leroy, Rita was bothered about the sleeping arrangements. Her parents' house was a three bedroom modern terraced on a council housing estate. It had two decent sized bedrooms and a further bedroom that was only big enough for a single bed. She had hoped that she and Yansis could share one of the large bedrooms, and that Jenny wouldn't mind staying in the single room temporarily. In fact, as her parents had been aware of her imminent arrival, she hoped they had already arranged this. Rita therefore broached the subject when her mother returned carrying a tray of drinks.

"You have a seat here, Mam. Me and Yansis will take our cases up and, if you want, we can fetch a couple of chairs from the kitchen. Are we in the front bedroom?"

"The front bedroom's already taken by me and Jenny," growled Leroy, with an air of menace, which took Rita by surprise.

She turned to her mother, "Are we in the small bedroom then?"

Rita was trying to visualise how she and Yansis would manage with a single bed in a room that measured no more than 10 foot by 6 foot, but she figured it would have to do. After all, her sister was pregnant so it was only fair that she and Leroy had more space.

As she was mulling over the possibilities, Joan replied, "Ooh, that's something I need to have a word with you about, Rita. There isn't a bed in that room anymore. We didn't see a need for one after you'd left. It's been such a long time since you've been home so we use it for storage now. You're welcome to the settee, though, and I can fix you up with a sleeping bag, if you like, so Yansis can kip down next to you."

"You're joking! We could be here for months. How can we manage for months on the settee and the floor? And where will we put our stuff?"

"You ought to be bloody grateful we're putting you up. We've not seen hide nor hair of you for donkey's years," Ged chipped in.

Rita was about to retaliate; she and her father hadn't always seen eye to eye, but Yansis changed the subject in order to defuse the situation.

"It's no problem. We can find somewhere to stay, Rita. Manchester is a big city. There must be lots of hotels."

"That'll cost us a bloody fortune," Rita replied before a thought occurred to her. "Oh don't worry, we'll find somewhere."

A few minutes of uncomfortable silence followed before the phone rang in the dining room and Joan went to answer it.

"Leroy's expecting an important business call," boasted Ged.

"Oh, what is your business?" asked Yansis.

"A bit of everything, this and that," came the guarded reply.

"Leroy, it's for you," announced Joan, on returning to the living room.

At last, Leroy prised himself from the sofa to take the call.

"So what exactly is 'this and that'?" asked Rita, once Leroy had left the room.

"Leroy's a business man, and a well-respected one too. He deals a lot in imports and, before you go sounding your mouth off, he's been very good to us," said Ged.

"I haven't said anything," Rita snapped back.

It was obvious she wouldn't gain anything by continuing to probe, so Rita cleared the finished cups from the living room instead. Although it gave her an excuse to get away from her father's goading, she was also curious about Leroy's 'important business call'.

The kitchen of her parents' home was next to the dining room, and while she carried the cups through to the kitchen and placed them in the sink, Rita strained to hear Leroy's conversation. He seemed angry about something, and his voice was becoming louder. She was glad she wasn't the person on the other end of the phone. As Leroy became increasingly agitated, she stopped what she was doing, realising that it might be best if he didn't realise she was there. She crept towards the dining room where she could overhear what he was saying more clearly.

"I want the fuckin' goods. They should have been here yesterday. I've got customers waiting, and if I stop supplying, they'll get them from someone else. I can't afford to have them taking over my turf."

There was then a brief pause while Leroy listened to the person on the other end of the line, before adding, "No, the usual, H."

The call ended abruptly and Rita panicked. If Leroy saw her in the kitchen, he would surmise that she had overheard his conversation. Then she heard him make another call. He had calmed down a little by now so she couldn't hear everything he was saying, just brief snippets … "It's sorted … promised tomorrow … It's sweet … should be a few days … be sorted then … somewhere to store them."

Rita could sense that the call was ending, so she ran quietly from the kitchen to the living room, on the pretext of checking for more cups. She made sure she was still there when Leroy returned to the living room. Once she was satisfied that he had noted her presence in the living room, she made her way back to the kitchen to finish what she had been doing.

When Rita walked in the living room again, the atmosphere hadn't improved much. While her mother was asking Yansis about life in Greece, her father was discussing some sort of business deal with Leroy. Rita couldn't hear everything because of her mother's chatter, but she got the impression that Leroy was providing goods for her father to sell somewhere. From the tone of the conversation, she could tell that her father held Leroy in high regard. Meanwhile, Jenny stayed silent, snuggled up to Leroy while passively observing.

There was something about the whole scene that didn't feel right to Rita and, after a short while, she made her excuses and prepared to leave. While she and Yansis were in the hallway saying their goodbyes, her mother announced, "I hope you get fixed up love."

"We'll sort something out," said Rita.

"Well let me know if you don't. Our Jenny will be getting her council house next week, and Leroy will be moving in with her, so we should have some room then."

"Now you tell me."

"Ooh, sorry love. I forgot with all the excitement."

"Good luck with it, Jenny. I hope it all goes well."

"Thanks," Jenny replied.

Rita hugged her mother and sister, said goodbye to her father and shouted goodbye through to the living room for the benefit of Leroy, who remained seated. Although she assured her mother that they would be back if they didn't find somewhere to stay, she noticed the look that flashed across her father's face. She knew that as long as Leroy was around, she and Yansis would be about as welcome as a dose of flu.

Chapter 2

The scene at her best friend Julie's house was in complete contrast to the one Rita had left behind half an hour earlier. Before she and Yansis even got inside Julie's home, the differences were apparent. Rita's parents lived on the Riverhill Estate, a deprived area of Longsight, situated a couple of miles from Manchester city centre. Rita had been glad to leave the estate when she had gone to live in Greece five years previously. The Riverhill Estate had become increasingly run-down.

During the years that Rita lived there, she had grown accustomed to the abundance of litter, overgrown gardens, graffiti ridden walls and stretches of worn grass used as dumping grounds for old furniture. The latter doubled up as play areas for small children who used the bug infested mattresses and sofas as trampolines.

She hadn't been home for four years, although she had paid for her parents to come to Greece once. The visit hadn't been successful, thanks to her father's loud mouth and bad manners. Her mother's behaviour, on the other hand, would have been endearing if it hadn't been so embarrassing. She had been in awe of everything; it was as though Rita was the first person on earth ever to have owned a restaurant.

Rita had intended to visit home more frequently, but the restaurant was often busy, and somehow the time never seemed right. Now it was different though; she was here through necessity rather than choice. Much as she loved her life in Greece, the health services were inadequate, so it was back to the chilly UK and the good old National Health Service.

Four years on from her last visit home, and the view had shocked her. As she caught sight of the drab streets, she wondered how she had ever lived like that. Then, as if that wasn't bad enough, she had encountered the hostilities indoors against the backdrop of mismatched furniture, clutter and general chaos that was her family's home. And all this while she was still reeling from the theft of her purse.

Julie had moved on from Longsight as well. Her husband Vinny's building business had benefitted from the late 80s housing boom, and they were now living in their second home together. It was a four bedroom Victorian semi in the leafy suburb of Heaton Moor, which they had bought eighteen months previously. The tidy, tree lined avenue was a welcome relief for Rita, and the room dimensions inside Julie's tastefully decorated home were impressive.

Rita took in her surroundings. The room they were in was a good size, with a dado rail around the walls, which were papered below the rail and painted above in a complementary, lighter shade. The curtains were dramatic with fashionable swags, tails and a pelmet. In a smaller room they would have been overbearing, but in a room this size they were a stunning focal point. The plush furnishings had been selected to match, with a careful balance of plain and patterned. Overall the room was light and airy as well as cosy.

After Rita and Yansis had made a fuss of Julie's two-year-old daughter, Emily, they settled into the comfy leather suite. Rita then recounted her recent visit to her parents' home over a cup of percolated coffee while Emily played at the other side of the lounge amongst hordes of toys.

"It's so good of you to put us up at such short notice Jules. You're a life saver. I can't tell you how glad I am to get out of my mam and dad's house."

"What happened? You said something on the phone about them not having enough space for you."

"Ooh, that's not the worst of it. What's pissed me off is the reason they didn't have any space. And to top it all, I had my purse snatched while I was trying to pay the taxi driver."

"Oh, no! How did that happen?"

"Some kid on a bike. He flew by before I hardly knew what had happened."

"Poor you, that must have been awful!"

"It was; it gave me a right bloody shock, I can tell you. Then we walked in, and there was this meanest looking black guy you've ever seen parked on my mam and dad's sofa, acting like he owned the place. The cheeky bastard didn't even stand up to be introduced. He just started weighing me and Yansis up like we were the shit under his shoes."

"Shshsh," pleaded Yansis, in reference to Rita's bad language, as he nodded towards Emily.

Rita lowered her voice. "Apparently he's called Leroy and he's Jenny's boyfriend. It looks as though they've been getting on pretty well too, judging by the size of her stomach."

"Oh, I wondered if you knew about that, but I didn't think it was my place to mention it."

"Oh don't worry, I'm not blaming you, Julie, but you would have thought one of them would have had the decency to tell me. The best of it is, I just know he's a bad sort. He's smoking cannabis in front of my mam and dad in their own home, so what's he up to when they're not around? And my dad's carrying on as though he's the next coming of Christ. He hangs on his every word. Not only that, but I overheard him on the phone, and I didn't like the sound of it one bit."

"Who, Leroy?" asked Julie.

"Yeah, I think he's dealing in drugs or summat. He said something about goods and his turf, and then H. You know what H is, don't you? It's heroin." she whispered.

"I know that it can refer to that, Rita, but it might not be. It could be anything."

"Well anyway, I think he's bad news, and he definitely didn't want us round there."

"D'you know, one of the lads that works for Vinny lives on the Riverhill estate? He's called Rob. If you want, I can have a word with Vinny when he gets home from work, and get him to see what he can find out about Leroy."

"Would you, Jules? Tell him to be careful though. I'm telling you, that Leroy looks like a nasty piece of stuff and I don't want him to find out we've been asking questions. You never know what he might do."

"I will, don't worry. Anyway, let's change the subject. That's not what you're over here for, is it? When are you going to see the doctor?"

"As soon as possible. I'll be on the phone on Monday, as soon as they open."

"Oh good. I hope you manage to sort things out. Good luck with it anyway."

"Thanks Jules. I think we need all the luck we can get at the moment."

"How long will you be over for?"

"I've no idea. It all depends on the treatment, but I'll let you know as soon as I find out. If it's not convenient though, we can always find somewhere else to stay."

"No, I wouldn't dream of it. Take as long as you want; there's plenty of room here."

"Thanks, Julie, that's really good of you."

Yansis then went over to join Emily, and the girls watched as he crouched down to her level so he could show an interest in what she was playing. Although she was guarded at first, she was soon showing him each of her toys, pointing to them, and describing them as best she could with her limited vocabulary.

"Sweet, isn't it?" Rita whispered to Julie.

After a moment's silence, Julie asked, "How are things in Greece? Are you still loving it?"

"Yeah, the restaurant gets busy at times, but I wouldn't swap it for the world. I love it, and the people are great. His mam and dad are darlings. Aren't they, love?" she shouted to Yansis, but he was engrossed in watching Emily play.

"Oh, I'm glad for you," said Julie.

"Yeah, there's only one problem," Rita whispered. "I can't bleedin' swear in front of them."

In between giggles, Julie replied. "Oh, Rita, you don't change, do you?"

A Gangster's Grip

***

It was a few hours since Rita had left her parents' home with Yansis, and Leroy and Jenny had gone out for the evening. Ged and Joan were sitting in their living room, discussing the day's events while the background noise of Michael Aspel & Company droned on the TV.

"That's all we need is our Rita stickin' her nose in where it's not wanted," complained Ged.

"Why, what are you worried about?"

"I just don't want her asking questions. You know what she's like. I've been making a packet since Leroy came on the scene. He sorts me out with some really good stuff."

"She wouldn't say owt. What do you think she's gonna do, tell the coppers or summat? Our Rita wouldn't do that."

"You never know. Me and our Rita have never seen eye to eye. Anyway, it's best you keep your mouth shut. The least she'll do is give me a load of earache, and I can do without that. If she doesn't know, then she can't say owt, can she?"

Ged was referring to the constant supply of stolen and counterfeit goods that Leroy had been providing him with over the last few months. Ged had been a petty crook for years; it was one of the reasons he and Rita didn't get along. When Leroy started going out with Jenny, Ged was already familiar with him because he lived in the local area. They each knew a little about the other's reputation, so it didn't take long until they fell into a mutually beneficial arrangement.

Because of Leroy's regular trips to Cheetham Hill, it was easy for him to get hold of low cost goods of many types; the area was known for trading in counterfeit and stolen merchandise as well as mainstream legal trading. Leroy had lots of contacts in Cheetham Hill so he knew who to go to for specific products. He would pass them on to Ged who sold them to his cronies in the local pubs, and Leroy would take a good cut of the profits. Leroy didn't bother with selling on any of the goods himself; he dealt in other products that gave him much higher profit margins.

After she had watched Aspel & Company for a few minutes, Joan asked, "How come Leroy doesn't sell the stuff himself anyway? How come he gets you to do it?"

"I don't know, do I? Anyway, you're not complaining are you? At least we're not skint anymore. Keeps you in booze and fags, doesn't it?"

"Suppose so."

"Right, well then. Anyway, why are we watching this shit? Let's go down the pub; I fancy a pint. What d'you say?"

"Go on then, but only if we stop off at the Chinese chippy on the way back."

"Course we will love. You can have a beef curry and rice if you like. I told you, I can get you whatever you want now, can't I? Only if you're nice to me though. The money's rolling in, and there's plenty more where that came from, as long as you keep your mouth shut."

Inside, Ged was heaving a sigh of relief, knowing he had skilfully deflected his wife away from a topic of conversation he wanted to avoid. He had a good idea why Leroy didn't sell the dodgy goods himself; it was just a side-line for him. Ged had heard the rumours about Leroy being a drug dealer, and by all accounts he was vicious too. But what could he do? He was in over his head now, and he wasn't daft enough to challenge someone like Leroy. Not a chance!

Anyway, life was sweet. He'd not been this well off for years; his dole didn't go very far by the time he'd tipped up for the housekeeping and bought a few pints. No, Ged Steadman was nobody's mug; he knew when to keep his mouth shut.

Chapter 3

Leroy was at the wheel of his black BMW, driving along the busy Cheetham Hill Road, on his way to a meeting with his suppliers. He cruised through this vibrant multi-cultural area where new architecture mixed with old, and industrial units, furniture stores and car showrooms stood alongside churches, mosques and synagogues. He'd left early intending to collect some other goods before his meeting.

Cheetham Hill is an area to the north of Manchester where Sunday trading was a regular occurrence long before the Sunday Trading Act of 1994. Leroy drove past the proliferation of wholesalers, retail shops and fast food outlets lining the streets and adding to the eclectic mix; their bright, garish signs advertising their wares. Here the shops sold a vast array of goods from food and clothing to electricals. As someone in the know, Leroy visited traders that were a little off the beaten track; the illegal traders who supplied counterfeit and stolen merchandise at knock down prices.

Leroy was accustomed to the area, so he knew where to go for the best prices, and how to drive a hard bargain. He parked his car next to one of the back alleys, out of view of the main drag, so he could visit a number of his contacts. Once he had cut the engine and opened the car door, the sound of excited bargain hunters and the aroma of fast food assailed his senses. Leroy obtained a selection of cheaply priced goods that he knew he could sell on through his network of associates, including Ged. He would put a high mark-up on the cost of the goods, and take the bulk of the profit for himself.

After stashing the merchandise in the boot of his BMW, Leroy glanced at his Gucci watch. There was still half an hour to go before his meeting, so he passed the time in a back-street café, drinking coffee and smoking weed. The café owners knew Leroy, and therefore knew better than to complain about him smoking illegal substances on their premises.

The meeting place was an old derelict building approached via the back entrance, through a maze of alleyways. Leroy was there five minutes before the arranged time, eager to obtain the drugs, which were already two days overdue. After a couple of minutes his contact arrived.

"About fuckin' time," complained Leroy. "What you got?"

He was pleased that his contact had brought a good supply with him, enough to keep Leroy going for a while. Despite his satisfaction, he was careful not to give anything away, negotiating a reduced price because of the delay. His justification for this was the loss of custom.

"Now don't forget, not a word about our arrangement to anyone," said Leroy.

"You worried about Mad Trevor?" asked his supplier.

"I ain't worried about no-one! It's just best that the rest of the gang don't know, that's all. You know how they feel about you lot. But me, I don't have any problems with you, man; we go back a long way. Besides, if the MSC hadn't got everything sewn up for themselves, we'd still be getting H from our other sources, and I wouldn't have to come to you. Now that ain't my fault, is it? If you ask me, Mad Trevor's been upsetting too many of the suppliers. They're not as friendly with us as they used to be, but the fuckin' MSC have got 'em eating out of their hands."

After a brief discussion, they were about to do the exchange when they heard footsteps scurrying down the alleyway. Leroy stepped into the backyard of the property, opened the gate a few inches and peered out. He could see two men running down the passageway, carrying leather jackets, fake designer clothing and cardboard boxes containing other goods. He bent his head around the opening in the gate to see what the men were running from, and noticed a policeman dashing across the top of the alley.

"Shit, it's a raid!" he told his contact.

They quickly completed the exchange then left the yard, running in the same direction as the other two men. It was fortunate for Leroy that he was familiar with the labyrinth of passageways; this enabled him to dodge the police and reach his car, which was parked just a few minutes away. He climbed inside and concealed the drugs in a special compartment built into the car, underneath the dashboard.

There wasn't much he could do to hide the counterfeit goods, but that was a chance he was prepared to take, knowing that the penalties were far less severe than those he would face for carrying heroin with a street value of several thousand pounds. He started his engine and continued along the length of the back alleyway, taking a circuitous route that avoided the main Cheetham Hill Road until he was out of the area and well on his way to Manchester city centre. He heaved a sigh of relief as he passed through the centre on his way to the Riverhill Estate in Longsight. That had been a close call, but at least the drugs were safely with him. Now all he had to do was find somewhere to conceal them until he moved into his own place with Jenny.

**

Tuesday 12th March 1991 - evening

Rita and Yansis had been staying with Julie and Vinny for three days, and were feeling very much at home in the spacious guest bedroom. Rita had arranged a doctor's appointment for the Tuesday evening, and by the time she and Yansis returned from the doctors, Vinny was already home from work.

"Ooh, just in time," said Julie. "The tea's ready. I was going to give it a few more minutes, and then we would have had to start without you."

"You should have done anyway; don't spoil your tea on our account," said Rita.

"No, it's fine. We want to have a chat with you anyway. Vinny's found out something today about you know who."

Rita stared wide-eyed at Vinny in anticipation. She hadn't expected to find out anything about Leroy so soon; not after Vinny had told her that his employee, Rob, had been off sick on the Monday. Evidently, he must have returned to work already.

"Let's eat first, before it gets ruined, and then he can tell you. How did you go on at the doctors, anyway?" Julie asked, as she strapped Emily into her high chair.

"Not much to tell really. He's made a hospital referral, so we've just got to sit tight and wait a few weeks. We won't know anything till after that."

"Oh well, at least you've made a start. I hope you don't have to wait too long, and that you manage to get things sorted out."

"Me too, Julie." Rita looked across at Yansis, and gave him a hesitant smile as she spoke.

Vinny tucked into Julie's home-made shepherd's pie with such relish that Rita felt guilty quizzing him before he had finished. Rita hardly tasted the food though; she was too eager to find out what he had learnt about Leroy. She didn't have to ask any questions; Vinny picked up on her air of expectancy as soon as he had eaten his last morsel and placed his knife and fork down onto the empty plate.

"Do you want a pudding?" Julie asked.

"Not for me," Rita quickly interjected before Vinny could reply. Then, seeing the expression on Julie's face, she added, "Oh sorry, go on, Vinny; you have your pudding if you like, then tell me about Leroy after."

Her tone and manner made it obvious that, although she was feigning politeness, she didn't want to wait any longer, and she was thankful when Vinny acquiesced.

"It's alright, Julie, I'll have it later." Then, turning to Rita and Yansis, Vinny added, "Come in the living room, and I'll tell you what I've found out."

He led her and Yansis out of the dining room, and left Julie feeding Emily the remainder of her tea. Rita surmised that this must be serious if he didn't want his two-year-old daughter to overhear any of the conversation.

A Gangster's Grip

As soon as they settled down in the lounge, Vinny began. "Right, one of the lads from work has been doing a bit of fishing, and I don't think you'll like what I've heard."

"Go on, I'd rather know."

"Well, apparently Leroy Booth and the rest of his family moved to the estate from Moss Side about a year ago. He's been in loads of trouble with the law. He has a few younger brothers and sisters; a couple of his younger brothers are tearaways as well, but not as bad as him. Leroy has a really bad reputation and he's not bothered who knows it. In fact, from what I'm told, he loves the fact that people are scared of him. They reckon his mam's a nice lady, but she's on her own, and she just can't control him."

"So, what sort of trouble has he been in?"

"Hang on, Rita, I haven't finished yet. For starters, he deals in dodgy goods. From what I've heard, your dad's well in with him and is one of the people who sells the stuff in the Brown Cow."

"That doesn't surprise me. What sort of stuff?"

"Electricals mostly. Video recorders, CD players, cheap CDs and video tapes; that sort of thing."

"OK, so what about drugs? Was there any mention of that?"

"I'm coming to that … Oh, don't worry; your dad's not selling drugs, not from what I've heard anyway. I think Leroy might be though. Have you ever heard of the Buckthorn Crew?"

"Not really, why?"

"It's a gang that's named after the Buckthorn Estate in Moss Side. That's where Leroy used to live before he moved to Longsight. There's a pub on the estate as well, called the Buckthorn Inn. Apparently, there are a few gangs in Moss Side; some are worse than others, but from what I've been told, the Buckthorn Crew are really bad news. They're into drugs in a big way, and violence.

"That's why all the locals are so frightened of him, not just because of how he acts, but because he's part of the Buckthorns. There have been a few shootings in the press that are connected to drugs. The police can never find out who did it, but it's all supposed to be connected to gang wars over drugs and turf, that sort of thing."

"Jesus, I don't like the sound of this! Why move to Longsight though? It makes no sense."

"That's what I thought. Unless he has a good reason for it; maybe he's hiding from something or someone. I don't know."

Just then Julie walked back into the lounge, but Rita was too hyped up to take heed of the fact that she was accompanied by her daughter Emily.

"Julie, I don't like the sound of this," Rita repeated. "I can't believe my sister would be daft enough to run around with a bleedin' gangster. I suppose the drugs go without saying then, if he's involved with that lot?" she asked Vinny.

"Well, I haven't heard anything specific, but your guess is as good as mine."

"Right, well there's only one way to find out. Yansis, we're going to this bleedin' Buckthorn Inn at the weekend to see what we can find out about him."

"Oh no, Rita; it's too dangerous," said Vinny. "And you don't want to be dragging Yansis there either."

Once Rita had her mind set on something, however, there was no stopping her. "Not half as bloody dangerous as the mess my sister has landed herself in. He's gonna be moving in with her, for God's sake! We've got to do something. If you don't come with me, Yansis, I'll go on my own. Anyway, we're only asking a few questions, what harm can that do?"

"Alright, Rita, I will come with you. You know I wouldn't let you go alone, but I don't like that you put me in this situation."

"For God's sake, Rita, be careful!" pleaded Julie.

Rita and Julie's friendship went back years. Rita knew that Julie wouldn't even bother trying to dissuade her from going; she would be wasting her time.

"Don't worry, Julie, I will," said Rita. "I'm only going to see what I can find out. Maybe when Jenny learns what a scumbag she's going out with, she might come to her senses. I just want to get her away from him, that's all."

"What if she doesn't want to get away from him, Rita? It might be harder than you think," said Julie.

"Well I won't know till I try, and if something happened to our Jenny, I couldn't live with myself, knowing that I hadn't done anything to try to help her."

She then lit up a cigarette to calm her nerves.

Chapter 4

Vinny had been kind enough to let Rita and Yansis use his Vauxhall Cavalier to travel to the Buckthorn Inn in Moss Side on Friday evening, although Yansis would be driving as Rita didn't drive. He didn't need much persuasion from Julie. Vinny had got on well with Yansis whenever he and Julie had visited Greece, and he considered him a friend. Besides, as Vinny mainly used his work van, his car was often available.

During the week, Rita had checked the Yellow Pages to find the address of the Buckthorn Inn, then she and Yansis had mapped out the route in the A to Z. She was thankful that they could use Vinny's car because it would be easier for them to leave quickly if there was any trouble. She didn't like the thought of having to wait for a taxi if it was kicking off; that's supposing she could find the number of a local taxi firm. Worse still, they could end up wandering around the Buckthorn Estate late at night with no idea how to get back to Julie's.

When Friday night arrived, she was a little apprehensive, but she assured herself that she was doing the right thing. She needed to find out more about Leroy if she was to have any chance of persuading her sister Jenny to split up with him. As Yansis drove, Rita studied the A to Z and followed the street signs. After a while, they turned off the main road and into a housing estate.

It was similar to the estate where her parents lived, but worse; full of modern but shabbily maintained houses crowded into a confined space. Some of the gardens were not only overgrown but littered with refuse. Although it was evening, she could see huge patches of mould growing down some of the walls, and painted areas that were cracked and peeling. Several of the windows were boarded up.

She wondered how these properties could have become so

dilapidated in such a short space of time. The weather worn bricks on corner properties bore evidence to the fact that the houses were built with second rate materials. There were a few smarter homes amongst the decay, and she sympathised with the house-proud owners, having to live amid such despondency.

When they arrived at the Buckthorn Inn, it seemed innocuous enough from the exterior, apart from the fencing, which might have given a clue as to the omnipresent danger. It was another modern building, but better maintained than some of the houses they had passed. There was a yard at the back of the pub surrounded by a high, sturdy-looking metal fence topped with barbed wire. The top floor had an outdoor roof terrace, which was also protected by the same high fencing. As they stepped out of the car, a Rottweiler ran onto the terrace and snarled at them, while straining at the fence.

"Bleedin' hell! They know how to welcome their customers, don't they?" Rita commented, trying to hide her increasing unease.

She caught Yansis's nervous glance, but she was here now, and wasn't about to back out. She took the initiative and grabbed hold of Yansis's hand, leading him towards the entrance.

"Take no notice of that bleedin' thing. It can't get out, and you know what they say – its bark's probably worse than its bite." Because Yansis was from Greece, this saying was lost on him, as were a lot of the old adages that Rita used.

The only people they noticed at first were some teenagers further up the street, on mountain bikes. Then, as they approached the doorway, they saw a young couple. They were tucked into the side of the porch, so Rita didn't notice them until she was a few metres away. Once they were in view, though, it was obvious they were getting very amorous and their antics were a bit much for public consumption. Rita tried to avert her eyes as she passed them. Although she was broad minded, this overt display embarrassed her.

Rita pulled the door handle and the atmosphere engulfed her. The air was heavy with smoke but from more than cigarettes. Rita recognised the sweet, sickly smell of cannabis. The place was full of it, and the atmosphere wasn't just to do with the smell either. Now she knew what Clint Eastwood felt like when he rode into a strange town. Jesus! Talk about hostile. People were actually pausing their conversations to examine them as they walked past. The only welcoming sign was the music as the sound of 'Groove is in the Heart' by Deee-Lite was blasting through the speakers.

The walk to the bar seemed to last forever until she compared it to the time waiting to be served. That must have broken a new record. When the barman deigned to serve them, Rita ordered a pint of lager and a double whisky. Somehow she thought she was going to need it, and for extra succour she lit up a cigarette too. Poor Yansis had to make do with a Coke as he was driving and didn't smoke.

She looked around the room, trying to decide where to go. The seats all seemed to be taken, so it looked as though they would have to stand. However, the place was crowded and there were some mean looking characters eyeing them up. She didn't fancy being accused of barging into anyone, so she led Yansis to a side of the pub that seemed calmer. They positioned themselves next to the wall and Rita glanced around, planning a strategy while avoiding eye contact with anyone. Meanwhile, Yansis stood uncomfortably sipping his Coke.

Rita noticed a group of girls sitting around a table. They looked younger than her but might be friendly if she approached them in the right way. There were a couple of seats empty between their table and the next one. The people at each table had spread themselves out, so anyone wanting to sit there would either have to prise themselves in or ask them to move up. Rita, having appraised the situation for a few minutes, and after gulping down the last of her double whisky and a good measure of lager, decided it was worth taking a chance.

"Come on, Yansis, let's get a seat."

Before Yansis could protest, Rita made her way over to the table full of girls.

"Hiya girls, d'you mind if we grab them two seats, only my bleedin' feet are killin' in these stabbers?" she asked, indicating her shoes as the source of her discomfort.

A Gangster's Grip

"Er yeah, go for it," one of them replied, and they shuffled closer together while Rita sat down next to them, leaving the seat at the other side of her free for Yansis. It was a tight squeeze for him, and the people on the neighbouring table weren't as accommodating, but he coped. Meanwhile, Rita struck up a conversation with the girls.

"Ooh that's better, you're a life saver," she said loudly to the girl sitting next to her, who had encouraged the others to make room. Then, while she had their attention, Rita continued, "I've only just got them. I knew they were a bit high but I couldn't resist." She lifted her right foot and turned it at an angle to show off the shoes.

"They're gorgeous," said her new found friend and the others joined in.

"I'm Rita by the way, and this is Yansis."

The girls introduced themselves, and Rita found out that the one sitting nearest to her was called Alesha.

"It's alright here, buzzin' isn't it? Is it your local?" asked Rita, playing the role of loquacious drunk.

"Yeah, we come here all the time. We've not seen you in here before though."

Rita picked up on the air of suspicion but she was prepared. "No, we were supposed to come with my sister and her boyfriend, but she backed out at the last minute, so we thought, sod it, we might as well come anyway. It'll make a change."

Alesha turned away, ready to resume her conversation with her friends. '*Shit, I've lost her,*' thought Rita. She knew she had to think fast to keep the conversation going, so she leant over to the girl and whispered conspiratorially. "Actually, I think they've had a row; I'm not sure he's good for her. I don't wanna say too much in case you know him, 'cos he's from round here, but people keep telling me he's bad news and she should finish with him."

Rita knew she would have piqued the girls' interest, and Alesha was quick to respond. "What's his name?"

"Leroy Booth," whispered Rita.

There was a definite shift in the girls' attitudes as soon as Rita spoke his name. She sensed it straightaway despite the double whisky she had drunk. She hoped they weren't close to him; they might have been related for all she knew. But that was why she had been careful not to call him; instead she had implied that it was other people who were saying bad things, and had feigned ignorance. With that in mind, she carried on prodding.

"Do you know him then? I don't know much about him myself. We've just come back from Greece, so I wouldn't mind finding out if all these rumours are true."

"Shshsh," whispered Alesha, as she looked around her. Rita then understood that the reason for the change in the girls was down to fear. When Alesha was satisfied that no-one was listening to them, she continued quietly. "You wanna be careful, coming in here, asking things like that. It's dangerous asking questions about Leroy Booth."

"Why?"

Alesha nodded towards a young woman standing a few metres away from them, and said, "You see that girl over there, in the blue top?"

Rita looked across the room and noticed a slim, pretty young woman in profile, with smooth, caramel coloured skin. "Yeah," she replied.

"She used to go out with Leroy, and she got too involved in what Leroy was up to. Do you wanna know what happened to her?"

Rita looked at Alesha, unable to answer straightaway as a feeling of dread descended on her.

"Laura!" Alesha called to the young woman.

Laura turned around to look at them. She was a stunning young woman, with beautiful brown eyes and full lips, as well as the smooth caramel coloured skin. In fact, if it hadn't been for that one imperfection she would have been flawless. Unfortunately, the ugly scar running down one side of her face ruined her flawlessness.

"I didn't know you were out tonight. How long you been in here?" asked Alesha.

"About half an hour."

A Gangster's Grip

"Oh, I've only just seen you. Be over later for a chat."

The conversation was soon over. It was only a pretext to let Rita see Laura's damaged face. Alesha lowered her voice again as she turned back to face Rita. "That's what happens if you get too involved in Leroy's business. You probably wish your sister could finish with him, but let me tell you; she can't. The only way she'll be finished with Leroy is when he's finished with her. If you've got any sense, you'll leave her in the mess she's made for herself, and piss off out of it. I'd be off back to Greece if I was you."

For once Rita was speechless. She quickly downed the remainder of her lager, and stood up to leave. "Come on, Yansis, we're going."

They dashed from the pub without uttering another word to the girls. When they got outside, they noticed that the group of five or six teenagers on mountain bikes had now moved down the street, and were circulating around the pub. Rita and Yansis had left the car on the pub car park, so it didn't take them long to notice that the front windscreen was smashed.

"Oh shit, that's all we need!" cursed Rita, who was already feeling agitated following Alesha's revelation.

Her reaction was bait to the group of youths, who began to taunt.

"Looks like someone did your windscreen in lady."

"Tyre's lookin' a bit flat too, bitch."

The youths followed these comments with laughter and jeers. Rita's first impulse was to give them a piece of her mind. The cheeky little bastards! She glared at them, the fury building up inside her. As she made eye contact with them, they stayed still and silent, surveying her, waiting for a response. She could feel Yansis pulling her arm, trying to lead her towards the car.

There was a time when she'd have leapt at them and vented her anger. But she'd changed during the last few years, and developed an instinct for danger. She noticed they were even younger than she had at first deduced, ranging in age from about 10 to 14. Nevertheless, they looked menacing, especially as a few of them were carrying large baton-like lengths of wood, which they were switching from hand to hand in a threatening manner.

She knew that retaliation would have been foolish; she would have been like a gladiator slave stepping into the arena. But unlike the gladiator slaves, Rita had a choice. This was one time when she would have to swallow her anger, and concentrate on getting home safe. She and Yansis continued towards the car, noticing the flat tyre on the passenger side. Yansis unlocked the doors and Rita got in immediately, despite the shower of broken glass all over the seats. She could see the gang of youths making their way towards them. Yansis was standing with his back towards the youngsters, and was preoccupied with the state of the car. He leant in, and began brushing the glass away with his hands.

"Oh, Rita. What can I do with the car like this?" he asked. "I don't know what I will tell to Vinny."

Rita, her patience running thin, and aware of the gangs' increasing proximity, yelled, "Just fuckin' drive, Yansis!"

***

Saturday 16th March 1991 - afternoon

"Just get hold of the bleedin' thing will you?" Ged shouted, as he lifted one end of a two seater settee that had seen better days.

At the other end of the settee was Joan. They had been helping Jenny to move house for over two hours now, and Joan was getting tired. Ged was in a foul mood. He could have been in the pub, flogging his gear, and making sporadic trips to the bookies in between pints. Instead, he had been lumbered with helping to shift Jenny's furniture and smaller items, and he'd had it dropped on him at the last minute.

Up until yesterday morning, Leroy had supposedly been taking care of everything, but then he'd rung to say he couldn't do it because he had a bit of business to tend to, and he'd asked Ged to take over. And when Leroy asked you to do something, you did it, no matter what your other plans were.

A Gangster's Grip

Ged didn't even have a van, and he'd had to borrow a rusty old Ford Escort van from one of his mates. It wasn't the ideal choice of vehicle for moving house, due to its size, which meant they were having to make several trips.

Although the house was in the same area as theirs, it had taken them well over two hours, and they hadn't yet completed the second trip. There were only the three of them, and Jenny was in no condition to carry much. With the time it took to load the van, drive it there, unload it, put everything in place and drive back, it seemed that they would be at it all day Sunday as well.

The state of the furniture was annoying him too. He'd been sick to death of hearing Jenny boast about the things that Leroy was getting for her. Fair enough, he had got hold of a 28 inch Phillips TV, and a top notch stereo player, but they were knock-off. The rest of the stuff either came from second-hand stores, or were bits they could spare. The trouble was, he wouldn't dare complain to Leroy, so he was taking his bad mood out on his wife.

"Our Rita would have helped if we'd have asked," said Joan.

"You must be bloody joking! I've told you, the less she knows the better."

"She's bound to want to visit Jenny in her new house. She'll see the tele then, and you know our Rita; she's bound to ask where it's come from."

"Aye well, let her ask her questions when I'm not around. I can do without the earache. Let's get the rest of this stuff inside, then we can have a sit down while you put the kettle on."

They struggled into Jenny's new two bedroom house, with some loaded cardboard boxes, then Ged took a seat while he waited for Joan to make the drinks.

After a while, he heard Joan shout from the kitchen, "Did anyone pack the kettle?"

'Jesus,' he thought, 'all bloody weekend wasted and I can't even have a brew. I'll be glad when this is over.'

Chapter 5

Following the revelations of Friday night, Rita had been desperate to get hold of Jenny. She needed to warn her about Leroy, before he moved in. She wasn't sure whether Leroy was planning to move in with Jenny as soon as her house came through, but she presumed so. It sounded as though he had already been staying with Jenny regularly, at her parents' home, so she couldn't see any reason he would hang around once Jenny got her own house.

Rita gathered, through her mother, that the property was listed under Jenny's name. That made sense, because if Leroy wanted to make himself scarce, then he would avoid having his name listed on public records.

It was important for Rita to warn Jenny about Leroy as soon as possible, then perhaps she could get her away from him before it was too late. The trouble was, she'd been ringing her parents' house all weekend, and had no luck. When she got up on Monday morning, she tried the phone again. If there was no answer this time, she would go round and find out what was going on. Rita was amazed when her mother answered after a few rings.

"Jesus, Mam, I was beginning to think you'd emigrated or summat."

"Why, what's wrong?"

"I've been ringing all weekend, and there's been no answer. Has the phone been out of order, or has my dad not been paying the bills?"

"No, don't be daft. We were helping our Jenny move house."

"Move house? You mean, she's moved already?"

"Yeah, I told you she was getting the house in a few days."

"I didn't know what day she was moving, though. You might have told me; I could have helped out."

"I wish I had have done, love; we've been at it all weekend. I'm bloody knackered."

"All weekend? Why, where's she moved to, Land's End?"

"No, Royle Way, but your dad borrowed this knackered old Escort van, and it took us umpteen trips to shift everything."

Rita couldn't help but laugh. "An Escort van to move house? I can just imagine the scene; I bet it was like summat out of bloody Steptoe and Son."

"Aye, except their cart could carry more than the Escort, and it was in better nick too."

When they had finished laughing, Rita told her mother she wanted to get in touch with Jenny, but she didn't reveal why. Although Rita had a relatively good relationship with her mother, she knew her parents were close, and that her father was the dominant one in the relationship. She wasn't sure how much her mother knew, and thought that perhaps she wasn't even aware of the dodgy goods that her father sold.

Her mother had always seemed naïve, but maybe it was all an act. Could anybody be that gullible? Maybe she knew what Ged got up to, but didn't want to see it. There were times in the past when Rita had criticised him, and her mother had usually made excuses for him, or jumped to his defence. If she was unaware of what was going on, then Rita decided it was best to keep it that way for now. If, on the other hand, she knew about the stolen and fake goods, and had a good idea about Leroy, what would Rita gain by getting her involved? Her father was the one with the influence, but Rita wanted to speak to Jenny before she discussed the matter with anybody else.

***

Monday 18th March 1991 – late morning

After coming off the phone with her mother, Rita asked Yansis if he would go with her to see Jenny at her new house. Having waited all weekend, she didn't want to waste any more time, so she was anxious to get there as soon as possible. The insurance company had already sent someone to replace the windscreen on Vinny's car that morning, and Vinny and Yansis had changed the damaged tyre over the weekend. Although Rita and Yansis felt bad about the damage to the car, Vinny had insisted that it wasn't their fault, and he was happy for them to carry on using it.

They said goodbye to Julie, who wished Rita good luck. Once they were in the car, Rita had a quick glance through the A – Z. Unlike the trip to the Buckthorn Estate, she had a good idea where they were going. She recognised the name Royle Way, and knew that it was part of the Riverhill Estate in Longsight, but on the opposite side of the A6 to her parents' house.

It was situated a mile or so from her parents', and she had walked around the area several times as a girl. A problem with these estates, though, was that they all had limited access by car, so she wanted to check the route before they set off.

When they arrived, she was relieved to notice that there were no other cars parked outside. Hopefully, that would mean Leroy was out, so she would have chance to talk to Jenny alone. It took a couple of sharp knocks on the door before Jenny answered.

"Oh, it's you."

"Lovely to see you too!"

"Sorry, I didn't mean owt. I just thought it might be my mam and dad. They said they'd help me sort everything out. There's still stuff all over the place."

"Or maybe you were expecting Leroy. He'd soon have this lot shifted, big lad like him."

"No, he's got a key. Anyway, Leroy's busy."

"Bloody hell, it's not taken him long to get his feet under the table, has it?"

"We live together. Anyway, what have you got against Leroy?"

"Nothing. I'm not having a go, but he wasn't exactly friendly when we met the other day."

"That's just the way he is. He's alright once you get to know him."

A Gangster's Grip

Rita stopped herself before things went any further. She couldn't believe that she and Jenny had got off to such a bad start. They had always got on so well as kids. Despite the age gap of four years between them, they were always close.

Maybe the age gap was part of the problem. Because Rita was older than Jenny, she had always protected her and stuck up for her. When Rita had gone to live in Greece, Jenny was still only 17, and although she got up to mischief, she still had a lot of respect for Rita and would listen to her advice. Besides, at that time, Rita wasn't averse to getting up to a little mischief herself.

Now though, as she assessed the situation, Rita realised that things had changed between them over the last few years. Jenny was a young woman of 22 who was making her own decisions, and her own mistakes, as far as Rita could see. Their grandparents had long since passed away, and with Rita no longer around, and their brother John away in the army, it left Jenny with no moral compass. Much as Rita hated to admit it, even to herself, her father's morals left a lot to be desired, and her mother was weak-willed. She wasn't a bad person; she was just easy to manipulate, and content to bend to her husband's will.

Once they were inside the living room, Jenny went to the kitchen to make drinks, leaving Rita and Yansis sitting on the worn sofa. While she was away, Rita looked around the room, taking in the flash TV and multi-stack stereo system, which seemed incongruous next to the shabby furniture. The house was freshly painted and papered, although the floors were bare, apart from the standard dingy brown tiles that the council fitted in all the houses on the local estates.

She could still smell the fresh paint, but there were other odours that hung in the air; the smell of marijuana mixed with a strong, dirty stench she couldn't quite identify. She guessed that it was some form of waste matter, although whether it was human or animal, or a mix of the two, she wasn't sure. It was usual for the council to do a full repair and redecoration if the previous residents had left the property in a state. That generally took care of most things, but some stenches you just couldn't shift.

Rita also noticed how overcrowded the room was. Jenny was right, there was stuff all over the place. A few feet in front of her and Yansis were boxes stacked on top of each other, which looked as though they still needed unpacking. At least someone had had the foresight to write the contents on the box in black marker pen. It would take several hours to put everything in place, and Jenny was in no fit state to do much. There was also some upstairs furniture still in the lounge, including a chest of drawers, which was chipped on the corners and had felt tip pen scrawled across one of the drawers.

Jenny's absence gave Rita a chance to rethink her approach, and by the time she heard the cups clinking in the hallway, she had primed herself. It was important to regain Jenny's trust if she wanted to get through to her.

"Thanks," she said to Jenny, as she took a mug of coffee from her. Then, after a brief pause, she added, "I doubt whether my mam will be here today; she said she was knackered when I was on the phone to her earlier. I tell you what, me and Yansis haven't got much on today, so why don't we help you? When we've finished this drink, you could show Yansis what wants putting where, and then he could make a start while me and you have a chat." Then, as an afterthought, she said to Yansis, "That's if you don't mind love."

"No, I don't mind at all, Rita. Like you say, we have nothing else to do today."

"OK," said Jenny. "As long as you don't mind."

They then spent a few minutes making polite conversation while they drank their coffee, with Jenny asking where they were staying, and Yansis asking about the stereo. Rita was only half listening to Yansis's questions about the stereo's technical capabilities as her mind was occupied with thoughts of her imminent conversation with Jenny.

It didn't take Yansis long to finish his drink. Rita had already made him aware of her concerns, and she knew that he wouldn't want to stay in the same room while she tackled Jenny.

His first task was to carry the chest of drawers upstairs, which he managed by removing the drawers and taking them up first, then carrying the empty carcass. Next, he shifted some boxes into the kitchen, and Jenny showed him which cupboards and drawers she wanted him to put things into. Once Rita was sure he would be occupied in the kitchen for a while, and she and Jenny were unlikely to be disturbed, she broached the subject of Leroy.

"Jenny, there's something I want to talk to you about. I don't think you're going to like this, but it needs to be said."

When she had captured Jenny's full attention, she continued. "The other day, when we were at my mam and dad's, I overheard Leroy on the phone, and I think he was arranging some sort of deal. He was talking about goods, and he mentioned turf, and something about his customers going elsewhere if he didn't get the goods."

"So what? Leroy's a businessman; he deals in goods all the time."

"What sort of goods, Jenny?"

"All sorts. Electricals mostly, but other stuff as well. Why, what's the problem?"

"The problem is, I think he's dealing in drugs."

"You what? Oh, I get it, he's black and from Moss Side, so he must be a drug dealer. Is that it?"

"No, that's not it, Jenny; you know I'm not like that! I heard him say H on the phone ... and there's rumours about him in the Brown Cow."

"Come off it! H could mean anything. What the hell were you doing listening to his phone call anyway? And how do you know what's being said in the Brown Cow? You haven't been home five minutes. I thought you were stopping at your mate Julie's. She lives nowhere near the Brown Cow."

"A mate of Vinny's does. He told us."

"And you just happened to bump into him, did you, or have you been snooping around? Just what is your problem with Leroy, for God's sake?"

Rita didn't like the way this conversation was going. She was trying to tread lightly, but there was no avoiding the facts. The trouble was, the more she told Jenny, the more irate her sister was becoming, but unfortunately, Jenny's anger wasn't directed at Leroy. Why couldn't she see through him? At this point, Rita could have left things alone, but as she'd already come this far, she figured that she might as well tell Jenny everything. Maybe a few shock tactics would get through to her.

"Jenny, my problem with Leroy is that I think he's dangerous. I found out something else that I think you should know."

"Go on," Jenny sighed.

Rita moved further along the sofa, positioning herself adjacent to the armchair where Jenny was sitting. Taking hold of Jenny's hands, and looking into her eyes, she began, "Me and Yansis went to a pub called the Buckthorn Inn in Moss Side. It's on the estate where Leroy used to live."

Jenny was now staring at her, with a mixture of anger and confusion, but Rita was determined to continue. "We got talking to some girls, and they pointed out Leroy's ex-girlfriend, a girl called Laura. She was really pretty, except for a scar that ran down one side of her face."

Rita took a deep breath before uttering the next words. "The girls suggested that the scar was something to do with Leroy. They said it was because she got too involved with Leroy's business, whatever that means."

Jenny swiftly drew her hands away from Rita's, her right one reaching to cover her mouth as her breath came in gasps, "No, they're lying! Leroy wouldn't do that."

Rita could tell that, although Jenny was saying one thing, her eyes were saying something else, reflecting her fear through wide-eyed shock and dilated pupils.

After a few seconds absorbing this news, Jenny responded, "What the hell were you doing in that pub, Rita? Why are you spying on Leroy? Just what the hell have you got against him? I can't believe you! Just because he's not that friendly to you when you meet him, you get some crazy idea in your head, then go around spying on him."

"Alright, calm down. Maybe the girls were wrong, I don't know. I just thought it was best to warn you, that's all. I mean, he isn't completely innocent, Jenny. He is dealing in dodgy goods, and he's got my dad selling them down the pub for him."

"I know all about the dodgy goods, Rita. Big deal! That's what everyone does round here. That's how we live. How else do you think we could afford stuff? Your trouble is, you're so used to mixing with your stuck-up customers in Greece that you've forgotten what it's like in the real world. Life's not just one long fuckin' holiday, you know."

Rita had tried to stay calm up to now, hoping that she could regain Jenny's trust, but as Jenny became increasingly angry and started to criticise her lifestyle, there was no way Rita was going to just sit and take it.

"Hang on a minute, Jenny. Those people you call stuck-up, most of them are decent hardworking people who've saved all year to go on holiday. And, for your information, me and Yansis put a lot of bleedin' hours into running that restaurant. We hardly ever have any time off."

"Yeah well, it's alright for those that can get good jobs, isn't it? But round here, we haven't got much choice other than being stuck on the dole."

"I come from round here, and I worked for a living."

"Yeah, at some crappy factory, and you'd still be at some crappy factory if you hadn't met Yansis."

"Look, I don't need you having a go at my personal life."

"Why not? You're having a go at mine!"

Just as the argument had reached its peak, Yansis walked back into the living room, jolting Rita back to her senses. She felt ashamed for losing her temper; Rita didn't like Yansis seeing this side of her character. She had come here to warn Jenny about Leroy and try to help her, but all she had done was turned Jenny against her, and made matters worse.

Rita quickly backtracked. "Look, Jenny, I don't want to fall out with you. Let's leave it, eh?"

Yansis's presence was enough to deter Jenny from carrying on the row, and she nodded her head, looking shamefaced.

"We came here to help, Jenny, not to have a row. I've not seen you for years, for God's sake. Come on, let's get some more of those boxes emptied while we're here."

"That's just what I come back to ask," said Yansis, affable as ever. "Where do you want me to put these boxes, Jenny?"

For the next couple of hours, they worked in relative silence. They put all the boxes in the right places, although some of them still needed emptying. The atmosphere was strained, and when they left, Rita asked for a pen and paper to write down Julie's phone number, so that Jenny could get hold of her.

She then put her arms around Jenny, and said. "Don't forget to let me have your number as soon as you've had your phone connected. I'm not going to say anything else, Jenny, and I'll try to get on with Leroy, but all I do want to say is that if you ever need me for anything, I'll always be there for you, OK?"

Jenny nodded. The fight had now left her, and Rita dashed to the car with Yansis, reluctant to prolong the embrace and let Jenny see the tears that were starting to form. She was surprised that she had become so emotional. Her, Rita, the feisty one who nothing ever seemed to touch. But she knew what had upset her. It was the fear she had seen in Jenny's eyes.

Chapter 6

The visit to her sister, Jenny, had unsettled Rita more than she cared to admit. She had hoped that, by talking to Jenny, she might convince her to break free of Leroy's clutches. But after Monday, there didn't seem much chance of that. Rita's memories of Jenny were of a naïve little girl who hung onto her every word. Boy had things changed! Jenny had definitely inherited the same feistiness as her; that was for sure.

Rita couldn't work out what kept her sister tied to Leroy. Was it because she was so smitten that she couldn't see the bad in him, or was it down to fear? Jenny certainly seemed smitten when she had seen them together at her parents' house, but then she had noticed the fear in her eyes on Monday. That had unnerved Rita more than anything. Perhaps it was like the girls in the Buckthorn Inn had said; once you was in a relationship with Leroy, it was difficult to just walk away. Their words had shocked her, but there was a part of her that still didn't quite believe them. There might have been an element of truth, but it smacked of the melodrama of youth.

The trouble, as far as Rita was concerned, was that the longer Jenny was with Leroy, the deeper she would become embroiled in his shady world. That being the case, Rita wasn't prepared to give up just yet. She therefore decided to visit her dad in the Brown Cow. She wasn't sure what she expected to achieve, but she knew that her dad was involved with Leroy, so perhaps he could wield some influence, or at least tell her what was going on.

Rita anticipated that her discussion with her father might become heated, and she didn't want Yansis to get involved. She always felt embarrassed when Yansis saw that side of her. He'd been brought up differently, and wasn't used to this way of life, so in some ways she felt as though she wanted to shelter him from it. Fair enough, she had dragged him along to the Buckthorn Inn, but what choice did she have? She wasn't exactly inundated with offers to accompany her.

Anyway, she knew the Brown Cow, and she'd go at lunchtime when she felt safe going in on her own. It wasn't her favourite pub. She and her friends had preferred the Flying Horse when she lived on the estate, mainly because the Brown Cow had always been the pub where her dad hung out. Another reason was because there was generally a better clientele in the Flying Horse, although this wasn't always the case. The Flying Horse was nearer to Julie's former home, which was where the council housing estate met with the older style properties where Julie had lived.

Rita hoped to catch her dad in the pub now, as it was still the place where he spent most of his spare time.

When they pulled up in the carpark of the Brown Cow, Rita persuaded Yansis to wait outside in the car, as she didn't expect to spend too long in the pub. She told him it was best if he kept an eye on the car and, in view of the recent events outside the Buckthorn Inn, he didn't take a lot of convincing.

Inside the pub, Rita recognised a few faces, but she hadn't been to the Brown Cow for years, so there were a number of strangers too. She walked around the pub lounge, searching all the tables to see if she could spot her dad, but there was no sign of him. It had been wishful thinking on her part; she knew that he was most likely in the vault, but the vault of the Brown Cow wasn't the most inviting place for a woman. Nevertheless, she wouldn't let that deter her.

Rita strode into the vault to the sound of whistles and jeers from several of the men. It was nothing less than she expected, and she tried to ignore them and focus on the matter in hand. She spotted her father straightaway, sitting at a table with a few of his cronies, and walked over to him. "Can I have a word, in private?" she asked.

A cacophony of taunts and suggestive comments ensued from the men sitting with Ged, until he shut them up by announcing, "Give over, it's my fuckin' daughter!"

It didn't take Ged long to leave the table, and Rita guessed that he wouldn't want his friends to hear what she had to say, any more than she wanted to be overheard. He would know that she hadn't come here to have a nice friendly drink with him, but her visit had still piqued his curiosity. She led him away, through the door and into the large pub foyer.

"What you doing here?" he demanded.

"I told you. I want a word."

"Well what's wrong with having a word with me at home, instead of coming here showing me up in front of all my mates."

"I don't think you'd want my mam to hear what I have to say. It's about our Jenny and Leroy." She whispered the last word.

"Oh yeah?" he sneered.

"Yeah, I'm a bit worried about our Jenny. I think she's in danger … with him. I think he's bad news."

"What the hell you talking about? He's alright; he's been good to us."

"Well you're bound to think that. He's fixing you up with plenty of fake and knock-off stuff to shift."

"So, what if he is? What's it to you?"

"That's not all he gets up to, is it?" She lowered her voice before continuing. "He's dealing drugs."

"Is he 'eck."

Her father's reply was instantaneous and defensive, and she could tell he knew more than he was admitting to.

"Look, Dad, I know he is; I've been told things. I think you know what he gets up to as well as I do. Now you might think it's alright to turn a blind eye, as long as he's seeing you right, but have you thought about the harm he can do? He's not just a dealer, he's a dangerous man. I know how he treats women. I've been to the pub where he used to live, and seen the scar on his ex-girlfriend's face …"

Before she could say anymore, Ged interrupted. "You what? Are you stupid, going down there?"

"No, I'm not stupid, but you are for dealing with him. Anyone in their right mind would run a mile. Instead, you've got your daughter shacked up with him. But never mind, eh," she added sarcastically, "as long as you're alright, that's all that matters."

Ged surprised Rita by grabbing hold of her arm and threatening her, "Keep your fuckin' nose out of things that have got nowt to do with you!"

"No, I won't!" she retaliated, trying to prise her arm from his grip. "Someone's got to help Jenny. You need to warn her, and stop selling his stuff for him so he's got no hold over you."

Ged was becoming increasingly agitated now as, still gripping her arm, he leant towards her. She could smell the alcohol fumes, as he snarled into her ear, "You just don't fuckin' get it, do you? Nobody tells Leroy what he can and can't do, not if they want to live to tell the tale anyway."

She tugged sharply, managing to wrench her arm away and he backed off, as if realising how menacing he must appear to any passersby. While Rita stared at him in disbelief, he added, "You know your trouble, Rita? You don't know when to keep your big mouth shut. You've always been the same. Now clear off back to Greece and leave things alone, before you really upset the apple cart."

He turned towards the pub door, but Rita hadn't finished with him yet. "You make me sick!" she yelled. "Thank God our John's out of it. No wonder he joined the bloody army; he probably didn't want to end up like you!"

She didn't get a chance to say any more as he was already on the other side of the door, cursing her under his breath as he went back to join his friends. Rita stepped out of the porch and onto the pavement, taking a moment to compose herself before she returned to the car.

She was thankful she hadn't taken Yansis with her. Although he wasn't one for trouble, she knew that he wouldn't have stood by while her father behaved in such a way. If Yansis had retaliated, the whole thing could have escalated, and it was bad enough as it was. The experience had left her shaken, and she took her cigarettes from her handbag and lit one up with trembling hands.

Rita was standing outside the Brown Cow, taking furious drags on her cigarette and trying to calm herself down, when she felt a prod in her ribs. She spun round, primed for a repeat performance with her father, but was surprised to see a face from the past. It was a young woman called Tracy, who used to be a regular in the same local pubs as Rita, years before.

"Rita Steadman. Bloody hell, I thought it was you! I thought you were gonna do me some damage for a minute. I haven't seen you for years. How are you?"

"Oh, I'm sorry. I've just had a barney with my old man. I thought he'd come back to give me some grief. I'm alright. It's Rita Christos now, actually. How are you?"

They soon fell into conversation, catching up on the years since they had last seen each other, and it helped to take Rita's mind off her current predicament. Rita hadn't been close to Tracy in the past, but she provided a link to an old friend that Rita had lost touch with. That friend was called Debby, and Rita had been thinking about her a lot since she returned to Manchester. She had wanted to visit her, but Debby's family had moved off the estate, and Rita's mum didn't know where they lived.

When Rita had asked her mother about Debby, she told her that, as far as she knew, Debby hadn't moved away with her family. She now had a young family of her own, and a house on the estate, but her mother didn't know any more than that. Unfortunately, Joan didn't know Debby's new address. Rita was therefore pleased to find out Debby's address from Tracy, and it wasn't too far away.

After saying goodbye to Tracy, Rita went back to the car. At least some good had come out of today, she thought, and she was looking forward to visiting her old friend, but she would leave it for another time. She had had enough excitement for one day.

Rita returned to Julie and Vinny's home with Yansis, and recounted her meeting with her father, firstly to Yansis in the car and then again to Julie. She left out some of the facts, not wishing to upset Yansis by letting him know how aggressively her father had behaved towards her.

When she spoke to Julie, she kept the facts brief; she was still feeling troubled by the encounter, and wasn't in the mood to rake over the finer details just yet.

***

Friday 22nd March 1991 – evening

Jenny and Leroy were having a night out in the Brown Cow. It wasn't the nearest pub to their home, but it had been Jenny's local when she lived at her parents' so they still went there sometimes. The landlord was running a disco on Friday evenings, which increased the pub's popularity. The place was packed, and customers were queueing three deep at the bar.

While Leroy was waiting to get served, Jenny scanned the room. She noticed how people regarded her and Leroy warily. Those who were acquaintances became over-friendly, and people who had never bothered with her kept their heads down and whispered amongst themselves. They knew of Leroy's reputation.

Leroy didn't have to wait long before he was served; he never did. That was another advantage of him having such a bad reputation.

"Right, where do you wanna sit?" he asked Jenny.

"There's no seats. You have to come early if you want a seat."

"I said, where do you wanna sit?"

"Oh."

Jenny soon interpreted his meaning, and looked over at the crowd sitting in the corner. She had already seen them when she walked in. Kelly Brady, with her boyfriend and some other mates. Kelly bloody Brady! She'd known her for years, been to the same school as her. But they'd never been friends. She was the ultimate mean girl who'd picked on her at school, and Rita had even had to step in once or twice when things escalated. Nowadays, she left her alone, but Jenny hadn't forgotten what she'd put her through. Kelly bloody Brady.

"I fancy sitting in the corner over there, away from the speakers, but all those seats are taken."

"Not for long, come on. You carry the drinks, and I'll sort the seats."

She tried to keep up with Leroy as he strutted across the pub.

"Which seats d'you fancy?" he asked Jenny, once they reached the table where Kelly Brady was sitting.

Jenny pointed to Kelly Brady and her boyfriend. "Those two."

Despite a slight feeling of apprehension, Jenny took delight in the expression on Kelly's face when she caught sight of over six feet of towering aggression, looming over them. Leroy slapped his hands on the back of Kelly and her boyfriend's chairs.

"These two are taken," he said. "Get your drinks and go."

"Yeah, taken by us," said the boyfriend, laughing to his friends in a desperate show of bravado.

"Not anymore they ain't. My woman's pregnant and wants to sit down. Now have some respect, and fuck off and find somewhere else to sit."

Kelly chipped in. "There's no other seats. Besides, we came here early to get these seats. If you want to sit down, then you should come early like the rest of us."

"Shut it bitch!"

"You what? Andy, are you gonna let him talk to me like that?"

"You're out of order, mate," said Andy. "These are our seats. You can't just walk in and expect us to shift out of 'em."

"Who says?" Leroy leant over to Andy and whispered in his ear. "You ever heard of the Buckthorn Crew? You know what my lads do to guys who disrespect me?"

"Look, I don't want no trouble, mate," said Andy. "We just came for a good night out with our mates."

Jenny watched the look of disgust on Kelly's face, at her boyfriend's lack of courage.

"If you don't want no trouble, then you best do as you're told," said Leroy. "You don't wanna be lookin' over your shoulder every time you leave the house, do you? In fact, even inside your house you're not safe these days. You see that story in the paper the other night? Three masked men with guns raided a house in Salford."

He then held two fingers to his head, in the shape of a gun, and imitated the sound of a gun discharging.

"Nothing to do with me, but there's some bad bastards around these days. You gotta watch who you're dealing with. Now, I ain't making no threats," he stated, to the rest of the group. "I'm just telling you what some people are like, that's all."

"Come on Kelly, let's go," said the boyfriend, who left his seat without finishing his drink, pulling Kelly behind him. Kelly fixed Jenny with a scowl as she passed her, and Jenny responded with a sarcastic grin.

Kelly's group of friends followed her and her boyfriend, eager to get out of the pub as soon as possible.

"Take your pick," Leroy said to Jenny. "You need room to spread out in your condition."

They moved into the corner, taking advantage of the space around them. Leroy dragged one of the stools towards him, and used it to rest his oversized feet on. As she gazed around the pub, noting the reactions of the anxious customers, Jenny felt like royalty.

"Thanks," she said.

"It's alright. They should have got up for you anyway. Scumbags shouldn't expect a pregnant woman to stand up, especially *my* woman. They need to learn respect."

Despite the implication that she was Leroy's possession, Jenny was pleased to be linked to him. Nobody messed with her when she was with Leroy. She felt a fluttering in her stomach; it was the baby moving around. It triggered thoughts of how proud Leroy was about the fact that he was to become a father. He had been delighted when he found out she was pregnant, and was determined that his child would have everything he never had.

Jenny knew that things hadn't always been good for Leroy. He'd told her about it one night after a few drinks, in one of his rare vulnerable moments. He was the oldest child, but he'd never known his father, who had split from his mother even before Leroy was born. For a few years his mother struggled to bring him up alone, occasionally leaving him with relatives while she went for nights out. They'd got along well while there were just the two of them. Then, when he was seven, his mother got married, and had several children to Leroy's stepfather.

Leroy and his stepfather never got on. He resented his stepfather for coming between him and his mother and, as a young child, he failed to hide his feelings. Many stepfathers would have been patient, and built up a relationship. Leroy's stepfather wasn't like that. Instead, he repaid Leroy's resentment with a ferocious venom. Leroy wasn't his child, and he found ways to remind him of that at every opportunity.

Not only did his stepfather leave him out of treats he bestowed on his own children, he blamed him for everything. If one of Leroy's younger siblings tormented him, and he reacted, he was to blame because he was the oldest. As he got older, Leroy lashed out against his stepfather, verbally at first, but when his stepfather punished him physically, Leroy retaliated. He always came off worst against a grown man. When he tried to enlist sympathy from his mother, she told him he had brought it on himself for being disobedient.

Then, when Leroy was 16, his stepfather returned home drunk one night and picked a fight with Leroy, who was a big lad by then. Although his stepfather had the age advantage, he underestimated how much his drunkenness had slowed his reactions. When he swiped Leroy round the head for back-chatting him, Leroy responded with a powerful blow to his stomach, followed by a swift uppercut. While his stepfather was winded and doubled over, Leroy grabbed a breadknife and held it to his throat.

"You ever touch me again, and I swear I'll finish the fuckin' job off," he threatened, as his stepfather stood trembling.

After that night, his stepfather never touched him again, and it was a few weeks later when he packed his bags and left. Leroy swore from that moment onwards that nobody would ever pick on him again. With his stepfather gone, he took on the role of protector for the rest of his family, on an estate where it was vital not to show any signs of weakness.

Chapter 7

Rita and Yansis had arranged to go out with Julie and Vinny on Saturday evening to a few of the pubs in Heaton Moor. Julie's parents were looking after Emily overnight, so the four of them were free to relax, and didn't have to rush back. Rita was glad of the chance to let her hair down, and take her mind off her recent stresses.

Perhaps because of her current frame of mind, Rita was downing drinks at a rapid pace, and before long she was worse for wear. The alcohol loosened her tongue and, as the evening progressed, her troubles came spilling out. It was while Vinny and Yansis were engrossed in a discussion about Vinny's building business that Rita confided in Julie. Up to this point, she had told Julie some of what had been happening, but it wasn't always easy to divulge everything, when Julie was busy looking after a two year old, and taking care of the bookkeeping for her husband's business.

Julie was aware of what had happened in the Buckthorn Inn in Moss Side, and she also knew about Rita's conversation with her sister. At this point, though, Rita hadn't told Julie about her row with her father the previous day. As much as she loved Yansis, she didn't always find it easy to open up to him the same way as she could with Julie. For one thing, it would set him against her father if he knew fully how Ged had treated her. For another thing, he didn't understand her family like Julie did. Rita and Julie had lived near each other since they were children, so Julie was familiar with Rita's upbringing, and knew about many of the things Rita had put up with as a child.

"I'm really worried about our Jenny, you know, Jules. That's why I went to see my dad yesterday."

"Do you want to tell me what happened, Rita? You still haven't told me everything, have you?"

"That's because he was a right nasty old bastard," she whispered. "Wait till the lads go to the bar, and I'll tell you."

This gave Rita reason to down her drink even quicker and, when Yansis saw her empty glass, he took the hint and went to the bar with Vinny. While they were gone, she told Julie all about her run-in with her father, adding, "I've tried telling my dad she's in danger, but I'm wasting my breath. He's enjoying lording it over his mates in the pub too much. Since Leroy came on the scene, he's been acting like he's bleedin' Al Capone, and my mam just agrees with everything he says. Honestly, you'd think it was still the dark ages, the way she lets him rule the roost. She could do with standing up to him once in a while."

Once she had started, there was no stopping her. As well as wanting to offload herself, she also wanted to analyse the facts, desperately trying to draw conclusions, "My dad's not as daft as he makes out, you know. All this time he's been making out that he's taken in by Leroy, and just wants to bask in the reflected glory, when really it's all about protecting himself. He knows how dangerous Leroy is, so he doesn't want to do anything to upset him. That's why he makes out that he likes being a part of it all. What really pisses me off, though, is that he doesn't mind seeing Jenny in danger, as long as he doesn't stick his own neck out. If that cowardly old get won't do anything about Leroy, then it looks like I'll have to do it."

"What can you do, though, if Jenny refuses to break away from Leroy?" asked Julie.

"I don't know, I'll think of something. I've got to get Jenny away from him somehow. My granddad would be turning in his grave now if he knew what a shithouse my dad had turned out to be."

By the time Yansis and Vinny returned from the bar, Rita was reminiscing about the good times she had spent with her grandparents. They were her father's parents who had looked after Rita and her brother and sister for much of their childhood, while her mother and father had spent most of their evenings in the pub. It was through her grandparents that Rita had gained her strong moral fibre, and because of this she had come to disrespect her father as she had grown into adulthood. Throughout most of his adult life, he had shunned work in favour of spending his time between the pub and the bookies, and he financed these occupations through a series of dodgy deals.

Once she had finished reminiscing, Rita made light work of her next drink before returning to the subject of her concerns over Jenny, recapping on her visit to the Moss Side pub. "What worried me, Julie, was the way the girl in the Buckthorn Inn said, 'when Leroy is finished with her', because it wasn't said as though she was referring to finishing a relationship, but as though it meant when she had served her purpose. I've been wracking my brains trying to think what he wants her for ..."

"Are you sure you're not overreacting, Rita? She probably just meant finished with her, as in, when he's had enough of her. Maybe he's a bit of a womaniser."

"No, no, you're not listening to me, Julie." Rita's voice had risen, the force of the alcohol taking over, and Yansis and Vinny had now halted their conversation to listen to her. "Remember what we said about him coming to Longsight to escape from someone or something in Moss Side?" Before anyone could answer, she continued. "Well that might be why he's moved in with Jenny."

"Yeah, but why now? He's been living in Longsight for a year," said Vinny.

"I don't know. Maybe they found out where his mam lives, or his mam got wise to what he's up to, and doesn't like him having drugs in the house. Maybe he thinks he can get away with more at Jenny's than he can at his mam's. After all, they're supposed to be living together, so maybe he thinks it's his own house, even though, from what my mam told me, the house is in Jenny's name. Now why would that be? So it's harder to trace him?"

"I suppose you have got a point," said Julie. "She would get a council house more quickly as a pregnant woman on her own, as well."

"And another thing," Rita added. "Our Jenny might have refused to believe what the girls told me about the scar on his ex-girlfriend's face, but you should have seen the look on her face. She was shitting herself!

That can only mean one thing; if she was that frightened, then she must think Leroy is capable of doing something like that."

This last line was a conversation stopper, which changed the atmosphere between them. After a few seconds of uncomfortable silence, Vinny offered to go to the bar again, and Yansis accompanied him, leaving Julie with Rita.

"Let's change the subject Reet. I think we've scared the lads off. How are things in Greece? Are you still getting on well with Yansis's parents?"

"Oh yeah," Rita replied. "I couldn't wish for better in-laws, but I just wish they'd stop going on about grandkids all the time. It hasn't half put some pressure on me and Yansis."

"It can't be easy for you. They're big on family aren't they, the Greeks?"

"Don't I know it?"

By the end of the night, Rita had drank so much that she was making little sense, and she had scant recollection of getting back to Julie's. When she got in bed, the room was spinning so much that she was thankful when sleep took over.

***

Sunday 24th March 1991 - morning

Rita woke up on Sunday morning with an urgent need to get to the bathroom. She couldn't remember how much she had drunk the previous evening, but she was paying the price for it now. For most of the day she was ill, and spent the time either lying in bed, willing her banging headache to go away, or rushing to the bathroom to empty the contents of her stomach. It was three o'clock in the afternoon before she felt well enough to go downstairs; even then, she couldn't face anything more than a cup of coffee.

She had intended to visit Debby that day and, when she went

downstairs, Julie reminded her of her plans. Apparently, she had told Julie about her encounter with Tracy in the Brown Cow on Friday, and how she was planning to visit her old friend. Julie hadn't been as close to Debby as Rita, so she had decided not to accompany her.

The way Rita was feeling, she knew that any trip outside was out of the question for the rest of the day. She therefore decided to put it off until Monday. Rita learnt from Yansis that he had offered to do some labouring for Vinny the following week, which she thought was a good idea. Part of his wages would be in lieu of rent, which eased her conscience, and made her and Yansis feel as though they weren't putting on Julie and Vinny so much.

Because Yansis would be at work the following day, and Rita didn't drive, she caught the bus to Debby's house. It wasn't too much bother as Julie lived within walking distance of the A6, which ran through the Riverhill Estate, on the way to the centre of Manchester. That meant Rita could be there in no time.

Chapter 8

Rita scarcely recognised the woman that answered the door. Debby had always been a big girl in a voluptuous, bubbly way. But she must have lost at least two stone, maybe three, since Rita last saw her. Her drab clothes hung on her like discarded rags, her lank and untidy hair dangling in clumps around her shoulders. Rita spotted the remains of a black eye on a face that was pale and drawn. "Ouch, that looks painful," she commented, after they had gone through the preliminaries.

"Yeah, bloody kids with their toys all over the place. I tripped on one, and banged it on the banister."

It was an unconvincing lie. The kids she referred to, clung to Debby, two of them, cautiously surveying Rita. Although both of them looked under four years of age, signs of desperation were already painted on their grubby little faces.

"Sod off and go and play, will yer?" admonished Debby and they scarpered.

Debby led Rita through to the living room. The place was filthy, the smell putrid. Rita moved some dirty clothing to one side so she could sit on the grimy sofa. As soon as she sat down, a mangy cat parked itself on her knee, and she pushed it away saying, "Sorry, I don't do animals." She immediately began to itch.

Rita and Debby made small talk, and Rita soon established that Debby was married to one of the lads off the estate. They had wed after Debby had given birth to her first child, and then another child had followed in quick succession. Because Debby's husband was local, Rita thought she might know him.

"What's his name?" she asked.

"Carl Carter."

"Carl Carter?" Rita couldn't place it at first, and she kept running the name over in her mind until an image emerged. "Oh God yeah, I remember him; thin lad, brown hair. Didn't he used to hang around with Dave Sutton?"

"That's right," Debby replied.

Rita didn't add anything else to her recollections of Carl Carter. Some thoughts are best kept to yourself.

"Actually, he works with your Jenny's fella, Leroy," added Debby.

With what she remembered about Carl Carter as a teenager, that didn't surprise Rita, and she replied on impulse, "Oh yeah, got him selling knock-off as well as my dad, has he?"

A wry smile spread across Debby's face, "Yeah knock-off, that's right; gets us some good stuff. He gets loads of good fakes as well."

Her rapid admission to the stolen and counterfeit goods, led Rita to believe he was perhaps selling more than that, but she didn't comment. They chatted a little more, but the conversation was stilted. Apart from reminiscing about the past, they no longer had much in common.

During the time she was there, it seemed to Rita that Debby was becoming increasingly edgy. Eventually she got up and went to the toilet. She was gone a good ten minutes and, while she was away, the children crept towards Rita, hiding behind each other and giggling nervously. Rita's heart went out to them. Poor little things, forced to live in this squalor.

Rita was desperate for the toilet herself so, when Debby returned, she announced, "Right, I'll just nip to the loo too, and then I'm off."

She wished she hadn't been so desperate, as the bathroom was in as bad a state as she had anticipated. It was while she was hovering, trying to avoid contact with the soiled and stained toilet seat, that she spotted it. '*Oh no!*' she thought. '*Not Debby, not with them little 'uns in the house.*'

She finished in the bathroom, made her excuses and left, but not before she had delivered her parting shot. "By the way, Debby, you wanna make sure you leave your *knock-off* where little hands can't get hold of it."

Rita was relieved to breathe in the city air after the malodorous filth inside Debby's house, and the walk to the bus stop helped to clear the smell from her nostrils. However, when she reached Julie's house, she still felt as though the stench clung onto her clothing, so she stripped down to her underwear, threw her clothes in the washer and found something else to wear.

"Jesus, that was an experience!" she said to Julie. "You wouldn't believe how she's changed. The place was a tip, and it stank something rotten."

"Really?"

"Yeah, and you'll never guess what I found in the bathroom."

"Go on."

"Well, I'm hovering over this bloody manky loo, trying not to touch the seat, when I saw what looked like a syringe poking out of the top of the wash basket. I know ... I shouldn't have looked, but I was curious. It wasn't just because of what it looked like. She'd been acting strange while I'd been talking to her, all edgy, as though she just couldn't settle. So I went over to the basket when I'd finished, pulled the lid up, and I couldn't believe my bleedin' eyes! It was a syringe alright, sticking out of a supermarket carrier bag. There was a load of other stuff in the bag as well; some brown powder in a little polythene bag, a spoon, a cigarette lighter and some other things. It was like a bloody drugs factory!"

"Oh my God! Did you say anything?"

"Only in a roundabout way. I was too shocked to come straight out with it, but I think the other reason I didn't confront her was because of the connection."

"What do you mean?

"Her husband only works with Leroy, doesn't he? It got me worried. I don't know what the bleedin' hell to do, Julie. I think that's what made me suspicious, as well. She admitted that Leroy's got him selling dodgy goods, but it felt like she was laughing as me, as though she knew there was more to it."

"I can't believe it, Rita. She must be stupid, especially after what happened to Amanda."

"I know, and she's got two little kids there. They could easily have got hold of those drugs where she left them. I warned her about that on the way out, but not in so many words. I just hope she doesn't make a habit of leaving them where the kiddies can get at them; maybe she was rushing about because I was there."

Amanda had been a friend of Julie's, who had died of a drink and drugs overdose several years earlier. The experience had been particularly traumatic for the girls as her death had followed a night out with them, and Julie and Rita had been accused of her murder. As a result, they had been through a damaging period, especially Julie who had been close to Amanda.

Another thought occurred to Rita. "You'll never guess who Debby married."

"Who?"

"Carl bloody Carter. Do you remember him? A right sly little bastard, skinny, pasty looking, brown hair, a typical bully's sidekick. No wonder she's on drugs, if she's married to him, and he's working for Leroy."

"Yeah, he was always up to no good. Christ, Rita, it just gets worse, doesn't it? What are you going to do?"

"I haven't got a clue."

***

Wednesday 27th March 1991 - morning

Debby felt dreadful. She'd been awake most of the night, suffering from the chills and cold sweats. When she had nodded off, she had been woken again by stomach cramps and an urgent need to run to the toilet. The diarrhoea had persisted for several hours, along with muscular aches and pains. Now she felt exhausted and her craving was intensifying, bringing with it feelings of extreme anxiety and panic.

This was her punishment for standing up to Carl last time they'd had a row. She hadn't had a fix since Tuesday morning; he'd refused to give her any heroin from yesterday afternoon onwards, even though she'd begged him for half the night. His response had been to make her sleep on the sofa so she wouldn't keep him awake. This morning he still wouldn't let her have anything, and now he was out.

She'd scoured the house from top to bottom, but she couldn't find where he'd hidden the drugs. Maybe he'd taken them with him out of spite. The only thing she'd found was some cannabis, which had helped the anxiety a little, but not near enough. And it had done nothing to alleviate the other symptoms.

The children were becoming distressed because her behaviour confused them. When she lay on the sofa wailing, they wept too, without understanding what they were weeping about.

In her desperate state, she contemplated going to Jenny's to see if Leroy was there. Maybe he would help her, but then she dismissed the notion. He wouldn't be happy about her bringing business to his home. And it wasn't a good idea to upset Leroy. She didn't know if Jenny was even aware of him dealing drugs.

Oh God! What else could she do? She didn't even know where Carl got his supplies from. He wouldn't tell her. Maybe she should go to the Moss, see if she could buy some herself. But she didn't have much money. And she didn't have a clue who to go to. What could she sell? What did she have that was worth anything? Where could she sell it anyway? Damn! Damn! Damn!

She thought about her mother. Maybe she could drop the kids off with her, and see if she would lend her some money. But how could she go looking like this? What could she tell her? Her mother would know she was in a state, and she didn't want her to find out she was on drugs. It would kill her! She would hang on, just a bit longer. Perhaps she could manage for a short while. But if Carl wasn't back soon, she didn't know how she would cope.

***

Heather Burnside

Rita had gone up to bed. Her intention had been to read a few pages of her latest novel then go to sleep, but Yansis had other plans. She had been avoiding Yansis's amorous advances all week. Since her confrontation with her father on the previous Friday, lovemaking had been the last thing on her mind. The visit to Debby hadn't helped either. Rita had spent most of the week thinking about the situation; the danger her sister might be in, Debby's lifestyle, the threat to Debby's children, and her own father's involvement with Leroy. And the more she thought about everything that was happening around her, the more stressed she was becoming.

The problems with Rita's family were taking over her life to such an extent, she had almost forgotten why they had come back to Manchester in the first place. Yansis hadn't forgotten though. While Yansis wanted to concentrate on their problems, Rita wanted to thrash over the same ground that she had already covered tirelessly.

"Who'd have thought Debby would have ended up a junkie? Honestly, she was always a bit dizzy, but I never thought she'd have been that stupid. Mind you, I shouldn't be surprised, judging by the low-life she's married to."

It was rare for Yansis to lose his temper, but now he raised his voice to grab her attention and put a stop to her fretting.

"Rita, Rita, you need to stop this! You need to be happy, I want to make you happy. Come to me; for tonight, let us just think about us. I know you have problems, but just for one night I don't want to hear any more. You will make yourself ill, and I want you to relax."

His unusual outburst stunned Rita into silence. She turned and looked at him, his dark, chiselled features scrunched up in a mask of fury, and felt a pang of guilt. Her reaction calmed him, and his voice softened as he spoke to her. "Tonight you are mine, Rita; no Jenny, no Leroy, no Debby, just you and me."

His use of the English language had always endeared her. Even when he was exasperated with her, he still spoke in full sentences. After more than five years together, he hadn't adopted much of her Mancunian slang, and his accent was more appealing than ever. He moved over to where Rita was sitting on the edge of the bed, until he was crouching behind her. With practiced skill, he massaged her shoulders and the back of her neck, kneading the tight knots that had formed.

"Take off your top and lie down on your front," he instructed.

Rita wasn't the type to be dominated, but she could feel her tense muscles relaxing under Yansis's ministrations, and was enjoying the release. She followed his instructions, then waited as she felt him climb on top and straddle her from behind. He undid the fastening on her bra and let it drop to her sides, then took her arms and placed them above her head. She felt herself shiver as the cool air caressed her skin while Yansis made her wait for a few seconds, the anticipation heightening her desire.

Then he worked on her back, pummelling the muscles, ridding them of tension, and giving her the same release she had felt with her shoulder and neck muscles. When she was feeling more relaxed, the pummelling turned to soft caresses, as his hands skimmed down her sides and reached under her torso, feeling for the button and zipper on her jeans. He undid them and slipped them and her briefs slowly down while planting tiny kisses along the backs of her thighs.

Just when she wasn't expecting it, he flipped her over and began caressing the front of her body; touching, kissing, feeling, licking. Within no time she was overcome by sensation, and all thoughts of her troubles were temporarily pushed aside. She returned his caresses, lost in the moment. By the time he entered her, she was ready and he soon sent her body into spasms, making her gasp with pleasure and call out his name.

When it was over she curled up next to him, her head on his chest. After a few minutes, she was asleep, more relaxed than she had been all week. Unfortunately, it didn't last long. At four in the morning, she woke up to go to the bathroom. Once she was awake, she was again plagued by troubling thoughts, and found it impossible to get back to sleep. Like many nights since she had returned to Manchester, she lay by Yansis's side and worried.

Chapter 9

Rita was visiting her sister again. Yansis was out working with Vinny, and she was getting restless at Julie's, so she left the house and jumped on the 192 bus. She went to see her mother first, then caught a taxi to take her the short journey to her sister's home.

When Rita arrived, Jenny had company. She had noticed a red Audi parked outside, but didn't realise it was connected with her sister.

"This is Winston," said Jenny, indicating a young, good looking black guy sitting on the sofa. "This is my sister, Rita."

"Hi, alright?" enquired Winston. "Actually, I was just going," he added, standing up.

"Oh, don't go on my account," said Rita.

"No, honest, I was going anyway. I've got some business I need to take care of, but it was nice meeting you, anyway."

He rushed from the room, nodding repeatedly as he passed Rita, and she replied, "It was nice meeting you too, Winston. Maybe another time?"

He let himself out of the door and was gone within seconds.

"Who's that?" asked Rita. "He looked like a nervous wreck."

"Oh, he's alright, Winston. He's probably just worried because he's late."

"Late for what?"

"He's meeting Leroy … He works for him, OK? Selling goods! He's a bit late because he's been helping me sort the house out, and we didn't realise what time it was."

Rita's involuntary response was *'Jesus, not another one selling God knows what!'* but she didn't voice her thoughts. She was also tempted to ask why Winston was helping her with the house, instead of Leroy, but she held her tongue. She didn't want to turn this into an interrogation.

It was important to keep on good terms with Jenny if she was to maintain her confidence. That way, she might stand a better chance of getting her away from Leroy when the time was right. How she would do that, she wasn't sure, but she knew that falling out with Jenny wouldn't help.

Instead, she said, "It looks as though he's been doing a good job."

"Yeah, we're getting there," said Jenny.

Looking around the living room, Rita could see that things had moved on a great deal since she visited a week and a half ago. The room and hallway were now carpeted, and there were no longer any boxes scattered about. All the living room furniture was in place; there were ornaments on display, and pictures on the walls.

"Did you manage to empty all the boxes upstairs as well?"

"Yes, every single one of them. Winston's been a godsend."

"Great, it's looking really good." Rita couldn't resist adding, "I would have helped you move in if you'd have asked, you know. Just because I'm not keen on your choice of boyfriend, doesn't mean I'm not there for you."

"I know, but not to worry; it's all done now."

As the conversation dwindled, Jenny took the usual measure of putting the kettle on. Once Rita was alone, she heard a noise coming from the back garden and went to the window to find out what was causing it. On spotting her, a pit bull terrier bounded across the garden, barking ferociously. It launched itself at the window, stretched upright on its hind legs, and began growling at Rita, who leapt back in alarm.

She had come face to face with the dog, and been close enough to see the madness in its eyes. Even now, it was still leaping at the window, frantically trying to get at her.

"Jesus Christ, where the hell did that come from?" she asked.

On hearing the commotion, Jenny dashed back into the room.

"Down, Tyson!" she shouted, and after a few seconds, the dog's growls diminished. "It's Leroy's," she continued. "He used to keep it at his mam's, but now he's brought it here with him. Don't worry, it's trained; it's just not used to you, that's all."

A Gangster's Grip

"You didn't tell me he had a dog! How come it wasn't here last time?"

"He takes it out with him a lot. Don't worry, I know how you feel about dogs. I'll make sure I put him out the back when I know you're coming round."

There weren't many things that frightened Rita, but dogs always unnerved her, especially aggressive looking ones. She was relieved that it was on the other side of the window but, nevertheless, it took several minutes until her heart rate returned to normal.

"Doesn't it bother you?"

"No, it knows me. I used to see it when he lived at his mam's. You just have to make sure it doesn't know you're scared, otherwise you've had it."

"Well thanks for that, Jenny. If it ever comes indoors, I just hope it won't be able to hear my bleedin' heart going nineteen to the dozen, or see my knees knockin'."

When they were settled with a drink each, Rita broached the subject of her recent visit to her friend Debby's. She was careful to be matter of fact; just two sisters sharing a bit of gossip and scandal. Jenny was aware of Debby's unkempt appearance, having seen her around the estate, but she appeared shocked that she had been taking drugs. Thankfully, Jenny seemed as outraged as Rita on hearing that Debby had left drugs within easy reach of the children. '*Good*' thought Rita, '*at least that's a good sign that Jenny isn't taking them too.*'

Rita moved onto Debby's choice of husband but, although Jenny knew who he was, she couldn't remember him from years ago.

"Yes, he was always a cocky little shit," said Rita.

"Really?" asked Jenny. "He seems alright."

"Oh, do you know him then?"

"Yeah, through Leroy."

"Oh, of course. Debby mentioned that he works for Leroy. Bloody hell, Jenny, he's doing alright your Leroy, isn't he, with all these men working for him?"

Rita was playing out that old adage of 'flattery gets you everywhere' and, as the conversation was in full flow, she took the opportunity to find out as much as she could about Leroy. She was careful not to be too pushy but, instead, tried to make it sound as though she had a genuine interest in Leroy's business. It was difficult feigning curiosity bordering on admiration for someone who dealt in stolen goods and drugs, focusing on the former and deliberately omitting to mention the latter.

Her act paid off; by the time she left Jenny's, she had established that Leroy obtained his goods from Cheetham Hill where he made regular visits, as well as his visits to Moss Side. Rita surmised that these must therefore be the places where he both bought and sold drugs.

Rita lost track of time. She hadn't set off from Julie's until two o'clock in the afternoon, and she was surprised to find it was soon a quarter to five. Once she realised how late it was, she left Jenny's, knowing she would already have hit the rush hour traffic. While she walked to the bus stop, she mulled things over in her mind, thinking about the connection with Winston. And as for that dog! One thought that hadn't occurred to her until now was how Jenny expected to bring up a baby with a dog like that prowling around. It was all too much to take in.

As soon as Rita reached Stockport Road and noticed the traffic crawling along, she knew that the journey back would be slow. Although she didn't wait long for a bus, when it did arrive it was full, and she had to stand for most of the way. Because of the heavy traffic, the journey was stop, start, and she was thrown about the bus, finding it difficult to keep her balance in her high heels.

Her hands gripped the metal rails, as she tried to avoid eye contact with the other passengers, and tried her best not bump into them. Neither of these was easy to accomplish, as the passengers were tightly packed together, and there was nowhere-else to look because the windows were steamed up. The constant jerking motion, combined with a lack of fresh air, were making her feel nauseous, and the screeching of an overtired toddler wasn't helping matters. This was one experience she hadn't missed during the years she had spent in Greece, and she was thankful when she reached her destination.

"Bloody hell, Rita, we'd given you up for dead," said Julie, when she walked through the door.

"That's just how I feel after that bus journey."

Noticing how pale Rita looked, Julie beckoned her to sit down, and gave her a few minutes to recover before she served their evening meal. Vinny and Yansis were already home and, once Rita was feeling a little better, Yansis embraced her and asked her about her day. Rita knew that he probably felt guilty for being short with her the previous evening, but she didn't blame him in a way. She had been consumed with her anxieties over her family since they'd returned to Manchester. Nevertheless, things needed discussing, and she knew there was no way she could keep it inside. She was anxious to share the latest revelations with them all, so during the meal she opened up.

"I've been to see my mam and our Jenny again. There's not much to tell about my mam. Same old, same old, but at least my dad wasn't home when I went round, so that's one good thing. I found out a few things when I went to Jenny's though."

The rest of them listened in eager anticipation.

"There was a lad there when I arrived, called Winston, about Jenny's age. He didn't seem a bad lad, polite, not ignorant or aggressive like Leroy, but nervous as hell. In fact, Jenny was a bit shifty when I first got there too. Apparently he works for Leroy too, selling goods, according to Jenny, but I think we all know what goods means by now. Anyway, he couldn't get out of the house quick enough. She said he had to meet Leroy, and he was late. I reckon he must be frightened to death of him, judging by the rush he was in."

"You don't think Jenny had been taking drugs with him, do you?" asked Julie.

"No, I don't think she's on drugs."

Vinny raised his eyebrows, sceptically.

"Don't get me wrong, I'm not being naïve. It was her reaction when I told her about Debby. She was just as outraged as I was at what I found in Debby's laundry basket, especially with her having two little kids in the house. No, apparently Winston had been helping her sort the house out. It looked a lot better too. It's really come on since me and Yansis were there, although why Leroy has got this lad, Winston, sorting out the house, instead of doing it himself, is beyond me."

"I think it's about control," said Vinny.

"Yes, he likes everyone at his beck and call, all doing his dirty work for him," agreed Julie. "He's got your dad selling the dodgy goods, and probably this Winston and Carl selling drugs. That's as far as we know; there could be others."

"Yeah, and don't forget about his younger brothers," added Vinny. "They might be part of the Buckthorns too."

"I'm not sure, maybe they're a bit young yet, but you never know … Jesus, just what the hell has our Jenny got herself into?"

Yansis remained silent, but he reached out and put his arm around Rita's shoulder, in response to the anguish that was evident in her voice.

After they had eaten, Yansis asked if they would like to go out for a drink. Julie and Vinny couldn't go because they had to look after Emily, but Rita guessed that Yansis's intention was for them to spend time alone together.

On this occasion she tried not to have too much to drink, although a few drinks at a steady pace helped her to relax. It was a joy to talk about her life in Greece. So much had taken place since she'd returned to Manchester, just under three weeks ago, that she'd almost forgotten their stay was temporary. While they talked about Yansis's family, their friends, the restaurant and the characters that dined there, she could virtually imagine herself back in Greece. It was a good feeling, and it made her yearn for the day when she could return.

It wasn't that she didn't like Manchester. She loved seeing her mother and Jenny, and Julie and Vinny were great company, but she could do without all the hassle that seemed to surround her family.

By the time they returned from the pub, Julie and Vinny had gone to bed, and Yansis was getting frisky. Not wishing to be caught in a compromising position, downstairs, Rita suggested that they go upstairs. While Yansis went to the bathroom, she got ready for bed.

Despite the lovely evening she had just spent with Yansis, he was becoming insatiable, and after her recent stresses, she felt too tired to spend yet another night of passion. In the few minutes that it took to carry out his ablutions, Rita had slipped between the sheets and was feigning sleep.

Chapter 10

It was Easter Sunday, and Rita and Julie were in the kitchen, putting the finishing touches to the roast dinner that Rita had started earlier while Julie had been out visiting her parents. The tantalising aroma of roast chicken and vegetables drifted through the house.

"It's good of Yansis to keep an eye on Emily while Vinny sorts the car out," said Julie.

"Oh give over, it's no problem; try stopping him. What's wrong with the car anyway?"

"Something and nothing. He just said the anti-freeze and water wanted changing, and you know Vinny, he doesn't hang about if something wants doing."

"Did Emily have a good time at your mam and dad's?" asked Rita.

"Oh yeah, she was spoilt rotten. Have you seen how many eggs she's got? She'll be eating them till Christmas. I don't know if she'll manage any dinner because she ate a load of junk at my mam's, but at least she had a sleep in the car on the way back so she won't be cranky."

Julie went to the safety gate separating the kitchen from the living room, and had a quick look to make sure Emily was alright. Whispering to Rita, she beckoned her over. From the doorway, they could see Yansis crouched on the floor playing with Emily, and trying to engage her in the various functions of her activity toy. He seemed to be engrossed in moving handles, tooting horns and turning dials that made clicking noises. They moved away from the gate, smiling as they went.

"I don't know who's enjoying that more; Yansis or Emily," laughed Rita.

"One thing's for sure, he'll miss her when you go back to Greece."

"Him and me too; she's such a little darling and she's inherited her mam's good looks. I wonder if she'll grow up to be a leggy blonde too."

"Give over, you're not so bad yourself, Rita."

"Well, I'm not exactly model material but I managed to cop for Yansis, so that's good enough for me." She then lowered her voice so she couldn't be overheard from the living room, before continuing. "Mind you, he's driving me mad at the moment. He's bloody sex mad. I mean, he always had a good appetite, if you know what I mean, but lately he's insatiable."

"I've never heard you complain before," Julie laughed.

"Yeah but even I have my limits, Julie. Bloody hell, enough's enough!"

Maybe he'll calm down when you've got things sorted out. You'll know where you're up to then. I don't suppose you've heard anything further from the hospital, have you?"

"No, it's early days yet, but I'll let you know as soon as we do. Anyway, it's not just that; I'm that mithered with everything else that sometimes I just want to be left alone."

"I can understand that. All this business with Jenny and your dad is really stressing you out, isn't it? You could do with a break from it all. A few days away would do you the world of good."

"Yeah, I wish I could just nip back over to Greece but it's not that easy, is it?"

"No, but you could go somewhere local, maybe Blackpool or the Lakes. You probably wouldn't have got fixed up this weekend, with it being Easter, but next weekend shouldn't be too bad at this time of year. Why don't you have a ring around, see if there are any guest houses that can put you up for a few days?"

"Do you know, Julie, that's not a bad idea? I quite fancy Blackpool. Yansis has never been, so it should be fun, and there's always something to do there, even if it's raining. I'll have a word with him while we're having dinner."

Rita continued to stir the gravy while Julie spooned vegetables onto the plates.

"Ooh, I forgot to tell you," said Rita. "Jenny told me that Leroy gets his dodgy gear from Cheetham Hill, so I'm guessing he might get drugs there too. She said he goes there quite a bit, as well as Moss Side."

"I didn't think Cheetham Hill was known for drugs but Moss Side is. It's known for cheap goods though, and I bet a lot of them are knock-off or counterfeit."

"Yeah, that's what I thought; still, it's another piece of the jigsaw, isn't it?"

"I suppose so, but don't you be bloody dragging Yansis off to Cheetham Hill. You know what happened when you went to Moss Side. Don't get me wrong, I'm not having a go about the car. I was more concerned about you and Yansis. You could have got in a lot of bother with those teenagers."

"I know. Don't worry, I won't. I'm just biding my time, Julie, and treading carefully where Jenny's concerned. She'll come to her senses in good time. Leroy's bound to slip up, then she'll see him for what he is. And when she does, I'll be there for her."

***

Easter Sunday 31st March 1991 - afternoon

Ged and Joan were having a great time. The Brown Cow had taken a bulk delivery of meat at a bargain price a couple of weeks before, no questions asked, and the landlord had latched onto the idea of providing a roast dinner on Easter Sunday. Although the pub had cooking facilities and frozen food storage, the current licensees didn't normally provide cooked meals, just the occasional buffet for special occasions. However, this opportunity was too good to miss.

Within a few days, there were posters in the windows advertising Easter Sunday roast dinner at £3.99 a head. As the meat had been such a bargain price, and the vegetables were also cheap, the landlord knew that he would still have a healthy profit margin. The only snag had been having to get up at a ridiculous hour to buy his vegetables from

A Gangster's Grip

Smithfield Market.

The place was heaving. Word had spread about the bargain Sunday dinner, and it seemed as though half the estate had flocked to the pub. Many had also brought their children. With an eye for a bargain, lots of the mothers were sharing a meal amongst two or three of their smaller offspring.

Anticipating a good day of trade, Ged had arrived early, taking Joan with him. Between the two of them, they had managed a few carrier bags stuffed with video tapes and CDs. He had brought an assorted collection to the pub. It wasn't all of his stock, but it was as much as they could carry. He was thankful that they had included a number of children's videos in the selection, because the combination of pester power, drunken parents and Easter goodwill was doing wonders for his takings.

"Easter specials. Come and get your videos, £3.99 each or three for a tenner," Ged announced, as he worked his way through the crowds. Each time he saw a family with young children, he stopped to hold out the cases, watching the children's eager little faces light up as they studied the bright animations on the covers. He selected the princess ones for the girls, and others to suit the boys. His eyes would then flit to the parents, gauging their reactions as the children tugged at their sleeves and begged for these colourful Easter treats.

Because he was acquainted with many of the clientele in the Brown Cow, he knew who was good for a few pounds and who was a waste of time. He also knew those who preferred to keep their money for their own pleasures. Some of them wouldn't normally bother wasting good drinking money on their kids, but under public scrutiny, with the kids begging and pleading, they might just part with a tenner to save face.

As a result of arriving early, Joan had a seat at a good table with two of her friends. By taking turns going to the bar and the ladies, they had held onto their seats, despite the number of people that were standing up in the pub. Because of Ged's recent change in fortunes, Joan now drank brandy and coke instead of the lager and lime she used to drink, and she had even stood a few rounds for one of her friends, Big Bertha, who wasn't so well off. She was enjoying a chat and a laugh with her friends when Ged rushed over.

"Joan, I'm running out. You'll have to bring some more. Get some of the kids' ones; they're selling like hot cakes."

"Why me? I'm having a good time with my mates."

"Because I've still got some left to sell. I need you to bring me some more before I run out. I don't want to miss any selling time, do I? This is one of the best days I've had for ages."

He stooped down and took a long swig of her brandy and coke. Then he waited for her response, knowing she wouldn't say no. She wouldn't dare; he held the purse strings and she knew it.

"Come on love, I'll make it worth your while. Eh ..." he winked, "It'll be BCR for you tonight."

"Ooh," teased her friends, who then added a number of lewd comments, speculating on what the letters represented.

Joan stood up, staggering as she reached for her handbag. "Piss off," she giggled to her friends. "It's not what you think ... beef, curry and rice, that's what it stands for. The chippy will be shut anyway. It's Easter Sunday." She then tottered unsteadily towards the exit.

The landlord, who had been collecting glasses, walked over to them to find out what all the commotion was about. Spotting a carrier bag full of Ged's dodgy goods, he picked out a video tape and asked, "What's going on here then?"

"No harm mate, just trying to make a couple of quid," said Ged.

"You and me had better have a word," the landlord replied, leading Ged towards the vault.

Ged's heart sank. He couldn't understand this change of attitude. People had been selling stuff in this pub for years, and the landlord had always turned a blind eye. Ged wondered what could have happened; maybe the police were getting keener.

They entered the vault, which was quieter than the main room, and strode over to an empty corner where they wouldn't be overheard.

"Try to be a bit more discreet, will you?" whispered the landlord. "I've heard the coppers have been round a few pubs in the area, and the last thing I need is to lose my bleedin' licence." He then relaxed his manner as he asked, "How many you sold anyway?"

Ged couldn't resist bragging, "Loads, trade's been going really well. It was a great idea to put on some grub."

"Right, well as you've done so well out of it, I'll take a cut. Call it £30, and if the coppers do happen to come knocking, I know nowt about it, OK?"

Ged now understood the reason for the landlord's attitude. It was just a show so that customers would think he had reprimanded him. That would make it easier for the landlord to deny any involvement if the police investigated. Ged was a bit put out, but there was nothing he could do. Besides, considering how much he was expecting to make today, £30 wasn't too bad. As long as he could keep selling as fast, he should still do alright.

He was pleased to see Joan return, until he saw how few video tapes she had brought, and she hadn't brought any CDs. Ged was annoyed with her. The trouble was, she was too bloody drunk to think straight, and he was selling the goods so fast that he ordered her to go back again. Although Ged normally dominated Joan, the drink was making her difficult and he could tell she wasn't happy.

Ged was concerned, not on Joan's account, but because she couldn't bring fresh stock back quickly enough to replace the video tapes and CDs he had sold. Priding himself on his quick thinking, he offered her hard-up friend, Big Bertha, £10 to go back to the house with Joan while the other friend kept their seats for them.

Living up to her nickname, Big Bertha was five foot nine and well-built, and Ged figured that she should be able to carry a few bagfuls. She could also handle her drink better than Joan, so she would hopefully take control and make sure Joan got back with a decent amount of stock. He'd pay her once she returned to the pub, to give her a good incentive to return quickly.

His quick thinking paid off. After another trip, Ged had plenty of goods to sell, and Joan and her friends went back to having a good time. The adults in the pub got roaring drunk and had a sing-song; the kids got a good feed, and Ged and the landlord turned a healthy profit. Everybody was happy. In fact, as Ged commented to Joan on the way home later, it was the best Easter Sunday they had spent in the Brown Cow for years.

Chapter 11

Friday 5th April 1991 - evening

It was early Friday evening, and Julie and Vinny were standing in their doorway, waving off Rita and Yansis who were setting off for Blackpool. Vinny held Emily in his arms as she joined in the waving. After ringing round a few guest houses, Rita had found one that had a double room available for three nights, so they had booked in till Monday morning.

Once the car had fled up the street, and Rita and Yansis were no longer there, Emily's smile was replaced by a look of confusion, which was soon followed by tears. As Julie tried to comfort her, she couldn't help thinking what it would feel like when Rita and Yansis eventually returned to Greece. She had grown used to having them around during the last few weeks, and was enjoying their company, despite the problems that had accompanied Rita.

"God, it's going to be quiet this weekend without them two."

"You can say that again," said Vinny.

Rita hadn't always been Vinny's favourite person. At one time he had found her flirtatiousness and brash manner too much to handle. On occasion, he and Julie had had disagreements about her. However, she had mellowed over the years, and Julie was thankful that he could now appreciate what a loyal and true friend she had been. She felt sure that Yansis was part of the reason for the change in Rita.

As far as Julie was concerned, she was the same great girl she had always been, but her attitude towards men had changed. It was no wonder she had previously had such low regard for men, considering the role model she had for a father. Yansis was completely different to Ged though. He was respectful to Rita, and he and Vinny got along fine. As Julie became lost in thought about Rita's recent troubles, she shared some of her thoughts with Vinny.

"I hope this break takes her mind off things. She's had a lot to contend with since she came back."

"I know, but she shouldn't take it all on herself. Her sister's made her choice, so she should leave her to it."

"It's not that easy though is it, Vinny? I mean, imagine if it was our Clare."

"That's different. Your Clare's only thirteen; anyway, she wouldn't be that stupid. Rita's sister's a grown woman. How old is she, in her twenties?"

"Twenty two, but you don't understand. Rita's always looked out for her. Jenny isn't a bad person; she's just one of those people that rushes into things without thinking, then realises her mistakes when it's too late."

"Well she's had plenty of warning from Rita. I think she should just leave her to it now. After all, it's not doing Rita any good, is it? Or Yansis, for that matter."

Julie knew she was wasting her time arguing any further with Vinny. He had a point, but she could also appreciate Rita's point of view. Besides, she knew how strong willed Rita was, and if she had decided that she wanted to save Jenny from Leroy, then nothing would persuade her otherwise. Julie couldn't help but worry about Rita, knowing that none of this was doing her any good, and it was also potentially damaging for her relationship with Yansis.

***

Sunday 7th April 1991

Rita let out a scream as the train raced down the track leaving her giddy with nerves. When she reached the bottom of the dip, the carriage that Yansis was sitting in drew level with hers on the parallel tracks. She turned to smile at him, missing the sharp bend until the carriage swerved chaotically to the right, dragging her with it, and she lost sight of Yansis. Before she could recover, the carriage shot down the track again, then spun to the right. This time it was a prolonged turn, forcing her to one side of the carriage. She balked at the discomfort. To her relief, the track straightened out and she had Yansis in her sights again. She cheered as the two trains raced to the finish through a series of softer dips, and her train crossed the line seconds before his.

"Where to now?" asked Yansis, as Rita hobbled along the walkway next to the Grand National ride.

"Give me a chance," laughed Rita, rubbing an imaginary bruise on her arm. "I've got to get over that one first."

After a few minutes' thought, she said, "I know, let's go on the log flume."

They clambered into the log shaped boats, which meandered through the amusement park along a slow running river. Rita snuggled against Yansis, relaxed and contemplative, feeding him chunks of candy floss. It was the perfect end to their time at the amusement park.

They had been in Blackpool for two days. Yansis had never experienced anything like it, and Rita had enjoyed showing him the sights, such as the famous Blackpool Tower, Sandcastle Water Park and Blackpool Pleasure Beach amusement park. Rita had always been a white knuckle rider, and although Yansis had been reluctant at first, he was soon enjoying it. They went on all the major rollercoasters including the Big Dipper, Wild Mouse, Revolution and the Grand National until they were dizzy. When they needed a break from the rollercoasters, they had fun with the Ghost Train and the Dodgems.

After spending a great day at the amusement park, they found a Chinese restaurant tucked into the back streets, away from the main promenade.

"So, did your crazy rides take your mind off your troubles?" asked Yansis, once they were seated at a table.

"Definitely, I'm too busy thinking about my bruises to think about anything else after that Grand National," said Rita, "but at least my train beat yours," she added, grinning as she plunged her fork into a curried prawn.

Rita loved seeing Yansis's reaction to all the new experiences and sights. He was as thrilled as a young child when he spotted Blackpool Tower, and was intrigued by the old style trams that ran up and down the promenade. He insisted on having a ride on one just for the experience. The colourful piers had amazed him with their kiddie rides and fruit machines, and the tacky gift shops had enthralled him so much that she had bought him a 'Kiss Me Quick' hat for a laugh.

It was funny how something that seemed so tacky to people who had grown up with it, held a fascination for someone seeing it for the first time. The ability to see it all afresh though Yansis's eyes made it all the more special for her.

In the two days since they had arrived in Blackpool, she hadn't thought too much about her family troubles, and she wished that Yansis hadn't mentioned it because she didn't want it to mar their evening. She forced all thoughts of her problems to the back of her mind while she indulged in the delicious Chinese banquet. They had discovered a few good bars the previous evening, one of which had live bands playing most nights, so they were planning to visit there after the meal.

By the end of the night she was replete and content, but when she lay in bed listening to Yansis gently snoring by her side, the euphoria of the weekend started wearing off. She was due back in Manchester the following day, and she was thinking about what would await her on her return.

As had happened on many nights since she had arrived in Manchester, the thoughts swirled around in her head, causing her muscles to tense and making sleep futile. When her overworked muscles and overwrought imagination eventually gave in to exhaustion, it was four thirty in the morning.

***

Sunday 7th April 1991 – late evening

Ged was peeping through the lace curtains again. He couldn't help it. He'd been expecting Leroy for the last couple of hours, and he was late. It was now ten o'clock and he said he'd be there by eight. He'd had such a good day last Easter Sunday, and sales hadn't been too bad on the following bank holiday. The only problem was that it meant he was out of stock by Friday, and Leroy had promised to replenish him this evening.

"Why don't you sit down love and watch the tele?" Joan suggested.

"Alright!" he snapped. "I'm just checking."

"He must have been held up. Maybe he'll be here tomorrow. Why don't you give him a ring in the morning and find out when he's coming?"

"Oh yeah, I hadn't thought of that," he replied sarcastically.

He pulled the lace curtain to one side, taking a last look before returning to his armchair, and was rewarded by the sight of Leroy's shiny BMW roaring up the street. The sound of the high-powered engine caused a few curtains to twitch, which always made Ged swell with pride.

"He's here," he announced.

Ged turned away from the window, his facial expression changing to one of joy, with the frown lines melting away. He was at the front door before Leroy had reached the end of the path.

"Jesus, you're keen, aren't you?"

"Always keen for my favourite son-in-law," quipped Ged. Before Leroy could react, he added, "Well, almost son-in-law ... you know what I mean."

Leroy stepped inside the house, wearing a look of contempt. He threw two loaded bin liners down on the floor while Ged rubbed his hands together in anticipation.

"Ooh, let's have a look," said Ged, tipping the bags up and kneeling down to rummage through the contents.

When he had worked his way through both bags, he stood up, disappointed. "There's no kids' ones; I asked you to get me some kids' ones!"

Leroy reacted angrily, thrusting his chest out and pulling his shoulders back, as he shouted, "You what?"

"I told you, the kids' ones are selling like hot cakes down the pub. Some of these won't sell; you'll have to go back."

"Are you having a laugh? You'll get what you're fuckin' given! This is all top gear." He grabbed at the video tapes and shoved them in front of Ged's face, one by one, as he named them, "Die Hard 2, Pretty Woman, Home Alone, Dances with Wolves. Haven't you heard of any of these, you moron?"

Leroy was a picture of undisguised aggression, with the tendons straining in his broad neck and his eyes bulging. Noting his threatening manner, Ged tried to placate him, "Alright, alright, I don't mean any harm. Yeah, course I've heard of them. I might not be as switched on as you, Leroy, but if you say they're top gear, I'll take your word for it."

Leroy wasn't finished, "Do you realise the risks I take to get you these? It's not like taking a trip to Asda, you know! Not that I get any fuckin' thanks."

"Sorry, I didn't realise. These'll do. I'll have a go, and see if they'll shift."

Ged nervously scooped up the video tapes and other goods, putting them back inside the bin liners.

"How much do I owe you?"

"I ain't had chance to work it out yet. Them popular ones are gonna fetch more. You know, Ged, you wanna get hold of the Evening News or summat, and have a look what films are out. You're clueless, man." Sitting himself down, he added, "Pass me the bags and we'll sort it now, and I wouldn't mind a beer while you're at it."

Joan trotted off to the kitchen to fetch a can of lager from the fridge, which they kept available in case Leroy should call. Meanwhile, Leroy lit up a spliff and instructed Ged to arrange the goods into piles so they could count them out. He also made suggestions to him as to which were likely to be the best sellers, and should therefore be charged at a higher price.

Joan returned with the can of lager, and handed it over to Leroy.

"How are Jenny and the baby?" she asked.

"What you talkin' about, woman? There is no baby, not yet anyway."

Ged knew she was trying to smooth things with Leroy, knowing how proud he was of the fact that he was about to become a father. But she was making matters worse. What a stupid question to ask when he'd just calmed him down!

For the next twenty or thirty minutes Ged hovered precariously, worried in case Leroy lost it again. He'd heard about his reputation but this was the first time he had encountered it first hand, and the man was scary. He couldn't get his head round the way Leroy had gone from zero to raging bull in a matter of seconds, and it made him worry about who he was dealing with. Thankfully, once the cannabis had kicked in, Leroy calmed down and they settled the deal.

"Thank Christ for that!" he said to Joan once Leroy had left.

"I know, I couldn't believe it. Do you think something's upset him before he came here?"

"I don't know, but one thing's for sure; he's got a hell of a temper. I thought he was gonna have me for a minute. He was alright once I'd managed to calm him down though."

"It's worrying though, Ged. D'you think our Jenny will be alright with him? I hope he doesn't lose it like that with her."

"She should be. It's not as if he loses it all the time, is it? Like you say, something probably upset him before he came here … I think with people like Leroy, you've just got to know how to handle them, keep 'em calm."

"Maybe we should have a word with her, and warn her."

"Eh, don't you be sticking your oar in. It was bad enough when you started going on about bleedin' babies. What a daft thing to say! You nearly got him going again."

"I didn't mean any harm. I was just trying to make normal conversation, take his mind off the videos."

"Well, in future, leave it to me."

"Will you have a word with Jenny then?"

"If you want."

Ged had no intentions of having a word with Jenny, but it wouldn't do any harm to let Joan think otherwise. It wasn't worth the risk. What if it got back to Leroy that he had been sticking his nose in? No, if Jenny had any sense, she'd know how to play things with Leroy. Besides, everyone knew that you didn't go interfering in other people's relationships.

Chapter 12

Rita and Yansis had returned from Blackpool the previous day. One of Rita's first questions to Julie and Vinny was whether she had received any phone calls while they had been away. Julie reassured her that there hadn't been any, and that everything had been quiet.

Julie had taken the Tuesday off work. She assured Rita that all her bookkeeping was up-to-date, so they agreed to go into Manchester and have a look around the shops. It was a long time since Rita had been shopping with her best friend, and she was looking forward to it.

They parked Julie's car in the Arndale carpark and had a good walk round. Julie had taken the buggy because she knew that Emily's little legs would tire after a while. After exploring some of the fashion shops, they passed Boots the chemists, and Rita said, "I've just remembered, I need to nip in there for something."

"Go on then. I'll wait outside and push Emily up and down till she goes off to sleep. She's getting a bit cranky."

After a few minutes Rita came out of the shop.

"What did you treat yourself to?" asked Julie.

Rita opened her handbag a little, and edged open the Boots' polythene bag to reveal a tube of Lanacane cream.

"I take it you had a good weekend then?" asked Julie, giggling.

"You could say that. At least I was feeling a bit more up to it, once I'd got away from all the problems. He's worse than ever though."

"Maybe you should set some ground rules; limit him to so many times a week or something."

"No, it would only hurt his feelings, and it's a bit of a touchy subject at the moment. I just have to hope that bloody hospital appointment soon comes round, so we can get everything sorted."

"Ooh look," said Julie. "Emily's nodded off at last. Come on, let's go and grab some lunch, and have a good chinwag before she wakes up again.

***

Saturday 13th April 1991 - evening

Carl was on the Buckthorn Precinct, selling drugs in the darkened shop doorways. He had picked a spot that was renowned for drug dealing. The shopping precinct was set back from the main road, and remained unlit once the shops had closed for the night. Although he knew that he could have stayed closer to home, there was more money to be made down the Moss. And things were going well since Leroy had been getting the new supplies of heroin from Cheetham Hill. The druggies couldn't get enough of it.

Moss Side was so well-known as a drugs base that it brought in plenty of custom, and the money he could make here would have taken him three nights in Longsight. He therefore considered it well worth the ten minutes it took to reach there by car.

He spotted a couple walking along, and homed in on their naivety straightaway. They were looking around, cautiously observing the young lads that rode around on mountain bikes. Their body language couldn't have spelt out apprehension more clearly, unless they had been carrying a giant placard with the word emblazoned across it. Carl grinned as he watched them twitch and stiffen every time the lads came within reach of them. He could tell they were definite first timers to Moss Side, who didn't have a clue where to go, so he decided to make himself known.

It was a quick and easy sale, and once the drugs and money had exchanged hands, the couple were on their way back to the main road. Carl called over the lads that had been circling around on their bikes. He knew them, of course.

"Hurry up, you bunch of dicks, before they're gone. Did you see

A Gangster's Grip

them? Yeah? Right ... same as before, and I want it all back."

The lads hastened after the couple, eager to carry out his instructions. They were new recruits to the Buckthorn Crew, anxious to please the older gang members, and eventually command the same level of respect and earnings. Carl knew they wouldn't let him down; they knew better than to cross an established member of the Buckthorns. Nevertheless, he wanted to check and make sure. Aside from that, he derived a certain pleasure from his latest side-line.

He hurried after the lads, and was just in time to see them in action. They had surrounded the couple with their bikes and, as Carl approached, he could see the gestures of the lads as they made demands from the couple. For a moment it looked as though the man was going to play the hero, but the sight of a blade soon changed his mind. The woman started screaming.

Carl was now within twenty metres of them, and her screeching was loud enough to reach him. He was relieved when one of the lads jumped from his bike, grabbed her from behind, and forced his hand across her mouth to muffle the sound. Carl continued to approach, keeping himself hidden, until he could hear what was taking place.

"Shut your fuckin' screeching or he cops for it," said one of the gang, prodding the knife into the man's side. "Just hand over the drugs and we'll let you go."

The knife hadn't drawn blood; they were just a few warning jabs, enough to make him co-operate. As the man reached into his pockets to recover the drugs, his girlfriend's fear overwhelmed her. A torrent of urine gushed down her thighs, splashing the pavement, and soaking both her shoes and those of the lad who was restraining her from behind.

He jumped back and yelled, slapping her across the face, "You dirty bitch! These are my new trainers. You've ruined 'em."

His friend stashed the drugs inside his coat, and they leapt on their mountain bikes and sped away to the sound of the woman's distressed cries. Her partner was trying to comfort her, holding her close to him with trembling arms.

Satisfied that they had carried out his instructions without getting caught, Carl made his way back to the shop doorway where he knew they would expect to find him.

"Nice job lads," he said, when they handed the drugs back to him. "Now, do a couple more for me tonight, and I'll see you straight later … Oh, and Mikey?" he called, just as they were heading away.

Mikey turned around in response, and they all waited to see what Carl had to say.

"Try not to get piss all over your trainers next time," sniggered Carl, and the other two lads laughed at his cruel joke.

Later, Carl went to meet Leroy in a shebeen, one of Moss Side's illegal drinking dens.

"You have a good day?" asked Leroy.

"Tops, man, look at this," boasted Carl, showing Leroy a wad of notes, "and I've still got loads to sell tomorrow night."

"How d'you manage that?"

A smug grin spread across Carl's face, "Recoveries, innit?"

In response to Leroy's look of confusion, he explained how he sent the three young lads on mountain bikes to recover some of the drugs he had just sold to unsuspecting customers. He stayed hidden so the customers didn't realise his involvement, and they therefore thought they had been victims of an unconnected mugging.

"You sly bastard," said Leroy, with a hint of amusement in his tone.

"That's not all. You should have seen what happened to this couple. The woman was going fuckin' hysterical, so Mikey put his hand over her gob to shut her up. Her boyfriend was a bit cocky, so they showed him the blade just to let him know who was boss, and she pissed herself, man, all over Mikey's trainers."

They both thought this was hilarious. Carl accompanied his laughter with thigh slapping gestures, and wanted to embellish the story while he had Leroy's rapt attention.

"They were his new Nikes and all. He was well pissed off – ha ha, *pissed* off!"

The laughter continued, but suddenly there was a change in Leroy.

As his laughter subsided, he flicked Carl's face. It was a slow, calculated motion. "Hey, best not do too many of them recoveries, man. We don't want the punters to stop coming."

Carl flinched, surprised by Leroy's change in temperament as much as the slight sting to his face. "OK, I won't … God, man, I only did three or four! It's no big deal. The punters don't even know it's me; the Moss has always been full of muggers."

"Fuckin' shut it!" Leroy commanded.

An instinct for self-preservation told Carl to avoid saying anything that might annoy Leroy even more. Then, as though regretting his outburst, Leroy added, in a lighter tone, "Just do as I say, man, and everything will be cool."

"Yeah, sure," Carl replied.

"Another thing," said Leroy. "You and Winston are gonna have to start dealing in Longsight."

"Longsight, why?"

"It's 'cos of the H; it's gettin' too risky. None of the other Buckthorns are gettin' hold of much heroin now. The fuckin' MSC has got it all stitched up. If anyone hears we're shifting loads of the stuff down the Moss, there'll be trouble. The rest of the Buckthorns will want to know where we're gettin' it from. If we stick to Longsight, no-one will know what we're up to. They'll just think it's another crew that's sellin' it."

"I won't grass."

"I know, it's not about that. They're bound to know summat's wrong."

"But there's not as many punters in Longsight."

"There will be; you gotta give it time. Word will soon get round."

"But that could take ages."

"Did I say you had a choice?"

Carl knew when it was best not to push his luck, so he had to accept Leroy's orders, even though he wasn't happy about it. In the charged atmosphere that followed, Carl struggled for something else to say. He observed Leroy cautiously, wondering how to play him, and was relieved when he saw Mad Trevor walking over with two other members of the Buckthorn Crew.

As Carl had now been with the Buckthorn Crew for several months, he knew all the gang members. Although he worked closest with Leroy, there were many times when the gang worked together, for instance, when they had a score to settle with a rival gang.

The Buckthorn Crew didn't have a leader as such. Each of the members looked after his own business interests, but they all took advantage of their gang connections to give them access to supplies of drugs and weaponry. There were also members who had extended interests, such as Leroy, who used other people to sell drugs and stolen and counterfeit goods for him, and then took a mark-up from the profits.

Despite the lack of an appointed leader, certain members of the gang were regarded as natural leaders. These were the hard men who struck fear into anyone who came into contact with them, and commanded respect. Leroy and Mad Trevor were typical of this type of gangster. Their reputations were well-known both within the gang and outside it.

Both Leroy and Mad Trevor were rumoured to have killed men in the most vicious means imaginable. When Carl had been told by another gang member, in graphic detail, about one of Leroy's particularly ruthless killings, he hadn't believed it at first. Then another gang member had confirmed it, and he had first-hand knowledge, having been a witness to the violent scene. The more Carl got to know Leroy and his rapid mood changes, the more he became convinced that he could be a cold-blooded killer.

Leroy and Mad Trevor never came into conflict with each other; instead they maintained a cordial camaraderie, as though aware of the dangers of any disagreement. They each had their reputation to protect at all costs.

Carl watched Leroy switch back to his affable persona as he greeted the other members of the gang. He observed the two dominant figures, Leroy and Mad Trevor; big, brutal and each with an inherent mean streak, and he couldn't help but wonder what the outcome would be if anything should ever happen to damage the delicate bond that connected them. Something as phenomenal as trading with known enemies of the Buckthorn Crew would be one such instance that could cause devastation.

Once the gang members had finished greeting each other, they settled down to discuss business.

"How's things?" asked Leroy. "Is Tony OK?"

Tony was a member of the Buckthorn Crew who had recently run into problems with a member of their rival gang, the MSC. Leroy had heard about him being attacked, but didn't yet know the full details. Mad Trevor enlightened him.

"He's not doing too bad, but the bastard gave him a good smacking and fuckin' kneecapped him. And all because he eyed up his woman."

"They're not getting away with that. We need to sort it."

"I know. That's what we're here to talk about. We know who did it, and we know where he lives and hangs out."

"Nice one. What you got planned?"

"We'll just go for him this time, but it'll send a warning to the rest of the MSC not to fuck with us. He ain't getting away with a kneecapping though. We need to take him out. Do you know anyone who'll be good for the job?"

Leroy looked across at Carl. "What about Mikey?"

"Yeah," laughed Carl. "He'd go for it. He's a bit young though."

"That's even better," said Leroy. "He's dying to prove himself. You told me he wanted part of the action. Now's his chance."

Carl had reservations, but he wasn't the one making the decisions. If Leroy decided Mikey was up to the job, then who was he to argue? It didn't make any difference to him. However, he knew Leroy had younger brothers who were also anxious to prove themselves, and he noticed how Leroy hadn't been too eager to put their names forward.

"As long as he's prepared to take him out. That's all that counts," said Mad Trevor.

"Dead right," said Leroy. "If he wants a piece of the action, he's gotta prove he's up to it. Everyone's gotta prove themselves some time.

D'you reckon he's still out there, Carl?"

"Might be."

"Go and have a look. You can fetch him in, and we'll have a little word with him."

Carl did as Leroy ordered, then stayed for the remainder of the meeting while Leroy and Mad Trevor gave Mikey his instructions. The young lad looked out of place in a room full of adults. Carl guessed that he was about 15 or 16, and he noted how Mikey listened impassively as the other Buckthorn Crew members outlined a plan of action.

He wondered what emotions Mikey must be concealing; fear, dread or even perhaps pride and excitement at this acknowledgement. Whatever he was feeling, Carl was relieved it was Mikey they had selected and not him. While he was content to deal in drugs, he'd rather leave this sort of stuff to someone else.

Chapter 13

"Right, that's fine, Mrs Christos. You can get dressed now."

Rita was relieved that it was over. She had never liked smear tests. What woman does? But then she had to go through the added humiliation of an internal examination. She was always tempted to make polite conversation when faced with a situation she was uncomfortable with, but what could you chat about when someone was rummaging about inside your vagina?

The doctor was an Asian lady who Rita guessed was aged somewhere between late thirties and early forties. She had a pleasant demeanour, and was one of those people Rita took to instantly. In some ways that made it more difficult though. Once Rita was on that examination table with her legs spread, the doctor's manner became brusque and business-like, as though familiarity was forbidden under such circumstances.

The questions had been bad enough, most of which Rita had to answer while Yansis had feigned difficulty understanding the English language. Fair enough, some of them were directed at her, but even the others she'd answered for both of them.

When did you last have sexual intercourse?
What age were you when your periods started?
Are your periods painful?
What is your family medical history?
How frequent are your periods and how long do they last?

Talk about twenty questions! The most difficult one to answer, surprisingly, hadn't been of an intimate nature. No, it had been the question about whether she had a stressful lifestyle. She could hardly tell the doctor that her sister was shacked up with a drug-dealing, violent gangster who had her dad selling dodgy goods down the local pub. In the end, she told the doctor she was having a few family problems, and left it at that.

Despite the probing questions and invasive examination, Rita was thankful that their appointment at the hospital had finally come round. After almost two years trying to conceive, they were becoming desperate, and maybe now they could make some progress. The health services were so poor in their part of Greece that there had been little chance of getting the help they needed. They had therefore been patient, telling themselves it would happen eventually.

But it never had. So Rita had suggested returning to Manchester for a few months to find out what was causing the problem. Her hope was that if a problem was identified, it could easily be put right. Maybe then, Yansis would stop obsessing over the need to keep trying for a baby. The other bonus was that, once things were sorted out, they could return to Greece. At least, that had been her original intention, before she found out about the situation with Jenny. Now she wasn't so sure if she could leave things as they were.

Once she had finished getting dressed, she sat down next to the doctor's desk, and the nurse went to bring Yansis back into the room. The doctor reassured Rita that everything seemed in order as far as the internal examination was concerned, and asked to see them again in a few weeks' time, to discuss the results of the various tests she had carried out. She then gave them a temperature chart, and handed them over to the nurse who explained how to use it.

***

Wednesday 17th April 1991 – late morning

"Well, how did you get on?" asked Julie, when Rita returned from the hospital.

"God, it was awful! They started by asking us a load of

embarrassing questions about our sex life, which Yansis wriggled out of by pretending he couldn't understand English. They wanted to know all the ins and outs."

"I bet they did!"

"Well yeah, literally as it happens," laughed Rita.

They were sitting drinking coffee in Julie's kitchen. Yansis had gone to meet Vinny at work, after dropping Rita off, and she couldn't wait to tell Julie all about the hospital appointment.

"Then, once we'd finished answering all their questions, I had to have a smear test and an internal."

"Yuck."

"Dead right, but don't worry, Yansis didn't get off scot free. He had to go in another room to fill a plastic container with his sperm."

"What you mean?" Julie accompanied her question with hand gestures.

"Yeah."

"Oh no! I bet he was mortified."

"His face was a picture, Julie. He couldn't believe what they were asking him to do. I was dying to laugh. Anyway, the nurse has given me this chart to record my temperature, and she explained how I can tell when I'm ovulating. That's a relief in itself! At least Yansis won't be at it every hour of the bloody day and night now. I'll just whip my thermometer out and say, 'No, Yansis, wrong time. Sod off and wait!'"

"Rita, you're a card. I'd like to see his face when you tell him that."

"No, I wouldn't really be like that with him … but at least I've got an excuse if he gets too much. Maybe he'll calm down a bit when he knows that some days are a bit of a waste of time."

"Maybe. Anyway, I'm just glad you've moved forward with things. What happens next?"

"They'll call us back to the hospital in a few weeks and have a look at the chart, and give us the results of all the tests they took. Oh, and the other thing is, we've got to have sex a couple of hours before the next appointment, so I can be prodded and poked again for them to see how Yansis's sperm are reacting inside me."

"Poor you."

"I know. I tell you, Julie, between that and all the carry on with our Jenny, I'm beginning to wish I'd stayed in Greece."

"You might never have been able to have babies then though, Rita. At least this way you'll get to the bottom of the problem, and get it sorted."

"I know, I don't mean it. I just wish it wasn't so difficult, and we didn't have to go through all this, especially with all the other shit that's happening."

"Rita, I know it's not easy, but you've got to try and take your mind off other people's problems. All this added stress isn't helping. Try to focus on you and Yansis, and sorting your own problems out. That is what you came over here for, after all. You're well on your way to finding out the answers now. Before you know it, you could be back on that plane; you, Yansis and your little bump."

"Don't, Julie!" Rita had answered more sharply than she'd intended, but Julie had touched on a sensitive topic. "I'm sorry, it's just that I can't afford to get carried away. If I set my sights on it too much, I'll only be let down if it doesn't work out."

"It'll work out, Rita, you'll see."

Rita wasn't so sure. It wasn't that she didn't want this baby. She wanted it just as much as Yansis, but not in the same obsessive, all-consuming way. That approach was for people used to getting what they wanted from life. For her, it was different. She'd been let down so many times in the past that she took a more philosophical approach. The way she'd learnt to look at things was that if you set your sights on something, it would never happen. Therefore, you were best not to expect it and just regard it as a bonus if something good came along. And if it did, then you had to grab it with both hands, like she'd done with Yansis.

She'd suggested returning to Manchester for Yansis's sake, more than her own. It was becoming increasingly difficult seeing his face each month when she confirmed that, yet again, they hadn't conceived. She could have accepted it, but Yansis's look of ineptitude only underlined their failings. Rita felt it left her with no choice but to take some form of action that could put both their minds at ease. However, she realised that it might produce a negative outcome, and how would they cope with that? What would Yansis's reaction be if she had to tell him she wasn't able to give him the children he desperately craved?

She could see that Julie was ready to hug her, but she resisted. As had happened so many times before in her life, Rita refused to give in to emotion. She'd fight it like she always did, and if things didn't work out, she and Yansis would just have to cope with it as best they could. In typical Rita fashion, she dealt with her burgeoning emotions by burying them and changing the subject.

Chapter 14

Vinny and Yansis stepped out of the taxi on Deansgate, in Manchester city centre, where they were about to meet Vinny's workforce in the Sawyer's Arms. This was a favourite meeting place for them, and had been around so long that everybody knew where it was. Rumoured to be one of Manchester's oldest pubs, it dated back to the 1700s, and was amongst the many listed buildings in the city centre.

Now that Vinny was running several sites, he liked to get all his workers together every few weeks. Not only was it good for staff morale, but it was something he enjoyed too. Tonight he was looking forward to introducing Yansis to some of the lads who he hadn't yet met. They would have a drink in a few pubs, and then hit a nightclub, if they were still up to it.

Most of the crew had already arrived, and a loud cheer went up when Vinny walked in the pub. He responded to their enthusiasm by ordering a round of drinks for his workers. Yansis knew some of them who he had met at the site where he was working, and Vinny introduced the others. The conversation was the usual combination of work and football. Manchester was home to two major teams, Manchester City and Manchester United, so there was always friendly rivalry. Vinny did his best to make sure that Yansis wasn't left out.

Later in the evening, when Vinny had a chance to have a quiet word with Yansis, he pointed out one of the lads to him, "That's Rob, the one I told you about who lives on the Riverhill Estate, in Longsight. He's the lad who told me the rumours about Leroy."

He caught Rob's eye, and he came over, "Did you want me, Vinny?"

Checking that there was no-one listening, Vinny spoke quietly,

"Yansis is Rita's husband, the sister of the girl that's shacked up with Leroy. I told them about the rumours."

"Hi Yansis, alright mate?" greeted Rob. "Jesus, yeah, there's been some more said down the pub." Rob looked around before continuing. "We'd better go outside so I can tell you the rest. You never know who's listening."

Although it was chilly outside, it was easier to find a quiet spot where they were unlikely to be overheard, and it seemed to give Rob the confidence to carry on with his story.

"You know that Carl that hangs around with Leroy? He was in the pub the other night. He's a bit of dickhead. I don't know whether he'd had a skinfull or he was drugged up, but for some reason he was even more gobby than usual. He was mouthing off about the gangs. He reckons he's a member of the Buckthorn Crew too; seems to think that makes him summat special.

"He was telling anyone who was willing to listen that the Buckthorn Crew have their enemies. Not all the gangs get on. Apart from them having a rival gang in Moss Side, called the Moss Side Crew (or MSC), there's another gang in Cheetham Hill that they don't get on with. They're called the Cheetham Crew. The MSC gang are friends with the Cheetham Crew, but the Buckthorn Crew aren't. Carl's not very happy about it because he didn't know all this when Leroy enlisted him into the Buckthorn Crew. He'd be wise to keep his big mouth shut though. If Leroy finds out he's been sounding off, I don't think he'd be too pleased."

"Thanks for telling us, mate," said Vinny.

"Yes, thank you very much," added Yansis.

"You're welcome, any time, as long as there's no come back. I don't know if it will help, but there you go." He directed his next comment at Yansis, "Seriously though, mate, your missus wants to be careful who she's getting involved with. If I was her, I'd leave well alone. That Leroy sounds like a right nasty piece of work, if you ask me."

"I know, but what can I do?"

A shiver ran through Vinny, and he suggested that they go back inside. For a while, he turned these details over in his mind until his workforce noticed that him and Yansis had become a little withdrawn, and encouraged them to join in the banter. By the time they returned home, worse for wear, in the early hours of the morning, Rita and Julie were in bed fast asleep.

***

Sunday 21st April 1991 – late morning

"What time did you two get in last night?" asked Rita.

The four of them were in Julie and Vinny's dining room. Julie and Rita were standing at the table as they had been busy doing housework. Just as they were finishing sorting the last of the washing, Vinny and Yansis arrived downstairs at the same time as each other.

"Ooh, not too loud, Rita, my head's killing!" said Vinny.

"It serves yourself right for being a pair of drunken reprobates. You wouldn't catch me and Julie carrying on like that. We were tucked up in bed for twelve; weren't we Jules?"

"Yes, and not a drop touched our lips."

"What is this reprobates?" asked Yansis.

"Bad men like you two," said Rita. "Men that stay out till the early hours, getting drunk, while their wives take care of the house and children, and go to bed at a reasonable hour."

The girls couldn't help but laugh when they saw the wounded look on Yansis's face. When he realised they were poking fun at him, he joined in by tickling Rita into submission while repeatedly asking, "Are you saying I am a bad man?"

"Take no notice of them two," said Vinny. "Anyone would think they'd never been drunk. Anyway, we were back for half two. That's not bad going, considering we went to a club."

"Ooh, that's only about an hour later than us," laughed Julie.

"Yeah, that's more like it. I told you what they're like, Yansis. I bet you were both gossiping, putting the world to rights. It's a wonder our ears weren't burning. Anyway, I'm getting some paracetamols."

As Vinny walked through to the kitchen, Yansis ceased his playfulness with Rita, easing into a gentle embrace and she snuggled up to him, while asking, "What about you, love? How's your head?"

"It's not too bad. I think I didn't drink so much as Vinny but his friends were buying him lots of drinks. He was very drunk. You know, Vinny can be a very funny man when he has been drinking."

"Not so funny now though, is he, eh Julie?" she teased.

"Eh, look at this, Yansis?" Vinny called, as he returned with two empty wine bottles he had fished from the top of the bin. "Not a drop touched your lips?" he asked Julie. "What did you do, love, drink it through a straw?"

"I told you he is a funny man," said Yansis.

"Put them back in the bin, you dirty sod, and wash your hands. You'll have Emily copying you." Julie looked down at Emily who had picked up on the jovial atmosphere, and had diverted her attention from her toys to the adults in the room.

"Come on Emily, we'll go to play with your toys." Yansis broke away from Rita and, as he led Emily away to the living room, she was squealing with delight.

While Yansis played with Emily, Julie switched the kettle on and popped some bread in the toaster for Vinny and Yansis. Despite Rita's offers of help, Julie insisted that she was fine, so Rita and Vinny took a seat in the living room. As soon as they were sitting down, Rita could tell by Vinny's body language that he had some news to impart. He leaned over towards her, and adopted a serious expression as he began speaking.

"Rob was out with us last night; the lad that lives in Longsight."

"Oh yeah?"

"Yeah, he told us a bit more about Leroy."

He was about to carry on when Rita shouted Yansis over. "You might want to hear this love."

"I already know. I was there when Rob told us, but I will come anyway."

"I don't know if any of this will make any difference to you, Rita," said Vinny, "but Rob reckons that the Buckthorn Crew have got a lot of enemies. For one thing, there's another gang in Moss Side that they don't see eye to eye with, called the MSC, but there's also one in Cheetham Hill, called the Cheetham Crew. Apparently, the MSC gang trade with the Cheetham Crew, but the Buckthorns won't have anything to do with them. Rob found out through Carl who was mouthing off in the pub."

Rita stopped him before he went any further. "Hang on, let me make sense of this … Remember when you told me about Leroy coming to live in Longsight, and you said he might be hiding from something?"

"Yeah," agreed Vinny.

By this time Julie was back in the room, and they were all paying attention while Rita was trying to digest this latest piece of information.

"Well, it's no wonder he wants to get away if the Buckthorn Crew have got so many enemies."

"That's supposing it was his decision to move and not his mother's," said Julie.

"I doubt whether his mother has much say. He's the oldest; I bet he calls all the shots in that family." Rita was running her hands through her hair while thinking things through, a habit she had developed lately. "Maybe she was asking too many questions though, like mothers do. That'll be why it suits him better to live at Jenny's."

"Maybe," said Julie.

"Jesus, that's it!" shouted Rita. The others looked at her in alarm, Julie taking a swift glance at Emily to make sure Rita's shouting hadn't upset her.

"Sorry, I didn't mean to shout, but it's just hit me. Cheetham Hill! That's where he goes for his supplies, isn't it? The dodgy goods … I bet he's getting more than dodgy goods from Cheetham Hill." She ran her hands through her hair again and lifted her head, dropping her hands and looking upwards. "The bastard!"

Regretting her bad language, with Emily close by, she stood up and started pacing. Her frenzied steps led her to the hallway where she was no longer within Emily's hearing range. Julie and Yansis followed behind.

"What is it, Rita?" Julie pleaded.

"That bastard, Leroy! He's only playing both sides. Can't you see? It all makes sense now. That must be why he's going to Cheetham Hill, and if the Buckthorns hate the Cheetham Hill lot, how will they react if they know he's trading drugs with them?"

"Calm down, Rita. We don't know that," said Julie.

"It's obvious! The dodgy goods are just a cover. Why would he be dealing in dodgy goods when he can make a fortune selling drugs? Have you any idea how much these drug pushers earn selling heroin and crack? Our Jenny was telling me about it. Course, the silly cow probably didn't realise Leroy was one of them. That'll be why he's going up to Cheetham Hill. It makes no sense otherwise."

"Well, I suppose you could be right, Rita."

"Julie, I hope to God I'm not!"

"Why?"

"Because if I am right, then it means our Jenny is in even more danger than I thought."

Rita ran her hands through her hair once more before she went in search of her cigarettes.

***

Tuesday 23rd April 1991 – late evening

Mikey had been building up to this attack for over a week, and he was seriously scared. He intended to carry out Leroy and Mad Trevor's instructions, which meant that this experience would be a first for him. Mikey was used to pulling a knife; he'd used one a few times for muggings, but he was also used to choosing his victims. The sight of the knife would generally be enough to make them surrender, and part with their cash and other valuables. He'd even drawn blood, just a little nick once or twice to silence the cocky ones into submission. But he'd never killed a man.

He normally had his mates with him for back-up too, but this time he was alone. That was all part of his instructions. The fewer people that knew, the better, Leroy had said. That way there was less chance of any witnesses coming forward, if they were reckless enough to grass on the Buckthorn Crew.

He'd been watching the man, a member of the MSC, for a few nights. Every night he told himself that this would be the night he did it. Then he would bottle out at the last minute. Tonight, though, he had to do it. The pressure was mounting. Members of the Buckthorn Crew were asking why the job hadn't been done, and he was running out of excuses.

One advantage of him being chosen was that he wasn't yet recognised as a member of the Buckthorns, because he was new to the gang. Therefore, his presence in the area over the past few days hadn't raised any suspicions, or so he thought.

He'd been outside the house for the last twenty minutes. Watching, waiting. He knew that the man usually left around this time, either to go dealing, or to meet other members of the MSC. Mikey had decided that he would carry out his attack while the man was still alone.

It was late evening. The darkened paths and alleyways that wound around the estate made ideal places in which to stay obscured. Mikey was tucked behind an overgrown rose bush when he spotted the man leaving his home. The adrenaline pulsated through his body as he followed the man, taking care to keep to the shadows.

The man was approaching the end of a row of houses, and Mikey anticipated that he might turn the corner, which would lead to a gloomy alleyway. That was when Mikey would make his move.

Just as he had anticipated, the man turned the corner. Mikey sped up as quietly as he could, so he could close the gap. He entered the alleyway and caught sight of his intended victim, about five metres ahead. Mikey continued to move in on him, careful not to break the silence, so he could take him by surprise.

A Gangster's Grip

He was about three metres away when the man turned to face him. His challenging words caught Mikey unawares. "Come on then, boy, show us what you got," said the man, beckoning to him with upturned hands, like a warden controlling traffic.

Mikey was about to charge the man, his knife at the ready, when he heard heavy footsteps behind him. He turned to the side, keeping the man in his peripheral vision. He spotted the men to his right. Three of them, wearing hoodies. Mikey sensed straightaway that they were here for him. And they were getting nearer.

"What the fuck you up to?" the first one asked.

Mikey just stood there silent, the fear consuming him. Within seconds they had crowded in on him. "Not here," one of them said. "We don't wanna be seen. Get him in the car."

They grabbed Mikey's knife and frogmarched him to the end of the alleyway, where a car was parked. Then they forced him inside it. He was squashed on the backseat between two of the men, who searched him and seized the rest of his belongings. Another of them was driving, and the man he had followed was sitting in the front passenger seat. This was the man who Mikey had been instructed to kill. He turned around to face Mikey, and spoke.

"Right boy. I wanna know why the fuck you've been following me, and what the hell you think you're up to."

"I wasn't gonna use it, honest. It's just to make people gimme their cash."

"You must think I'm stupid!" shouted the man. "You wasn't planning no fuckin' muggin'. You've been following me for days. I wanna know who sent you, I want names, addresses, everything you know."

Mikey didn't say anything. Despite his fear, he couldn't afford to let the gang down. He would have to take whatever punishment they doled out to him, and refuse to give in.

"Don't play the smart guy with me," the man raged, leaning over the front seat to thump Mikey's jaw so hard it knocked him sideways. "I know that the Buckthorn Crew sent you, and by the time we've finished with you, you'll be squealing like a pig."

He turned to the driver. "Take us to the lock-up. It needs to be done where no-one can hear him scream."

Chapter 15

It was early Wednesday morning, and the postman was making his deliveries on the Buckthorn council estate. He liked this time of day; it was the only time when he felt safe in this area. The estate was notorious for gangs, and had a bad reputation for knifings, muggings and shootings. Although more than one gang was based on the Buckthorn Estate, each had its own territory. Rumour had it that this part of the estate was the territory of the Buckthorn Crew, and that many of the attacks were due to inter-gang rivalry.

This early in the morning the gangsters were still in bed, having stayed up late, dealing in drugs and involved in other nefarious activities. It was generally from midday onwards that the problems started. Once it was past midday, you couldn't guarantee your safety, but fortunately he didn't live in the area so, once his round was over, he got out of there as soon as he could. He'd been asking for a move for some time, but this was an estate where no-one wanted to work, and his employers knew it.

Until today he'd been prepared to put up with it, knowing how difficult it was to get another job if you were unskilled. Little did he realise that this would be the last day on his rounds. After today, he would never step foot on the Buckthorn Estate again. The sight that met him on that spring morning would stay with him forever.

It was a young man, although it was difficult to tell his age, his face was so badly beaten. There was no doubt in the postman's mind that the young man was dead though. Nobody could survive that level of injury without bleeding to death. He only took a quick look. He couldn't stand much more. But in those fleeting seconds he noticed that several fingers were missing from the body, and the torso was ripped open.

Shocked by the macabre scene, he dropped his sack of letters and fled. He didn't stop running until he reached his postal van. With shaking hands, he started the engine and drove to the postal distribution office, where he reported his discovery, and tendered his resignation straightaway.

***

Thursday 25th April 1991 – early evening

Jenny and Winston fastened their clothes and took up their usual positions; Jenny on the armchair and Winston on the sofa. There were two cups on the coffee table, which they had emptied earlier. It was a routine they had practiced on countless occasions. Sex for them was a frantic activity, with the risk of discovery adding to the thrill.

Like surreptitious teenagers sneaking behind their parents' backs, they had to grasp what opportunities they could. Jenny and Winston couldn't afford to undress fully. Instead they aimed for a quick recovery, in case Leroy should return home unexpectedly. They were chancing the odds, knowing he spent more time outside the home than inside it nowadays.

Winston leant forward, grasping Jenny's hands while they talked. From this position he could quickly sit back in the sofa if necessary, and Jenny could do likewise. It wasn't the same as spending hours, skin against skin, wrapped in each other's embrace, but for them it would have to do.

While their physical contact wasn't as intimate as they would have liked, they were getting to know each other intimately in the spoken sense. For Jenny, time had revealed the intrinsic differences between Winston and Leroy's personalities, and she was realising what a mistake she had made. The trouble was that, like Winston, she was now in Leroy's grip, and it was too late to do anything about it.

Over the last few weeks, Winston had told her how much he hated being part of the Buckthorn Crew. He had joined as a young lad when it had seemed the thing to do. At that time he hadn't given much thought to the trouble it would lead him into. He had also been under the influence of some of the older lads on his estate, including Leroy. What he hated most about the Buckthorns, though, was the brutality. Although he'd been pressured into committing his fair share of violence, it wasn't something he was proud of. However, he had avoided being involved in some of the more callous crimes by which the Buckthorns had gained their ruthless reputation. Now, as they sat facing each other, Jenny spoke.

"I wish it didn't have to be like this," she said, scowling.

"Me too, but he'd kill us if he ever found out."

"I know."

"Straight up, Jenny! I'm not just saying that. There are rumours, you know?"

Jenny shifted in her seat, and withdrew her hands from Winston's, in shock. "What rumours?"

"Him and a few of the gang were supposed to have killed a guy in prison. It was a few years back. They did it in retaliation, 'cos this guy killed someone who was working for Leroy. It was never proven though. They couldn't find no witnesses."

"You're joking!"

"No, seriously. I told you, we've gotta be dead careful. It's not the only one he's done either, from what I've been told."

"Jesus, Winston! I didn't think he was that bad."

Jenny was visibly shaken. The colour had drained from her face and, for a moment, she couldn't speak. She tried to focus on what Winston had told her, but her thoughts were a jumble and her heart was racing. She was glad when Winston leaned forward and took her hands again.

"Jen, are you alright?"

"Yeah … yeah, it's just a bit of a shock, that's all … Have you ever seen him hurt anyone?"

The revelations were too shocking to believe, and she found it difficult to accept that the man she lived with could be a brutal murderer.

"No, I've just heard it from the other guys," said Winston. "Mind you, I've been on the receiving end of a slap once or twice."

Jenny's face was full of concern, the deep furrows evident on her forehead, and a tight line forming around her lips.

"Oh, not for ages though," Winston added. "It was when I was younger. I was always cocking things up, but he trusts me a bit more now."

"It's a good job, isn't it?"

"Yeah, like I say, we've just got to be really careful, Jen."

It was fortunate for them both that Jenny had had time to compose herself when they heard the key turn in the lock. She flashed a brief, harried look at Winston before they prepared themselves, masks in place and bodies parted.

"Alright, mate?" asked Winston, as Leroy angled his head around the door. "I'd given up on you. I was just about to get off."

"Yeah, looks like you've been here for a bit," said Leroy, eying the empty coffee cups.

"I only stuck my head in to see if you were home, but Jenny offered me a coffee and we got talking."

"Well it looks like she treats you better than she treats me. Are you going to get me a beer or what, woman?"

Jenny was shocked by Leroy's angry outburst. Despite what she had been hearing from Winston, and although Leroy had changed since he had moved in with her, he had never spoken to her like this before. Then again, he was never in her company for long, as he spent increasing amounts of time away from home. She didn't know what he got up to; he only ever told her he had business to deal with.

She wasted no time heading to the kitchen, and returning with a can of beer. He hadn't offered a can to Winston, so she thought it best to follow his lead and not bother offering either.

"Here," she said, handing Leroy the beer.

"What about our visitor? Are you not gonna give him one too? Eh, that's an idea, Winston. How about a threesome?" Leroy laughed.

A Gangster's Grip

A look of horror crossed Jenny's face as she awaited Winston's response.

"Nah, not my scene, man. I'm greedy; I prefer my women all to myself."

Winston's attempt at bravado seemed to meet with Leroy's approval and he let out a loud guffaw, which he quickly recovered from, then asked, "Are you gettin' that drink for Winston or what, or are you just gonna stand around looking like a dick?"

"Alright, I'm going!"

When Jenny returned with the beer, Leroy asked, "What about the glasses?"

"But, you don't usually have glasses."

"Well, we're fuckin' having 'em now, so do as you're told!" he sneered.

Jenny was forced to leave the living room again, to the sound of laughter. As she returned, she could hear Leroy and Winston talking.

"So, what's up?" he asked Winston.

"Nowt, just thought I'd call and see my mate. Anything been happening?"

Leroy didn't reply. Instead he turned his attention to Jenny again, as he shouted, "Jenny, doesn't that fuckin' dog want feeding or summat?"

"No, he had something to eat not long ago,"

"Well find summat else to do then! Me and Winston have got business to talk about."

Jenny fled to the kitchen, where she busied herself washing the dishes while fighting back tears of humiliation. To speak to her in such a condescending way was bad enough, but it was worsened by the fact that he had done it in front of Winston.

When she finished washing up, she scrubbed the work surfaces, using brisk strokes. The swift, mechanical action helped her to work out her annoyance. Then she cleared a shelf of the cupboard and scoured it clean, moving on to another, then another. All the while her mind was in turmoil. How the hell had she got herself into this situation?

By the time she had calmed herself down, Winston was leaving the house. She could hear him saying goodbye to Leroy. Her first impulse was to run after him to say their farewells. But she wouldn't dare. It would be too suspicious. So she wiped her hands on the towel, and went to ask Leroy what he would like for tea.

"It's getting a bit late now. You don't have to bother cooking. D'you fancy a take-out? I'll treat you if you like, and we can have a nice night in together. You, me and a few drinks. Best not have too many though," he said, as he put one arm around her and patted her stomach with the other.

"Y-yes," Jenny replied.

Jenny couldn't believe the change in Leroy during the last half hour. At the same time, she was relieved that he was no longer in a foul mood. This was more like the man who had won her over when she started going out with him all those months ago. Seeing him like this made her think that perhaps the rumours Winston had heard were exaggerations.

She found it hard to believe that Leroy could be a killer. Alright, he wasn't ideal. He stayed out too many nights, she never knew what he was up to and he wouldn't tell her. But he couldn't be that bad. He lived with her, for God's sake! Surely she would know.

Jenny resigned herself to the thought that perhaps something had upset Leroy before he had come home. Nevertheless, she wasn't happy about the way he had spoken to her, so she decided to tackle him about it.

"You're in a better mood," she commented. "What was wrong with you before? Had someone upset you? Only, I won't stand for being spoken …"

Before she could finish speaking, his whole demeanour changed. His right arm tightened around the back of her shoulders, and his face moved closer to hers until it was only centimetres away. Acting on instinct, she pulled her head back but his arm tightened further, with his hips swivelling round to face towards her. He raised his left hand and gripped her throat, thrusting her head upwards then tugging her hair from behind. All she could see were his angry eyes glaring down at her.

She felt a rush of fear as her throat constricted.

"Let's get one thing straight!" he snarled. "You're my woman, and I'll talk to you how I fuckin' well like. And anything that happens to me outside this house is none of your business. You got that?"

He emphasised his last question by giving another sharp tug of her hair.

"Yeah," whimpered Jenny.

Leroy let her go, and pushed her away.

"Right, now get your shoes on and get round to the Chinese take-away."

Jenny rushed to put on her shoes and coat, thankful to get away from Leroy for a while, but dreading what mood he would be in when she got back home.

Chapter 16

Jenny hadn't kept to her promise. No sooner was Rita inside the house than the pit bull charged up to her, barking fiercely. The dog was excited by this new visitor, and leapt excitedly onto its hind legs, grasping Rita's tee-shirt with its front paws. Rita took this as a threat. All she could see was a mouthful of lethal weapons, poised to strike and stockpiled in a mean looking face. She felt her stomach plunge as fear gripped her, and the rest of her body stiffened.

"Get down, Tyson," said Jenny, with little conviction.

To Rita's relief, Winston appeared, and took control of the situation, seizing Tyson by the collar and leading him towards the back door. Within minutes the dog was in the back garden, and Winston had locked the door behind him.

"Thank you, Winston," said Rita. "I don't like dogs."

"I could tell; that's why I grabbed him quick."

"How come it doesn't bother you, anyway?"

"You've just got to let him know who's boss. If you let him know you're scared, he'll walk all over you."

"A bit like its owner," muttered Rita, noticing how Winston referred to the dog as 'him'. He obviously knew Tyson well.

"Anyway, I thought you were going to put the dog out the back when I came round?" she asked Jenny.

"It slipped my mind. I'll try to remember for next time. God, Rita, you're trembling!"

A smile was beginning to form on Jenny's lips, but a look from Rita stopped her from taking it further. There were some things Rita didn't find funny.

"Anyway, I'm going now," announced Winston. "It was nice

seeing you again, Rita."

"You don't have to rush off whenever I come round."

"No, it's fine. I was going anyway, honest."

It struck Rita as strange that Winston couldn't get out of the house soon enough whenever she came round. But a few other things about Winston and Jenny were strange too, and she was beginning to realise why.

"He's in a bit of a hurry again, isn't he?" she asked Jenny, after Winston had left.

Jenny shrugged.

"He seems to be round here a lot, Jenny. I can't understand why he's always helping you with the house, and not Leroy. I thought the house was finished now, anyway. What's going on?"

"Nothing. I've told you, Leroy's just busy, that's all."

"It still seems funny to me. He's round here every time I come, and he seems to know that dog very well. It's almost like he's the dog's master, the way he was with it."

"It's called Tyson."

"I'm not interested in the bloody dog's name. What's going on, Jenny?"

"Nothing. What you trying to insinuate?"

"I don't need to insinuate anything. It's bloody obvious! You're having an affair with him, aren't you?"

Although Jenny tried to deny the affair, Rita could see the guilt on her face.

"You are, you're having a bloody affair with him, right under Leroy's nose. You silly little cow! What do you think Leroy will do if he finds out? He doesn't strike me as the sort of bloke to take it lying down."

"He won't find out."

"Oh don't be so bleedin' naïve, Jenny! You're carrying on in the house that you share with him, and you think he won't find out. Are you stupid altogether?"

Rita had now taken to her recent habit of running her hands through her hair, accompanied by other manual gestures, each time she emphasised a point.

"I told you what happened to that girl in Moss Side, didn't I?" She paused for a moment, then asked, "Does he have a key?"

"Who?"

"Leroy, of course. Does he have a key?"

"Yeah, course he does. He lives here."

"Oh God, Jenny! So, he could walk in any time and catch you both at it. Jesus, he'd go ballistic!"

Jenny went silent. She looked like a defeated woman, sitting with her shoulders hunched and her lips curved downwards. Rita could detect a look of sadness in her eyes.

"Don't tell me you actually expect me to feel sorry for you?"

"You don't understand, Rita."

"Go on, tell me. I can't bleedin' wait to hear this!"

"Leroy's changed, Rita. I thought he was alright when I first started seeing him. I'd heard about his reputation as a bit of a hard man, but it seemed cool. Everyone in the pubs gave me respect when I was with him, and it felt good ... Oh, I know it sounds daft now, but it didn't seem like that at the time.

"And he treated me well. He was always buying me things, and calling me his woman and stuff. But now I hardly ever see him. He stays out all night sometimes, and when he comes in he doesn't always stay long. I think he only comes home for the odd meal, a change of clothes and sex. And he doesn't even talk to me with respect any more. Winston's completely different ..."

Her voice was trembling, and Rita could sense that tears were imminent. She actually felt sorry for Jenny. She had always been naïve, and Rita could see how someone like Leroy had found it easy to charm his way into her life.

"Come here, you daft sod," she said, taking Jenny into her arms. Rita let Jenny have a few minutes of comfort before asking, "Why don't you see if he'll go back to his mother's? Tell him it isn't working for you; he's not home enough."

"I wish it was that easy, Rita, but there's no way he'll leave here when I'm having his kid."

"Oh, like that is it? Shit, Jenny; you've got yourself in a right mess. You could always go back to my mam and dad's, I suppose."

"That's if my dad would have me. Don't forget, he thinks the sun shines out of Leroy's backside. Besides, how could I see Winston then? He lives in Moss Side with his family so it's not as if I could go round to his; Leroy would find out. And I can hardly bring him round to my mam and dad's. Anyway, I don't even know how Leroy would take it if I walked out on him."

"OK, well let's not worry about that at the moment; we'll have to think of a way round things. Try to take your mind off it for now. All this stress can't be good for the baby. How are you feeling anyway?"

"Not too bad," Jenny replied, stroking her rounded stomach.

"How many weeks now?"

"29."

"Well, you've not got too long to go. You just focus on looking after yourself and the baby. You never know, maybe Leroy might change once he's a dad. It sometimes happens."

"He might; he's still OK sometimes. I just wish he was like that all the time."

Although Rita had tried to reassure Jenny, she found it unlikely that Leroy would ever change. She had to give her some hope to cling onto though. At the moment Rita couldn't think of anything else to say that could offer her any assurances, but she'd have to come up with a way of helping her.

Rita stayed at Jenny's for a while, talking about a number of other topics to take Jenny's mind off her troubles. She felt as though she was succeeding in her attempts, until she heard the sound of the front door rattling, accompanied by the dog's barking. Leroy was home.

"Act normal," she whispered to Jenny, and she tried to think how she would act with Leroy under normal circumstances. It was the first time Rita had seen Leroy since she had first met him at her parents' home. That was seven weeks ago, and although she hadn't seen him since, she had found out a lot about him. None of it was good, but she remembered her promise to Jenny to be civil towards him. Besides, in view of what she had learnt, it was wise not to antagonise him. Her first impulse was to leave straightaway, but that would have displayed her aversion to Leroy, and she needed to put things right.

"Alright?" she greeted, as he walked into the room.

He briefly nodded his head in response, then disappeared.

"Where d'you think he's gone?" she whispered to Jenny, who shifted about in her armchair.

"I don't know."

They soon found out as the dog came bounding into the living room, with Leroy close behind.

"What d'you lock the dog out for?"

"Oh, Rita was a bit …" Rita's warning look told Jenny not to go any further. Letting Leroy know how frightened she was would be a big mistake. Jenny picked up on her warning and changed tack, "… he was being a bit of a nuisance, and we were trying to talk."

Rita was careful not to let her relief show, which wasn't difficult as she had tensed as soon as the dog approached her, and she now found it impossible to relax. Fortunately, the lure of his master was too good to resist and, as Leroy sat down in the remaining armchair, Tyson followed.

'*Mustn't show I'm scared, mustn't show I'm scared,*' she kept repeating to herself. She had heard somewhere that dogs can sense your fear, so she was determined to hide it from both the dog and Leroy.

"Come here, boy. Who's saying my Tyson's a nuisance?" said Leroy.

The affection was evident in his voice as he played with the dog, first of all lifting it and rubbing his head against its chest, then putting it back down on the floor. While Tyson was standing on his hind legs, Leroy took a soft toy, which he kept down the side of his chair. He put it inside Tyson's mouth and the dog reacted. Drawing back its fleshy lips to expose razor sharp fangs, it grasped the toy between its teeth. Leroy yanked at the toy, laughing and teasing. Tyson was becoming excited, panting heavily and wagging his tail. When the dog had worked itself up into a frenzy, Leroy released the pressure, let Tyson settle down a little, then pulled again. He did this repeatedly.

Although it was clear that the two of them were gaining a lot of enjoyment from this activity, all Rita could think was, '*Look at the size of those teeth!*' To her it appeared that he was goading the dog, and she was worried that it might attack. The dog was built for fighting; it was as ripped as its owner, with a broad expanse of muscle across its neck and chest. Its huge, jagged teeth were centimetres from Leroy's hand.

"It's a game they play," Jenny commented.

"He seems to be enjoying it," said Rita, the catch in her voice betraying her attempt at indifference. She hoped Leroy hadn't picked up on it. But he had.

"Enough boy, down now!"

Tyson was reluctant to give up his fun at first and hovered around Leroy's chair, panting.

"Fuckin' sound dog, Tyson; only dog you could ever want. I tell you what, he'd always have my back," he boasted to Rita.

"I bet he would. He looks strong."

"Yeah, loyal as well. If I told him to attack you, one word from me and he'd have half your leg off."

A rush of fear went through Rita. Her heart was hammering, and she could feel her stomach churning. All of a sudden, she became aware of a pressing urge to urinate, but she didn't dare get up to go to the toilet. To do so would attract the dog's interest, and she didn't want it approaching her, especially in such a heightened state.

"Leroy!" admonished Jenny, half-heartedly.

It was obvious that Jenny was wary of putting up too much of a protest, so Rita replied, "Yeah, but you wouldn't do that; would you, Leroy? I mean, I'm almost your sister-in-law."

Leroy roared with laughter, and she hated herself for sucking up to him. Here she was trying to flatter his overblown ego, in an attempt to hide her fear. She felt almost as hypocritical as her father, and loathed having to kowtow to him.

The mood became stilted, and Rita was thankful when Jenny announced that it was time for Tyson's feed. She guessed that Jenny had done it deliberately, sensing how uncomfortable she was in Tyson's presence, despite her brave act. Although she was glad to get rid of the dog, it left her alone with Leroy.

He made no attempt at small talk, but the way he stared at her was unnerving. She knew it was deliberate. He had taken an instant dislike to her at her mother's house, and now he was trying to make her feel uncomfortable. He was doing a damn good job of it too, but she wasn't going to let it show.

"So, Leroy, are you looking forward to being a dad?"

"Course I am. It's my first kid, innit? Why wouldn't I be?"

"Just asking, making polite conversation, like people do with their sister's boyfriends."

This met with silence again, so she tried a direct approach, "Look, Leroy, I know we got off on the wrong foot last time I met you. It's not that I've got anything against you personally. I was just a bit put out because I was expecting to stay at my mam's, and they never told me the score till I got there."

She knew that the reason they got off on the wrong foot was more his doing than hers, but perhaps he had noticed her distaste when she had seen him. Although she hadn't said anything against him, maybe he had gathered by her reaction that she wasn't impressed. Nevertheless, it was important to keep things amicable now; the last thing she wanted was to upset him and make matters worse.

While she was waiting for his reply, Jenny and Tyson returned to the room. Rita's need to go to the toilet was now becoming desperate, so she decided she must do something about it. She had stayed long enough to take some steps towards improving her relationship with Leroy.

"I must get going now, Jenny," she announced, "but I'll have to nip to the loo first."

She gave Jenny a few seconds to react, before standing up. To her relief, Jenny took hold of the dog. '*Thank Christ for that*,' thought Rita. '*For a minute I thought she was going to stand by and watch, while Tyson tucked in.'*

Rita headed for the bathroom, her legs quivering. She prayed that Jenny would have hold of Tyson when she came back out. Thankfully she did, so Rita popped her head back into the living room, wished them all a cheery goodbye and got out of the house as quickly as she could. As she walked to the bus stop, with her limbs shaking and her heart thumping, she decided that, in future, if she saw Leroy's car parked outside the house when she approached, she would turn around and go straight back to Julie's.

Chapter 17

The funeral procession crawled along Princess Road, en route to Southern Cemetery. In the first car following the hearse were Mikey's estranged parents, united by grief. His poor mother had no idea of Mikey's involvement with the Buckthorn Crew until it was too late. She knew about some of his escapades, having had to bear the shame and embarrassment when the police had hauled him in for shoplifting. But this!

Sitting next to his parents were Mikey's sisters, young girls still at school, whose memories would be tarnished forever by this day. In the second car were the grandparents, aunts and uncles who remembered Mikey as a cute, cheeky toddler not so long ago.

Leroy, Mad Trevor and the rest of the Buckthorn Crew followed the procession in their flash motors funded by drug money. They kept an eye out for any signs of trouble. It wasn't unknown for a rival gang to hit a funeral procession, knowing they could wipe out several of their enemies at once.

Throughout the service and the wake, members of the Buckthorn Crew were respectful. They commiserated the family and said all the right things. However, the sorrow of the day underlined the fact that revenge was imminent.

When the mourners started to go home, Leroy, Mad Trevor and the other Buckthorns also left the wake. They made their way to one of their regular haunts, a place where they could plan their next move.

Leroy was livid. "It's a fuckin' disgrace. The kid was only sixteen, for Christ's sake!"

"Someone's gotta pay for this," said Carl.

"That's obvious, innit?"

"Do we know who did it?" asked one of the other gang members.

A Gangster's Grip

Mad Trevor chipped in, relaying the message that someone had slipped through his letterbox. "We know it's the MSC. There were a few of 'em. They took him somewhere to torture him. That's how they found out my address, but we only know who one of 'em is. I've had to move my family into a rented place. It's a diabolical fuckin' liberty!"

"Right," said Leroy. "If there were a few of 'em, then I vote we take out a few of them."

"How?" asked Carl.

"We know some of the places they hang out. Let's get Mikey's little mates to trail 'em. They'll be dying to get involved; they'll want revenge."

"We don't want any more kids killed," said the gang member who had spoken previously.

Leroy could see that Mad Trevor was warming to his idea. This was confirmed when he spoke. "No kids need to get killed. We just use them to spy on the MSC. We'll do the big stuff, and we'll leave it a couple of weeks. Let's take 'em when they're not expecting us. It'll be a nice big fuckin' surprise."

The other gang members cheered and raised their glasses.

"To the Buckthorn Crew," said Leroy.

"To the Buckthorn Crew," echoed the other members.

***

Wednesday 1st May 1991 - evening

Rita didn't feel like having sex; she rarely did lately. It wasn't that she didn't want a baby, or that she'd gone off Yansis; she just had too many other things to think about. Since her hospital visit, she'd been filling in her temperature chart every day and, according to the pattern, she was ovulating. Yansis had been studying the chart too, so he knew it was the right time.

It was only nine o'clock, but they were having an early night. Yansis was so keen to make the most of the opportunity that she didn't have the heart to put it off any longer. By the time she started undressing, he was already in bed waiting, reminding her of an eager puppy. '*All I need now is for him to wag his tail, droop his tongue and pant,*' she thought. A vision of Leroy's dog flooded her mind, and she tensed.

"What is wrong, Rita? You need to relax. I keep telling you not to worry, this is our special time."

"I know. Sorry, Yansis."

Rita didn't elaborate, knowing that Yansis wouldn't want her going over the same problems at this particular moment. Instead she shook her head, as if trying to free her mind from the torment.

She climbed in bed beside Yansis and tried to respond to his gentle coaxing, yielding to his delicate kisses. All of a sudden, Rita heard the shrill ringing of the telephone in the downstairs hallway, and she sprang apart from him.

"For God's sake, Rita! It is only the telephone. Just relax."

He tried to continue but Rita sat up in bed, feeling on edge.

"Rita, what is wrong? It is only the phone."

"I know, it just made me jump."

She was tempted to light a cigarette but sensed Yansis waiting patiently, so she lay back down beside him. Just as he was about to resume, there was a knock on the bedroom door, and Rita sprang up once more, pulling the sheets around her naked breasts.

"Rita, it's me," Julie called from the other side of the door. "I've got your Jenny on the phone."

"Just a minute," Rita shouted back.

Intuition told her that Jenny wasn't ringing with good news at nine o'clock at night, and she leapt out of bed and put on her dressing gown.

"She sounds upset," Julie said, when Rita met her on the upstairs landing.

Rita raced down the stairs and picked up the receiver, which was dangling from the end of the phone's cord.

"Jenny? What's wrong?"

It was difficult to decipher most of her words. Jenny's speech was hurried and came spilling out of her, but Rita caught the words 'Leroy' and 'drugs'.

"Try to stay calm, I'll be right there. Ten minutes, tops."

Her brave words belied the way she was feeling. She slammed down the phone, shouting up the stairs before the phone had even settled in its cradle, "Yansis, we need to go, now! Something's happened."

While she was still speaking, she turned towards the stairs, about to go and get dressed. Yansis was already there, fully clothed.

"I am ready when you are, Rita."

***

Wednesday 1st May 1991 – late evening

Despite Rita's concerns, she was still mindful of the dog, and was relieved that it didn't appear to be home when she arrived at Jenny's. Although she had been expecting the worst, Rita was nevertheless shocked at the sight of Jenny. Her face was covered in blotches, her eyes red rimmed and swimming with tears.

"OK, I'm here now," Rita said, stroking Jenny's back until she felt her becoming calmer. "Let's sit down. Yansis can make us a cuppa, and then you can tell me all about it."

She looked beseechingly at Yansis over Jenny's shoulder, and he responded by heading for the kitchen.

"What is it; what's upset you?" asked Rita.

"It's best if I show you."

Jenny led Rita upstairs to an unused bedroom with a built-in wardrobe. Rita was full of dread as Jenny led her towards the wardrobe and opened the door. It seemed empty; at least, the bulk of it was. Jenny pulled up a chair and prompted Rita to stand on it and take a look.

The wardrobe had a shelf set at about 180cms high, which allowed for a recess at the top, approximately 30cms in height and the full depth of the wardrobe. Its height meant that anything at the back of the shelf would be out of view. Tentatively, Rita stepped on the chair, careful not to fall with her high heels. She could see an old blanket covering something set back in the recess.

"Pull the blanket back," said Jenny. "Be careful though."

Rita did as instructed.

"Oh my God! It's like a bleedin' junkie's paradise."

Tucked at the back of the recess, and obscured from view, was an assortment of illegal drugs and drug paraphernalia; pills, powders, syringes, cigarette papers and various other equipment that Rita didn't even recognise.

"Jesus, this lot must be worth a fortune!"

"Never mind that, Rita. What's it doing in my house?" Jenny wept. "If the police come here, I could be arrested. I could end up in prison, for God's sake! How could he do that to me?"

"Surely you knew he was dealing drugs?"

Jenny glanced at Rita, failing to meet her eyes, "Yes … I had an idea," she admitted. "But I didn't expect him to store them here. Just wait till I see him! He can clear off out of my house and take his drugs with him. There's no way I'm gonna risk going to prison. How would I cope with all them murderers and rock-hard lesbo's?"

Although Jenny spoke in the heat of the moment, and her words had no real substance, Rita still thought it best to warn her, "Now hang on a minute, Jenny. Don't do anything hasty. We don't know what we're dealing with here." Rita was running her hands through her hair again.

With all the drama taking place, Rita didn't realise that Yansis had followed them upstairs, until he spoke.

"Rita is right, Jenny. I think Leroy is a very dangerous man. You need to be careful not to upset him. He might be violent for all we know."

The look on Jenny's face, and the way she flinched, told Rita more than any words.

"Has he hit you?" she asked.

"Not really, well, sort of … He had his hand round my throat once, but he wasn't trying to strangle me or anything. It was just like a warning."

"Really?" asked Rita, the anger evident through the tight creases around her temple. "What else has been going on? You might as well tell us everything now, Jenny. If you want us to help you then there's no point keeping me in the dark. I want to know exactly what the bloody hell's been going on."

Jenny took a deep breath. "Let me put everything back first so he won't know it's been disturbed, then we'll go back downstairs."

Once Jenny had started, it seemed like she couldn't stop.

"Right, I'll start with Winston. He's been working for Leroy since he was 14. He lived on the same estate as him in Moss Side, and Leroy used to recruit younger lads into the Buckthorn Crew. If Leroy hadn't have recruited him, one of the others would have done. Besides, it was what all the lads did round there, and he didn't think he had any other choice. He saw all the older lads with loads of money, flash gear and cars, and he wanted some of what they had. So he went for it, but he didn't know what was involved. Now he hates it, and he'd love to get away."

"Well I can kind of understand him being taken in when he was just a kid, but he's not a kid anymore. So what's he doing still working for Leroy? Why doesn't he leave the gang and try and get a job?"

"Rita, you really haven't got a clue, have you? He's been in and out of detention centres and prison since he was a kid. Who's gonna give him a job with his record? Not to mention the fact that he hasn't got any qualifications or experience."

"But aren't there schemes to help lads that have been in trouble? Couldn't he get on a scheme and leave the gang? Then you and him could move somewhere else and get away from Leroy."

"Don't you think we'd have done that if it was that easy? Those sort of schemes are few and far between. Besides, you don't think Leroy would let us walk off into the sunset together and live happily ever after, do you?"

It was a rhetorical question and, after a brief pause, Jenny continued unburdening herself. "Winston's been telling me some bad stuff about Leroy, but I don't know what to believe. When I first met him, I knew he had a reputation as a hard man, and I knew he smoked dope and dealt in dodgy goods, but that's all I knew. I thought I could handle that, but not the rest, especially not what Winston's been telling me."

"Go on."

"Some of the lads in the Buckthorn Crew say they saw him kill someone … more than one. I didn't know whether to believe it; you know what these rumours are like. There was one in prison, apparently. They say he didn't do that one, but he ordered it and he was there when it happened. There was a gang of them, and they got away with it. Some bloke who had killed a guy that worked for Leroy."

Then Jenny gave the name of the man who was killed in prison. As soon as she heard the name, Rita ran to the bathroom. Her reaction was automatic, and she stayed there for some time, retching, until she had emptied her stomach. When she had finished, she straightened up and stood with her knees slightly bent and her hand propped against the wall to steady herself for a few moments. She took a few deep breaths to regain her equilibrium, before rinsing her mouth and swilling her face under the cold water tap.

"Are you OK, Rita?" asked Yansis who had followed her into the bathroom.

"A bit better now, thanks love. It was just a bit of a shock, that's all," she said, wiping her face with a towel.

"You mean these rumours that Leroy is a killer? It might not be true, Rita."

"I think it is, Yansis. That's why it was such a shock … Do you remember Julie's friend, Amanda, the one that died a few years ago, when me and Julie were suspected of killing her?"

"How could I forget, Rita?"

"Well, do you remember that guy that got killed in prison?"

"Yes, I remember."

"That's who Jenny was just talking about. They never found out who did it."

She didn't like the reaction on Yansis's face. The fear in his eyes was clear, and she hated doing this to him.

"Yansis, you shouldn't have brought me here tonight; I should have got a taxi. I don't like involving you in all this. It isn't fair."

"Nonsense, Rita," he said, placing his hands on her shoulders. "Your problem is my problem, and we will face it together."

Rita stifled a nervous giggle at his melodramatic response, but she appreciated his support, "Thanks, Yansis. Let's get back to Jenny. She'll be wondering what we're up to."

When Rita had heard Jenny relate the rumours about Leroy being a killer, she had written them off in the same way as Yansis. It was just an abstract theory, something nebulous that she didn't regard with any real belief. But when Jenny linked the rumours to an actual event, the murder of someone she was familiar with, then they took on a new meaning. It was now something tangible and more than a theory. Possibility became probability. The shock of this realisation had rocked Rita. As well as being a big time drug dealer, in all likelihood, Leroy was a murderer. And he was living with her sister.

Rita decided to be as frank with Jenny as Jenny had been with her, so she explained the situation regarding the killing in prison. Jenny hadn't made the connection, and she was almost as shocked as Rita. The problem was, there was a part of Jenny that still wouldn't accept it. Even though she had admitted how much Leroy had changed towards her, she still didn't seem ready to come to terms with the possibility that the man she had once loved could be a murderer.

"I'm sorry but we need to go back to Julie's now," said Rita. "Are you sure you'll be OK here?"

"Yeah. Don't worry, Rita. He wouldn't harm me, not while I'm carrying his baby. I'm more worried about having all those bloody drugs in my house."

"I hate to leave you, but I might be able to come up with a way out of all this. I want to get you away from Leroy as soon as possible. I need to talk to Yansis on our own first, though, so leave it with me."

As they said goodbye, Jenny held on tightly, the tears threatening to flow again. Rita found it difficult to prise herself away from her younger sister, but she knew that she had to. "Bye for now. Try to be brave, and

I'll get back to you tomorrow, I promise."

She kissed Jenny on the cheek and walked to the car with Yansis.

Chapter 18

Rita didn't mention her idea in front of Jenny the previous evening, because it would have put Yansis in a difficult position. With both Rita and Jenny present, he would have felt obliged to agree to her plan. As it was, she felt bad enough for asking him. For it to work, she wouldn't just need Yansis's co-operation, but that of his parents and his family and friends too.

Yansis had been a darling and had agreed straightaway, even though she had asked him repeatedly whether he was sure it was what he wanted. She could tell he was nervous about it, but he understood her need to protect her sister. Yansis needed to check that his parents were happy with the situation, though, so she waited while he made the call. Luckily they were in agreement, and Rita was relieved. Once Julie was out of earshot, she rang Jenny to tell her the news.

"Jenny, it's me. How are you? Good … Is Leroy there? Good. Right, here's the plan I was telling you about last night … I've had a word with Yansis and he's agreed for you and Winston to come and live in Greece after you've had the baby. Winston can work in the restaurant, and you can help out too once the baby's old enough."

"Rita, I don't know what to say … that's really good of you, but, but, I don't think it would work."

"Why not?"

"Leroy would come looking for us. He wouldn't stand for it; he'd want the baby."

"Well, we'll have to make sure he doesn't know where you are then."

"He'll know alright. My dad will tell him, for one thing. My mam and dad know your address in Greece. He'll soon get it out of them; they're frightened of him."

"We'll find a way round it, Jenny. You don't have to come out at the same time as us. We can stagger it a bit, and you can stay in a different area till the heat dies down. Yansis has got a massive family and loads of friends. Someone will put you up; they're all lovely people. We've already told his mam and dad so they'll be expecting you."

"What about my mam and dad? What do we tell them?"

"That's the only snag. We can't tell them, Jenny; it's too risky. You know as well as I do that my dad would tell Leroy straightaway."

"You mean, just disappear without telling them?"

"Yeah, it's the only way, Jenny. We can't afford to tell anyone. I'm not even telling Julie and Vinny, because it would put them at risk if Leroy came asking questions. He doesn't know where they live, anyway, and neither do mam and dad, so hopefully they'll be alright. Still, we can't afford to take any chances. Vinny knows lads that live on the estate, and you never know if he might let something slip. It's not that I don't trust them, but the more people that know in Manchester, the more of a chance there is of Leroy finding out."

Rita could hear Jenny sigh down the phone before she replied.

"Rita, it's really good of you and Yansis. I just wish there was another way, though; I can't stand the thought of how my mam's gonna feel when she realises I've gone missing."

Rita prepared herself for another emotional outpouring from Jenny, but instead she could tell that her sister was becoming resigned to the idea as she added, "I suppose I should say thank you."

"It's alright, Jenny. That's what sisters are for, to help each other out when they've got problems, but you'd better not let me down, the pair of you. Winston will have to work for a living and I don't want him getting into any trouble. If he does it'll backfire on me, and I'll bleedin' kill him if he does anything to harm any of Yansis's family."

"Winston wouldn't do that, Rita, I promise. He's a worker. He just needs a chance, that's all."

"Alright, well I'm trusting you on this, so don't let me down, and I want Winston's word for that as well. I'm probably being a complete mug, but I believe you when you say Winston's a good lad deep down, so I'm giving you both this chance."

"You're not a mug, Rita. I'll tell him; he'll be fine, honest. Thanks so much for helping us out."

"Right, well in the meantime, be careful. You've got over two months yet till the baby's born, so you'll have to make sure you don't do anything to upset Leroy. Are you sure you'll be alright with him?"

"Yeah, honest; he wouldn't touch me. He wants this baby too much, so he'd be frightened of harming it."

"Well, I'll have to take your word for it. Just act normal and, for God's sake, don't let him find out what you and Winston are up to!"

"I'll be careful, I promise."

"Oh and, Jenny, Yansis's parents don't know the full facts. They think your boyfriend is in hiding because he testified against somebody in court about a bank robbery. There's no need for them to know the truth. It would frighten the living daylights out of them, so you and Winston will have to keep to the story. We'll rehearse it all before we go over there, OK?"

"Yeah, fine … Thanks again, Rita; you're a life saver."

***

Sunday 5th May 1991 - afternoon

When Leroy walked through the door with Winston, Jenny's first impulse was to run to Winston and throw her arms around him. She knew she couldn't though. Rita's words of a few days ago flashed back into her mind, '*Be careful … don't do anything to upset Leroy … for God's sake, don't let him find out what you and Winston are up to!*'

So she exercised caution, treating Winston with polite indifference, like she would do with any of Leroy's friends and business associates. Although it would be silly to ignore him, she had to make sure that Leroy was the main focus of her attention.

The first thing Leroy did was walk up to her and kiss her fully on the lips. "Hi babe, you alright?" he asked.

This effusive greeting was unusual for Leroy of late, and Jenny suspected that it was for Winston's benefit. She caught a glimpse of Winston as Leroy moved away from her, and was concerned at how downcast he appeared.

"Do us a favour Jen and grab us a beer, will yer? I suppose you'd better get one for this loser too."

Jenny was surprised that Winston now seemed the target of Leroy's venom. She flashed a puzzled glance in his direction, and Winston responded by shrugging his shoulders.

When she returned they were deep in conversation, and Leroy appeared to be telling Winston off. "What's wrong?" she asked.

"Nothing for you to worry about. It's just that this dick wasn't man enough to do a job for me, so I had to do it myself instead. At least I had the balls for it."

"What sort of job?" asked Jenny, responding as she thought Leroy would have expected her to, despite Winston's discomfort.

"Never mind the details. It's sorted now anyway."

Leroy pulled open his can of beer and took a giant swig, smacking his lips, while Jenny and Winston sat in uncomfortable silence. She was used to this ploy by now. It was Leroy's way of making people suffer by forcing them to sit in an uneasy atmosphere. What should she say? Any questions about their day would encourage further criticisms of Winston. Where should she look? She didn't dare look at Winston, tempted though she was, but she could see Winston looking across at her, out of her peripheral vision.

Jenny had taken one of the armchairs, meaning that Leroy was sitting in the other armchair to the right of her, and Winston was sitting on the sofa, which was adjacent and to the left of her. In order to look at Leroy, Winston had to look past Jenny, making things very awkward. There was no other alternative because Leroy insisted on having his own chair, where he kept his cigarette papers, a small packet of weed and Tyson's toys, all stuffed down a hole cut into the upholstery underneath the cushion.

A Gangster's Grip

"I've got another job for Winston. That's why I've brought him back, so we can sort out the details. So you'll have to disappear for a bit while we talk business. I think this one shouldn't be too hard even for Winston." He laughed at his own misguided humour.

Jenny was about to leave the room when he stopped her. "Hang on. Sit down a minute."

She did as Leroy ordered, then he sat forward in his chair and shouted over to Winston, "Were you eyeing her arse?"

Jenny had a moment of panic, convinced that Leroy was going to confront them.

"No, was I 'eck," said Winston. Then, as if to add weight to his argument, he added, "What would I want to look at her arse for?"

"What you saying? Are you saying my missus doesn't have a nice arse?"

"Course I'm not. I mean, I wouldn't know; I don't look at it."

"You don't look at women's arses then. You a bum-boy?"

"No! I just don't look at other women's arses, I mean m-my mates' women, women's arses."

It was excruciating to listen to Winston becoming tongue-tied as he rushed to defend himself. Jenny couldn't understand the reason for Leroy's latest little game; whether it was because Winston had disappointed him, and he wanted to wind him up, or whether he suspected them, she couldn't tell. Surely, though, if he suspected them he would just come out and say it. Well, he'd do more than say it; chances were he'd give them both a good hiding.

Leroy laughed at Winston's discomfort, then ordered Jenny to leave the room. Thinking about it later, she wondered why he hadn't discussed the job elsewhere. Somehow, she didn't think that was the reason Leroy had brought Winston back to the house. There was something about the way he had set out to make them feel ill at ease in front of each other. She felt he knew more about her and Winston than he was letting on, or he at least he had an inkling. Then she shrugged it off. If that was the case, there was no way he would let them get away with it without having his revenge, and that would mean more than just humiliating them. The thought of what he might do to them if he ever found out was too frightening to even consider.

The next time she saw Winston, she asked him what the job was that Leroy had wanted him to do, but he refused to discuss it. Remembering how Leroy had humiliated him, she decided not to press him for more information. Instead, she was left to speculate. Knowing what she already knew, this caused her to worry more about what exactly Leroy got up to.

Chapter 19

Carl was busy at work. Normally he would be out selling at this time on a Friday evening, but he had another job to do. This was something that couldn't be done while the children were around, so he'd had to wait until they were in bed. He couldn't risk them getting their hands on the drugs, knowing that even a small amount could be fatal to a young child.

He covered the dining table with a plastic cover so that any spillage couldn't get into the wood grain. Then he sat down at the table and placed the packets of powder on either side of him. To his left he tipped out the packets of brown heroin and, to the right, the packets of another substance. It was a white powder, which the supplier in Moss Side had assured him would have a similar effect to heroin when mixed with it. The difference was that it had cost him substantially less than he was paying Leroy for his heroin supplies.

Next, he set down his scales in the centre of the table. He poured out a bag of heroin in front of the scales and a bag of the substitute drug, then he mixed them together in equal amounts. The result was a lighter shade of brown, but that suited him, because he could pass it off to his punters as higher grade heroin.

When he was satisfied that the two drugs were well mixed, he scooped small quantities onto the scales, keeping his eye on the dial to make sure that the weight didn't go over. He pulled a small polythene bag from a wad secured with an elastic band and spooned the contents of the scales into it. Then he sealed the top using Sellotape.

"What you doing?" asked Debby.

"What's it look like? I'm getting the supplies ready for the punters. Help us out," he said, passing her a handful of the small polythene bags and a second spoon. "I want to get it done so I can go out selling."

"You're mixing 'em, aren't you?"

"So, what if I am? It's not as if the junkies are gonna know the difference. Anyway, my takings are right down since I've had to start dealing in Longsight. I've gotta make up the money somehow. And your habit doesn't come cheap, you know."

"Leroy will go mad if he knows you're skimmin' the drugs."

"He won't find out, will he? And you'd better keep your gob shut."

"Don't do it, Carl; it's not worth it!"

He reacted by swiping her across the face with the back of his hand. "Don't fuckin' tell me what to do! I've been doing it for weeks now and nobody's noticed, so why's it a big deal all of a sudden?"

Debby pulled up a chair while rubbing her throbbing cheek with her other hand. "You shouldn't have done that, Carl."

"Well don't wind me up then. You asked for it … Are you gonna get some of these bags filled, or what?"

Debby obeyed him. He knew she would. She relied on him too much to feed her habit, so she was prepared to take whatever treatment he dished out to her, including the regular beatings. They sat filling the bags together until Carl broke the silence by going into one of his rants about Leroy.

"You know, that Leroy really thinks he's the dog's bollocks. He's got me and Winston dealing in Longsight while all the time he's still down the Moss every night. He's such a crafty bastard. He's getting rich pickings, a mark-up from us and, if Mad Trevor or any of the other lads find out about us selling the H that we got from the Cheetham Crew, he can act as though he knows nothing about it.

"So this is my little side-line, something he knows nowt about. He's not the only crafty bastard around. Word's getting around in Longsight about our gear, and by the time trade picks up, I should be quids in."

He looked at Debby for a response, feeling proud of his statement, but she remained silent.

***

A Gangster's Grip

Leroy was late for his meeting with Carl. He liked to keep him waiting; it kept him in his place, and let him know who was boss. As he approached Carl, he chuckled, noting the desperate look on his pathetic little face.

"Alright mate?" greeted Carl.

"Yeah, you?"

Leroy got straight down to business. He had called at Carl's home to collect his share of his earnings for the last week. When Carl handed over the wad of notes, Leroy counted it slowly while Carl waited. Satisfied with the amount, Leroy gave him a slap on the back, "Cheers mate; looks like it's not going too bad in Longsight."

Carl didn't reply, but Leroy could sense his festering resentment and decided he would have to keep an eye on him. If loyalty was going to be an issue, then he would have to set him a task that would test him. In any case, he'd already given it some thought and decided on the task before he came here. After all, there was no point in doing your own dirty work when you had other mugs to do it.

"It looks as though Cheetham Hill's working out for us, so we're gonna carry on getting the H from there. They give us a good price on some of the other gear too."

"OK."

"There'll be a bit of a change though ... I want you to buy 'em in."

"Me? Why me?"

"Because I fuckin' said so!"

"But what about Winston? Can't he do it?"

"Don't make me laugh. He hasn't got the bottle. He's frightened of his own fuckin' shadow. I sent him to give someone a good slappin' a few days ago and he bottled it. I ended up having to do it myself. I think Winston's got the wrong idea about what a good slappin' means."

He allowed Carl to take in this information, then added, "Or are you telling me you haven't got the bottle either?"

"No, it's not that. I'm just a bit worried about what would happen if

Mad Trevor and the others found out what I was up to."

"I thought you were tougher than that. Why do you think I'm asking you and not Winston? Now you're telling me you can't handle it? You're OK to sell the H that I get for you, but you don't want to get it yourself. What kind of a mug do you take me for?"

"No, no, I don't Leroy, honest. OK, I'll do it."

"You sure you can handle it?"

"Yeah, course I can; just tell me what you want me to do."

"There's nowt to it. I'll fix the meet-up. I'll agree the prices beforehand, so don't let him put one over on you. Then, you just go with the cash, and bring the goods back. Easy as that."

Despite the simplified instructions that Leroy was giving, Carl knew there was a lot more involved. In terms of risk, this was about as bad as it got.

Chapter 20

Although it was not yet eight in the morning, it was already shaping up to be an eventful day for Rita. She had just come off the phone with Jenny, and then noticed the post had arrived. As she sifted through the letters she saw one from the hospital, and knew it would be the one they had been waiting for. Yansis was just on his way out of the door with Vinny when he spotted the NHS sign on the envelope, denoting that it was from the National Health Service.

"Oh, Rita, why don't you open it now, then I can read it before I go to work?"

When Rita saw the eager look on his face, she knew he would be disappointed if she kept him waiting. She looked at Vinny for approval.

"It's OK, I can hang on for a minute," said Vinny in response. "I'll wait in the van."

She ripped the envelope open and scanned the letter. "It's our next appointment; Thursday 6th June."

"That's good news, Rita. It is not so far away," said Yansis.

"Yeah, only about three weeks."

She couldn't help her lack of enthusiasm. This latest call from Jenny was troubling her.

"I thought you would be happy, Rita. We will soon be able to find out what the problem is. Then perhaps we will be able to have babies."

"I'm sorry, Yansis. I am happy, but I'm a bit preoccupied at the moment. That call was from Jenny; she wants me to go round. She didn't sound right. I think there's something else troubling her."

"Why must you always go running round there, Rita? It isn't fair. We have our own lives to think of."

"I know that, Yansis, and I'm sorry, love, but you know she won't come round here. She doesn't want to bring any trouble to Julie's door. Things are bad enough as it is. You couldn't drop me off, could you, and then follow Vinny to work later? I want to get there as soon as possible. She hasn't phoned me this early for nothing … I know, I know, I shouldn't ask you but …"

She saw he was already regretting his hasty words. He didn't usually stay angry with her for long. "It's OK, Rita. I shouldn't shout at you; I know it is not your fault. Let me tell Vinny what I am doing. I am sure he won't mind."

"Thanks love," she said as she planted a kiss on his cheek. "Oh and, Yansis? I am chuffed about the hospital appointment. It might not seem like it, but it just came at the wrong time, that's all."

"That's OK, I understand. Now let me go and tell Vinny, otherwise he will be very upset with me."

***

Monday 13th May 1991 - morning

When Rita arrived at Jenny's, a quick scan of the cars in the street told her that neither Leroy nor Winston were in the house. She hoped that the fact Jenny had rung her meant she had had the foresight to put the dog outside if it was at home, and cursed herself for not mentioning it earlier.

Because of her concerns, Yansis came inside with her to make sure everything was OK. She wouldn't have asked him to do so; she felt bad enough for making him late for work, but she was relieved that he had come inside. At least if the dog was there, she wouldn't be on her own. Fortunately, it was nowhere to be seen. The only person there was Jenny, and once Yansis was satisfied that all was in order, he said goodbye and left.

"Where's Leroy?" asked Rita.

"God knows! I don't bother asking anymore. I'll only get told to mind my own business. He went out yesterday, and took the dog with him. He often stays out all night. I think he has other women."

"Doesn't surprise me. You alright?"

"Yeah, you know."

"You didn't sound too good on the phone."

"I'm not really but, well, it doesn't get any better, does it?"

Rita could sense that Jenny had something to tell her, but she wasn't the only one. Rita had been putting it off, trying to decide whether to open up. But the more she thought about it, the more it seemed the best thing to do. Jenny needed to know exactly what Leroy was up to so she could have her wits about her. Although it would frighten and upset her, she was already in this situation, so there was no point hiding things from her any longer.

"Jenny, there's something you need to know. It's about Leroy's trips to Cheetham Hill. I've known for a couple of weeks actually, but you were that upset the last couple of times I saw you that I didn't want to upset you even more."

"For God's sake, Rita, get to the point! What is it?"

"Well ... have you heard of the other gang, called the MSC?"

"Yeah, course I have. Winston said the Buckthorn Crew hate them. They're enemies."

"But did he tell you that the Buckthorns are also enemies with the Cheetham Crew?"

"No, why?"

"They're friends of the MSC and, from what I've found out, the Buckthorn Crew don't like dealing with them. So, it got me thinking about Leroy's trips to Cheetham Hill. Do you think he could be playing both sides off against each other?"

"I don't know. Why?"

"Well, maybe he can get drugs cheaper from them or something. I don't know why he'd want to deal with them, but my point is that he might be dealing with enemies of his own gang. And if he is, how d'you think that will go down with the Buckthorns?"

"Shit! I don't know."

"Don't get me wrong, Jenny, but it might be part of the reason Leroy was so keen to move in with you in the first place. Aside from being able to hide his drugs, he's out of the way in Longsight. If he was still on the Buckthorn Estate, there would be more chance of his gang finding out what he was up to."

Jenny's shock was evident from the taught lines on her face as she replied, "Yeah but, he was living in Longsight anyway, at his mam's."

"I know, but I bet he wasn't hiding drugs in his mam's house. There'd be too much risk of someone finding them in a houseful of people."

Jenny stayed silent for a moment.

"Are you OK, Jenny?" asked Rita.

Jenny clenched her teeth, and took a deep breath, before speaking. "Rita, I don't know how much more of this I can take. There's something else I need to tell you … I think Leroy suspects me and Winston."

"Jesus, that's all we need! What makes you think that?"

"It's the way he acts whenever me or Winston are in the same room as him. It's like he's deliberately trying to show us up in front of each other. He even accused Winston of eyeing up my arse the other day. He was trying to make him squirm just for a laugh."

"Yeah but, maybe that's just how he is. Surely if he thought it, he'd confront you both."

"I don't know, Rita; It's hard to tell whether he knows or not, but he seems to be enjoying watching us both squirm for some reason. Maybe he just thinks Winston fancies me, I don't know. But that's not all … There's something else …"

"Jesus, Jenny, aren't things bad enough?"

"You won't believe what I found in his hiding place, Rita."

"What?"

"Weapons. Guns, knives, a flamin' machete!"

"Oh Jesus Christ!"

Rita was back to running her hands through her hair, then she was up on her feet. "Come on, show me."

Seeing the evidence for herself didn't make any difference; there was nothing she could do. But she had to see it. She needed some form of authentication so she knew exactly what they were dealing with. But now she wished she hadn't asked to look.

Despite the amount of damage that guns could inflict, it was the sight of the machete that made her sweat. Its elongated steel blade curved menacingly towards a sharp pointed tip. As she stared at it, Rita had a mental vision of trips to the butchers when she was a kid. Watching the butcher hacking away at slabs of meat. Separating the joints. Sawing through bone. The thought that one of these weapons could be used in a similar way on a live human being was too much.

It was unusual for Rita to be speechless, but for several seconds she froze. Then, she became aware that her younger sister was looking to her for guidance.

"Jenny, I think you need to get out of here. Now! And we should report this lot to the police."

"The police! Are you joking? You don't grass up anyone to the police, Rita, especially gangs. How safe do you think we'd be if we did that? We wouldn't just have Leroy to worry about; the whole bloody gang would be after us! And I can't move out. Where can I go? This is my bloody home."

"I know, I know, I'm thinking."

At least, Rita was trying to think. But her mind was in turmoil. There was too much to take in, and danger at every level. Drugs. Guns. An illicit affair under a vicious gangster's nose! How much worse could it get?

"Right, OK … You can't go to my mam and dad's. We've already said that. It's the first place he'd look for you. What about friends?"

"No! He knows them all. I couldn't have Leroy going round their houses, anyway. It wouldn't be fair."

"OK, well Julie's is out of the question for the same reason. I've brought enough trouble to her door already."

Before Rita went any further, Jenny interrupted her.

"Rita, he wouldn't harm me, not while I'm carrying his baby. Don't you see? The weapons are to fight the other gangs. It's in the Evening

News all the time. I just didn't know he was part of all that. He might not even be the one that uses the weapons; he might just store them for the gang."

"Oh get wise, Jenny! Why the bloody hell would he risk keepin' them here if he wasn't gonna use them? You're still in danger, Jenny, even if the weapons are for the gang to use; especially if he knows about you and Winston."

"Maybe he doesn't know, otherwise, why hasn't he done anything? Honestly, Rita, he wouldn't harm me. If I thought he would, I wouldn't hang around, I promise you."

"Right, well you'd better make bloody sure he doesn't find out about you and Winston then! It's not just him I'm worried about, though. What if his gang find out he's been dealing with the Cheetham Crew?"

"We don't know that, Rita. Besides, if that is what he's doing, then, like you say, he might be keeping this address secret."

"What about a guest house? I'll help you out if you can't afford it."

"Where would I put my stuff for the baby? I'd never manage in a guest house with a baby."

"It wouldn't be for long; only till we can get you to Greece after the baby's born."

"No, we don't have to do that. I've told you, I'll be OK. I'll take care that he doesn't find out about me and Winston. And he's not stupid; if he's buying from Cheetham Hill, then he'll have been careful about telling people where he lives. As far as I know, there's only Winston and Carl who know this address."

"I just wish there was more I could do for you, Jenny, but it won't be for long. What are you now, 31 weeks?"

"Yeah, that's right."

"Well, let's hope it soon passes. In the meantime, you be extra careful. If anyone strange comes to the house, you'll have to be alert, especially if it's a group of guys looking for Leroy. If you suspect they might be after him, then you need to get out of here as quickly as you can."

A Gangster's Grip

"Course I will but, like I say, I don't think they'll know he's here. That's even if they are after him. We don't know that."

Rita knew she was wasting her time trying to reason any more with Jenny, who was determined to stay put till after the baby was born. When they had run out of conversation, Rita headed back to Julie's. Each time she left Jenny, she found it increasingly difficult.

As she walked to the bus stop, she mulled everything over in her mind. Despite Jenny's brave words, Rita was worried about her. She wasn't convinced that everything would be alright, and she wondered how much of Jenny's assurances had been bravado, and how much of them had been naivety. Did Jenny really still think that Leroy was OK, and that he wouldn't harm her?

It was incredible to think that Jenny had allowed herself to end up in this situation. But she had always been foolish as a child. Always hung around with the wrong crowd, and got up to things she shouldn't. Rita had lost count of the number of tricky situations she had helped her out of. Things were never black or white though. Jenny also had a sweet, loving side. And she was very trusting with people, although that might have been more of a fault than a virtue.

Rita deliberated about how much of this latest information she should share with Yansis. He would tell her she was getting too involved, and would think she was a fool for doing so. Yet he would still stand by her, because Yansis was like that. He loved her with all his heart, and would do almost anything to help her if she was having a bad time, even if he wasn't particularly happy about it.

But, at the end of the day, Jenny was her sister. As tempted as she was to go back to Greece, and put all this behind her, she knew she couldn't. Rita's conscience tugged at her; she wouldn't allow herself to abandon Jenny. If she did so, and something awful happened to her, she would never forgive herself.

Chapter 21

On 16th May 1991 at 9.41pm, two young lads walked into a Moss Side pub and headed to the bar. One of them asked if he could buy some crisps to take out. While the lad was being served his friend looked around the room, noting where certain people were sitting. They completed the exchange and left.

Ten minutes later, six masked men entered the same pub, their weapons concealed under long coats. Customers looked at them, confused, their minds not having chance to register what was happening. Two of the men approached the bar. The landlord, assuming they were after his takings, dashed towards the phone.

"Don't touch that phone!" ordered one of the masked men, withdrawing a revolver and aiming it at the landlord.

Meanwhile, his partner covered the customers that hung around the bar area, swivelling his gun from side to side, to let them know they were all within range. "If you all keep calm and don't do anything stupid, you'll be OK."

The customers stared, alarmed at the sight of the guns, and the pub fell silent.

The other four men took only seconds to get their bearings. Having been tipped off beforehand, they knew where their enemies would be situated. After spotting a few of the MSC members sitting around a particular table, they took out their weapons and opened fire. Customers gasped in horror, a couple of them dropping their glasses in shock.

Two minutes later it was all over. The gang left the pub and sped away in two stolen cars. The burnt out cars were found abandoned later, three miles away.

***

A Gangster's Grip

Friday 17th May 1991 – early evening

It was the latest in a series of anxious calls that Jenny had made to Rita. Leroy hadn't been home for two days and she was worried. It wasn't unusual for him to stay away for days at a time. She had no doubt that he spent time with other women, as she had already told her sister. However, in view of what Rita had told her about gang rivalry, she wondered what could have happened to him.

There had also been a report in the press about gangland killings last night. Several men wearing masks had walked into a pub and shot at a number of customers, who were believed to be gangsters, killing five. What if one of the dead was Leroy?

She hadn't failed to see the irony of her situation; if anything had happened to Leroy it would provide the perfect escape for her and Winston. And yet she was concerned. She guessed there was a tiny part of her that still cared. A part of her that still yearned for the charming persona she had fallen for when she first met him. Sadly though, that facet of Leroy was much in abeyance nowadays.

Jenny's brain was trying to process all the information that had come to light over the past few weeks. Things had deteriorated, and she somehow couldn't reconcile who Leroy was with who he had seemed to be. When she met him she had felt proud. To her he was tough, and respected by everyone, and he treated her like a princess. It made her feel special when she was out with him.

Then, as the weeks went by, his attitude changed. He became surly and preoccupied, and conversation was sometimes strained. She never knew whether he would be up or down. At first his good moods more than compensated for the down periods, so she learned to tread carefully when he was feeling irritable, and made the most of the times when he was upbeat. But as time went on, his mood swings increased, and she knew better than to tackle him about it.

Now, though, it was about more than coping with Leroy's mood swings. Could he really be a dangerous man? The man she had once loved? The man who had told her he loved her too? Surely not! Despite being frightened, she consoled herself with the thought that he wouldn't harm the woman he professed to love, not while she was carrying his baby.

Rita was once again trying to offer words of comfort when he walked through the door. Although Rita had told Jenny to act normal, due to her anxious state she jumped as the door opened, and the dog ran towards her barking. Realising that he couldn't overhear Rita on the other end of the phone, Jenny attempted to calm herself and turned to greet him. She knew as soon as she saw him that he wasn't happy. '*Best tread carefully,*' she thought.

"Hiya love, where've you been? Are you alright?"

He ignored her and walked past, so she tended to the dog. "Come on Tyson, down boy!" Then she whispered into the phone, "Rita, I'd best go."

"I thought as much. OK, you take care, and don't forget what I've told you. See you soon."

Jenny felt trepidation as she walked into the living room to encounter Leroy slumped in his chair. He was already clutching a can of lager. She had to say something. After he had spent two days away, how could she say nothing? Nevertheless, she was wary of being confrontational."

"Is everything alright?"

"Sure. Why wouldn't it be?"

"With you not being home, I thought something might have happened. I was worried about you."

"Just business," he said, as he levered the ring-pull on his can of lager.

"Oh, it was just … with you not ringing. I was worried."

"Stop fussing, woman." He pointed to her as he spoke his next words. "Just 'cos I moved in with you, don't mean I answer to you, right?"

"But, I was worried, Leroy."

"No-one tells me how to run my fuckin' life!"

She could feel his anger building, and knew she had to defuse it before it got out of control. "It's only 'cos I care about you."

A sly grin formed on his lips. "Right, well stop giving me grief then, and get me summat to eat."

To signal that it was the end of the conversation, he picked up the remote control and switched on the television. Jenny retreated to the kitchen, crestfallen. Her feelings were a mixture of fear, anger and humiliation, but she attempted to rid herself of the overwhelming emotions by the time she served up their meal.

As she washed and cleared away the dishes, Jenny wondered what the evening had in store for them. It was rare that Leroy took her out nowadays, so chances were that he would either go out again, as he often did after they had eaten, or she would have to sit through his choice of television programmes until it was time for bed.

"Load of shite!" he cursed when she walked into the living room. He was flicking through the television channels, rejecting each of them in turn. "Don't know why we bother with a tele. It's nowt but shite."

He looked at Jenny, for affirmation, she assumed. She was about to say something in support of his views when he announced, "Let's go up."

"What?"

"Upstairs. Nowt else to do; might as well go up now."

His demand took her by surprise. Any spontaneous lovemaking had taken place earlier in their relationship. Lately, he had settled for a quickie before they had both gone to sleep. This wasn't like the spontaneous lovemaking of a passionate relationship though. It was more of an order. It was on a par with 'make the tea', 'bring me a beer' or 'feed the dog'. There was no love involved, and the thought of this unnerved her.

"I don't really feel up to it tonight, Leroy. I keep getting bad indigestion 'cos of the baby."

"A bit of wind will do you no harm. Bit of action might get rid of it, as long as you don't fart on the job," he laughed. "Anyway, you'll soon come round to the idea. You know what a randy little cow you are when you get going."

"I don't feel like …"

Before she had chance to finish what she was saying, he put down his lager, stood up and was taking her by the hand and leading her from the room. At one time, his assertiveness would have been a turn-on, but now it was terrifying. She dawdled behind him, her heart pounding, as he led her up the stairs and into the bedroom.

He was soon undressed, and Jenny stared at his erect penis, fumbling at her buttons with unsteady hands. Even his honed body had failed to arouse her.

"Well, what you waiting for? Are you gonna get your kit off, or what? Anyone would think you were a virgin, not a woman who was seven months gone."

She finished undressing and slipped into bed, bracing herself while he slavered over her with eager kisses. She tried to respond but was finding it difficult.

"For fuck's sake, Jenny, what's wrong with you? It's like being in bed with a zombie. Sex doesn't do you no harm when you're pregnant, you know!"

Jenny didn't reply. If Leroy thought that was the reason for her reluctance, then she was prepared to go along with it.

He soon gave up on any attempts at foreplay, and roughly turned her over onto her front. Jenny knew what was required of her, and pulled herself to her knees until she was on all fours. She willed it to be over as quickly as possible. Her lack of preparation didn't make it easy, and she gritted her teeth as he entered her.

Not having any regard for her feelings or satisfaction, he soon finished, and she slumped onto her side, facing away from him once he had withdrawn. She heard him walk to the bathroom then return. To her surprise, he started getting dressed. She turned onto her back, her face questioning his actions.

"Oh, interested now, are you?"

"Where are you going?"

"Like you care."

She watched as he sat on the bed to put on his socks then stood up and pulled on his jeans. He was just about to walk out of the bedroom when he paused and turned back to her. "There's summat you need to remember, Jenny. I do what the fuck I like, when I like, and no-one tells me what I can or can't do. So stop asking questions if you know what's good for you."

Jenny listened to his footsteps walking through to the spare bedroom, presumably to collect something from the wardrobe. He wandered round the house for a few minutes, then he was gone. Once she was satisfied that he had left, her tears of relief drenched the pillow.

Chapter 22

The Buckthorn Crew were celebrating. They had carried out their attack on the MSC in retaliation for Mikey's death, and it had gone well. It was usual to carry out reprisals on members of the MSC. The two gangs had been enemies for years.

No-one was sure how it all started; it had been going on for so long. Some said it was over a girl, others said it began as an argument over territory. Everybody accepted it as the way things were. Usually, one of the gangs would attack a member of the other gang, which would result in death or severe injury. The opposing gang would then hit back.

Lately, the MSC had struck too many times, and the Buckthorns were determined to even the score, especially since Mikey's murder. Using some of the younger members of the gang, the Buckthorn Crew kept a track of the places where the MSC hung out. When they received a tip off that several of the MSC were drinking in a Moss Side pub, they knew the time was right. That had been two nights ago.

The police had difficulty gathering evidence. All the witnesses could tell them was that it was a group of men with masks, long coats and shotguns. They walked into the pub, carried out the shootings and dashed back out again. Nobody admitted to knowing the victims. Nobody knew of a reason for the killings. And nobody had seen the registration plates of the getaway cars.

The Buckthorn Crew later learnt through news reports that five people were dead, and two severely injured. As all the shots were aimed at the MSC, the Buckthorns assumed they were the victims. However, Mad Trevor later found out through his sources that two of the dead were members of the Cheetham Crew. This gave him a double cause to celebrate as he hated them as much as he hated the MSC.

Leroy wasn't quite as overjoyed as Mad Trevor. He too had a mean streak, but where Mad Trevor derived pleasure from gaining the upper hand in gang warfare, Leroy's motivation was more on a personal level. He liked to intimidate people and witness their humiliation and fear, especially if they had wronged him. For now though, Leroy was enjoying the camaraderie.

At the same time, Leroy was cautious; that was why he hadn't asked Winston and Carl to this meeting. They knew too much about his other operations. Instead, he had made excuses for them, and let Mad Trevor believe that he preferred it if this celebration was for the more senior members of the Buckthorn Crew.

They had picked this club for a reason. It was a place frequented by prostitutes who would help them continue their celebrations well into the night. Leroy and Mad Trevor were sitting in an alcove with another two Buckthorn Crew members who were already occupied with the local girls. They had several pints of lager on the table, and the smell of cannabis hung in the air.

"We sorted the MSC good and proper," said Mad Trevor, who then paused to take a drag of his joint. "Fuckin' bonus to take out two of the Cheetham Crew as well, innit?"

"Dead right." Leroy tried to muster some enthusiasm. He was relieved that he had suggested the masks, insisting it would protect them in case any witnesses were brave enough to come forward. Secretly, he hoped that one of the two men wasn't his contact, not that he held him in high regard, but it would impinge on his heroin supplies.

"They're gonna come back at us after this. Best make sure we're ready for 'em."

"I know that," said Leroy. "We've gotta make sure we're always armed and don't go to the same clubs all the time."

"They might team up now and try and hit us together."

"It don't matter. We can still take 'em, man. The MSC are clueless anyway. They're not organised. Most of 'em are kids."

"I know. Don't worry, we'll be ready." Raising his can of lager, Mad Trevor announced, "To the Buckthorn Crew, the top crew in the Moss."

Leroy responded by raising his can, and the dense clink of metal on metal could be heard as they bashed them together. This caught the attention of the other two gang members, who briefly joined in before returning to the girls' ministrations.

When Mad Trevor had exhausted the subject of gang warfare, he eyed up some of the girls who had been circling him and Leroy. The local girls knew of their reputations as members of the Buckthorn Crew, but they also knew about their willingness to spend large amounts of money when they were celebrating. Many of the girls were attracted to Leroy for the same reason Jenny had been. As well as having physical appeal, he could be charming and charismatic when he wanted. There was also a certain kudos in being linked to one of the prime gang members. Leroy looked around at the swarms of willing girls, and knew that he was in for a good night. And if the mood suited him, he might even extend his celebrations over a day or two.

***

Saturday 18th May 1991 - evening

Jenny knew she was taking a risk; Winston shouldn't be here with her, but what else could she do? She had to see him, and there was nowhere else they could go but her home.

"It's OK," Winston assured her, when she began fretting. "I've told you, Leroy's out celebrating with Mad Trevor. I know how these things go. They'll be out all night at least."

"God, I hope so," said Jenny.

"Don't worry. I won't stay that long, just in case."

They were lying in Jenny and Leroy's double bed, half-naked. It was unusual for them to take such a risk, but they had given in to temptation because of Winston's knowledge of Leroy's whereabouts. Now though, as the heat of their passion died down, Jenny was losing her nerve.

"Let's get dressed and sit downstairs, in case he comes back early."

"If you want, but there's no reason why he should."

"You never know with Leroy," said Jenny. "He might have a row with the other lads and storm out."

"Alright then, but we'll still have to think of summat to tell him if he comes in. I can't say I came looking for him when I know where he is, can I?"

"OK, we'll think of something. What are they celebrating anyway?"

"A raid."

"What kind of raid?"

"Do you really want the details, Jenny? It's not good. I'm surprised you ain't seen it in the news."

"What?"

"The pub shootings."

"Jesus, you're joking!"

Jenny had seen the newspaper reports but hadn't linked them to Leroy as a perpetrator. Despite all she now knew about him, she was still in denial to an extent. It was ironic that she'd been more concerned about him being a victim of the raid. But if he was carrying out this type of thing then there was no doubting that he was a full on gangster. She found it hard to accept that he could boldly walk into a pub full of customers and shoot people down. No matter who they were and what they had done, it didn't make it right.

"No, it's true. They went to get the MSC."

"You weren't there, were you?"

"No, thank God! Leroy reckons I ain't got the bottle for it. That's why he didn't invite me tonight; he said I don't deserve to celebrate. Suits me though. You know I'm not into all that kinda stuff."

"I'm glad you're not like that, Winston," said Jenny, stroking her cheek against his bare chest. "Thank God we'll soon be out of it. Only eight weeks now till the baby's due, then we can sod off to Greece. I can't wait. You never know, it might even come early." She was enjoying cuddling up next to Winston but before she got carried away, she said, "Come on, we'd best get downstairs."

Jenny shuddered as she pulled back the covers, although it was warm in the bedroom. She knew that the chill that ran down her spine was nothing to do with the weather; it was the fact that Winston's words had emphasised the fear that now stayed with her constantly.

Chapter 23

The man approached Carl, his face pale, gaunt and covered in blemishes. Carl recognised a repeat customer when he saw one, and was pleased that word was spreading in Longsight. Despite his desperate appearance, the man surprised Carl by his insistence on examining the goods before making a purchase.

However, Carl was used to dealing with junkies and treated them with the contempt he felt they deserved. He knew he had the upper hand. Most of them were so eager for their next fix that they didn't put up much of a fight. It didn't stop a few of them trying it on though. Dealing in Longsight also gave Carl an added advantage, because there wasn't the level of competition from other dealers that there was in Moss Side.

"You'd better come away from the main road if you want to look at them. I ain't risking being fuckin' pulled just 'cos you're being awkward."

He led the man down an alleyway, where he held open a bag of smack for the man to examine. The darkness of the alleyway made it difficult to see the drugs but, nevertheless, the man objected.

"It's a bit pale innit?"

"That's 'cos it's good stuff," said Carl. "None of that shit you get down the Moss. You can tell it's quality by the colour. Don't you know nowt?"

"Yeah, course I do, but a mate of mine bought some from Longsight and he said it was a bit iffy."

Carl pulled the bag away from the man. "Right, fuck off. I'm wasting my time with you. If you don't know good stuff when you see it, then go and find some other shit. I reckon your mate must have been so out of it he can't remember where he got the stuff from. All my customers know this is the best …"

Carl walked away as he continued his tirade, knowing he wouldn't get very far. It was obvious the man was in withdrawal, and wanted his fix as soon as possible. It was therefore unlikely that he would spend ten minutes driving to Moss Side to find another dealer.

"Wait! OK, maybe my mate got it wrong," said the man, as he dashed after Carl.

Not all of his customers were so awkward to deal with. Most of them weren't concerned with the colour. Maybe they suspected the heroin was mixed with something else but they were past caring; as long as it satisfied their cravings, they were content.

Although custom had increased in Longsight over the last few weeks, Carl's income still didn't compare to what he had made previously in Moss Side. He realised that a good proportion of his earnings came from sales of heroin, and Leroy did have a point about the risk of selling it down the Moss. Nevertheless, Carl felt bitter about the loss of income, and the way in which he always had to take orders from Leroy.

Tonight, in particular, his festering resentment was in abundance, because Leroy had arranged for him to meet his suppliers in Cheetham Hill. That meant that Carl had to finish selling early, on one of the busiest nights of the week. Why Leroy couldn't have organised it for another night, or day, he didn't know, but when he had questioned him, he had turned nasty again. Still, at least he was making extra money from the skimming, and that thought gave him a warm glow, knowing he was getting one up on Leroy.

Carl jumped in his white BMW, and dropped his remaining drugs and cash at home before setting off for Cheetham Hill. He would be calling to see Leroy as soon as he had collected the drugs, so he thought it prudent to keep his own supplies separate.

As it was late evening, the roads were quiet until he reached the centre of Manchester. He could have taken a right turn after Piccadilly Station and skirted around the city centre, but he decided to take in the buzzing Saturday night atmosphere. It was a mistake. Drunken revellers packed the streets, which slowed down his progress. He revved his engine in annoyance to disperse the drunken hordes who littered the roads.

Eventually he hit Deansgate, a busy stretch of road dating back to Roman times. Here the revellers mixed with the theatre crowd as the popular Opera House and Royal Exchange theatres were nearby. He guessed that a show must have finished at the Opera House, as crowds of well-dressed people were coming out of Quay Street. He had just passed the John Rylands neo Gothic library, heading towards the end of Deansgate in the direction of Cheetham Hill, when he noticed a few familiar faces, and his stomach lurched.

Standing outside a popular Deansgate bar were Mad Trevor and three other members of the gang. Carl was too late to do anything about it. What could he do anyway? He was in the driver's seat; he could hardly duck. As he sped past, he knew that one of the gang had spotted him.

That was all he needed! Having to explain himself to Mad Trevor and the others wasn't going to be fun. To tell them he was out clubbing wouldn't be convincing when he was in the car on his own. The fact that he had driven past the busy stretch of bars and clubs wouldn't help either. As he turned off Deansgate, he tried to think of an excuse he could give as to why he was driving through the centre of Manchester at ten o'clock on a Saturday night.

During the rest of his trip to Cheetham Hill, the thought occurred to him that it was unusual for members of the gang to be out in Manchester. But then he surmised that everyone had a night off now and again. Perhaps they fancied a change from the Moss. They might have even been checking out the other gangs that operated in the city centre. He'd have to mention it to Leroy and see what he thought.

While these thoughts were running through his head, he hit on a good reason for his presence there. He could say he had gone to pick Debby up. The silly cow had got herself in a state mixing her usual drugs with too much booze, and he had gone to fetch her home. He was circling around looking for somewhere to park when he had passed the lads. Hopefully, they would fall for that one; after all, everyone knew what a nightmare the one way system was.

Once Carl was back in Longsight, he called at Jenny's home, as Leroy was expecting him.

"Who's that at this time of night?" Jenny shouted from the living room, where she was watching television.

"No-one for you to worry about," Leroy replied. He then led Carl upstairs and checked through the drugs he had bought, to make sure everything was in order.

"Nice one," he said, giving Carl a hearty slap on the back.

Carl decided that it would be best to broach the subject of Mad Trevor and the other members of the gang straightaway, as it was playing on his mind. To his relief, Leroy didn't seem fazed by the situation at all.

"They go up to Manchester now and again. They like to flash the cash and impress the girls. I think it gives Trev a buzz if he can pull a bit of class. Whatever turns you on, I suppose. I couldn't be doing with some snobby bitch looking down her nose at me. Still, they usually shift some gear while they're in town, so it's a win, win for them. Anyway, mate, if anyone asks, just stick to your story about Debby getting pissed and you having to pick her up. I'll back you up on it."

"OK," said Carl whose relief was turning to suppressed rage. It was easy enough for Leroy just to back him up on his story, but he was the mug taking all the risks. He left Jenny's house as soon as possible. He didn't want to give Leroy a chance to see the anger in his eyes; it was becoming more and more difficult to keep his ill-feeling hidden.

After the events of the night, Carl was glad to arrive home. Although it was late, he counted his earnings before he went to bed. There were two reasons for doing it at this hour. The first was that he would be comparing his takings to the drugs he still had, and he didn't want to do that when the kids were around. The second reason was because it always gave Carl a thrill to find out how much money he had made.

Tonight he was disappointed when he counted his takings. For a

A Gangster's Grip

Saturday night, even in Longsight, it should have been much more. But it didn't help that he had had to spend part of the night driving to Cheetham Hill. He was also aware that a portion of his earnings had to go back to Leroy. In the early days, he had been happy with this arrangement, but now it angered him. What was Leroy's justification for his cut if he wasn't buying in the drugs? Carl was the one meeting with the suppliers.

He drew comfort from the fact that he still had a decent supply of drugs left, thanks to the skimming, so his profit margins were good in terms of the amount of drugs he had sold. What use was that, though, if he didn't have chance to shift the stuff? He had a good mind to start dealing in Moss Side again, and to obtain his own drugs direct from the suppliers. That would teach Leroy a lesson!

But he wouldn't do any of those things; he was too afraid of Leroy's temper, and he knew that the repercussions would be more than he could handle. Throughout the process of counting and bagging up the money, Carl's face contorted with rage and he cursed Leroy repeatedly.

***

Sunday 26th May 1991 – early afternoon

Rita and Jenny were sitting side by side in the back of Vinny's car, with Yansis driving. As soon as they had picked Jenny up, on the way to her parents' house, Rita had switched from the front passenger seat to the rear, to be next to her. Rita wasn't looking forward to this visit. Ever since her argument with her father, relations had been strained. She had visited her mother several times since then, but had rung her beforehand to make the arrangements. By doing so, Ged would find out she was coming and would make excuses not to be there.

Now though, they were out of excuses. Her mother wanted to have Sunday dinner with them all seated round the table together, just like old times (with the exception of John who was away in the army). It was a sweet thought, but Rita knew that the occasion would be about as sweet as a bottle of vinegar.

There was bound to be a bad atmosphere once she and her dad were sitting near to each other. Aside from that, she was worried about Jenny letting something slip. Jenny had already told her that Leroy wouldn't be there, so Rita wanted to make sure that this didn't lull Jenny into a false sense of security. The last thing Rita needed was for her mother and father to find out about her plans, which was why she was having a discussion with Jenny in the car.

"Right, listen to me, Jenny. You're not to say a word to my mam and dad about you and Winston coming to Greece. Right?"

"Yeah, I know. You've already said."

"I mean it, Jenny. You're probably not going to like what I'm gonna say now, but my dad can't be trusted where Leroy's concerned. If he finds out anything about our plans, he'll tell Leroy. He's frightened to death of him, for one thing, but he's a bit too bothered about protecting his own interests as well."

Rita expected Jenny to put up an argument to defend her father's reputation. After all, Jenny had always had a much better relationship with him. However, she accepted Rita's instructions without comment, and Rita surmised that Jenny was perhaps more aware of their father's failings than she let on.

"Don't tell my mam either, because no matter how much she promises not to say anything, she tells my dad everything. Even if she doesn't want him to know, he'll get it out of her. OK?"

When Jenny didn't reply, Rita repeated her question more loudly, "OK?"

"Yeah, OK."

"Right, well that's that sorted. Don't forget, act as normal as possible."

Rita was satisfied that she seemed to have got through to Jenny by the time they reached their parent's house. The effort that her mother had made was touching. She had already set the table when they arrived, and decided where everybody would be sitting. Joan had allocated the space at the head of the table for her husband, and the place at the other end for Yansis.

"You don't have to do that, Mam. You should sit there; Yansis won't mind," said Rita.

Secretly, she was relieved as it meant that she would be seated next to Yansis, with her mother acting as a buffer between her and her father. On the table for six, Jenny would sit on the other side of her father, opposite her mother, and there would be an empty seat opposite Rita where Leroy would have sat if he had attended the meal.

"Yansis is our special guest all the way from Greece," said her mother, "so I thought it would be nice for him to sit at the end of the table."

Rita smiled, thinking about how Leroy would have reacted to this announcement.

"Where's Leroy?" asked Ged, as soon as he walked into the dining room.

"Working," Jenny answered.

"What, on a Sunday?" Ged responded automatically, before correcting himself. "Mind you, he's a busy man, isn't he? And business doesn't take care of itself. Even when you're not selling, you've got all the stocktaking and bookkeeping, and all that stuff to sort out. I suppose it's understandable really."

Rita could feel his eyes shifting around them, and knew that his words were for the benefit of her and Yansis. Who did he think he was trying to kid? He already knew she had seen right through his pathetic façade. She tried to stay calm as the others took their seats, and she helped her mother to hand out the food.

"Ooh, I'd forgotten what a good cook you are, Mam," said Rita, as she tucked into her roast chicken, roast potatoes and veg with lashings of gravy.

"I'd forgotten, myself. I don't do a Sunday roast as often, now there's only me and your dad at home."

"You can't beat it, can you? Traditional English cooking. Do you remember that steak and kidney pie my grandma used to make,

Jenny?"

"Yeah, the meat used to melt in your mouth, didn't it? And the pastry was to die for."

This led to other memories from their childhood, and Rita and Jenny spent most of the meal recapturing the times they had spent with their grandparents. Whenever Rita had a chance to talk about her grandparents, it gave her a warm feeling inside. They had been so good to her, and being able to share her recollections with Jenny made them all the more special, especially as Jenny reminded her of some events she had forgotten about.

As their conversation progressed, she became aware of the fact that she had been excluding Yansis. "Oh, I'm sorry love. We're getting a bit carried away, aren't we? Grandma and Granddad Steadman were lovely, though. It's a pity you never got to meet them."

"Yeah, change the subject, for Christ's sake. Let someone else get a word in for a change," interrupted Ged.

Rita glared at him. She didn't respond, as she didn't want to cause a scene in front of Yansis, but her mother cut in instead.

"Ged, come on now. You can't blame the girls. Their grandparents were good to them, after all. I would have thought you'd have wanted to hear about them. They were your parents when all's said and done."

Rita noticed her father shuffle in his chair, and knew that sharp words would be exchanged between her mam and dad once they were all gone.

"I'm just saying, let someone else have a turn; that's all. We've got a special guest, haven't we? We shouldn't be ignoring him."

Rita had to keep her temper in check once again as he emphasised the words 'special guest' in a sarcastic manner.

Following her father's outburst, they ate the rest of the meal in relative silence but, thankfully, they had almost finished anyway. The end of the meal signalled a good excuse for Ged to announce that he was going to the pub, leaving the dirty plates for someone else to clear up. '*Thank God that's over,*' thought Rita, and she relaxed for the first time since they had arrived at her parents' home.

Chapter 24

Tuesday 28th May 1991 – late evening

Debby could tell that something was wrong as soon as Carl walked into the house, late on Tuesday evening. His face was pale and his expression sombre. Noticing how jittery he was as he sat down and lit himself a spliff, she looked at him inquisitively.

"I've just had a bit of bad news," he announced. "Someone OD'd over the weekend."

Despite feeling a little sadness at this news, Debby was almost relieved that at least it wasn't something that impacted on them, or so she thought. Overdoses amongst drug addicts were nothing new in the world they inhabited, and she had learnt to become detached from such events, unless they affected her directly.

"Oh, that's a shame," she replied, without conviction.

"You could at least act interested. You're a hard faced bitch at times!"

"Like you care. Had a bad day have you, and come home to take it out on me, as usual?"

He rose from his chair, but she was ready for him. Debby dashed behind the sofa, making it difficult for him to get at her. To her surprise, he sat back down. This was so out of character that she knew there was something amiss.

"It's nowt to do with having a bad day, so stop your fuckin' wise cracks. The punter bought his gear in Longsight. If Leroy thinks it's down to me, I could be right in the shit."

"Hang on a minute," said Debby, trying to process what he had told her so far. "Why would Leroy think it was down to you?"

"Because he bought it from the area where I deal."

As she stared back at him in shock, he failed to meet her gaze, and Debby knew there was more to come. "Go on, what else?"

Carl's voice dropped to an imperceptible mutter, as he added, "The punter's mate said the drugs were iffy. He reckons it looked as though the H was mixed with something."

"Oh no, you idiot! What did I tell you about skimming? You wouldn't be told though, would you? You're such a know all!"

Carl's ignominy was short-lived, his shame turning to annoyance as Debby continued to throw insults at him.

"Shut your fuckin' mouth, before I shut it for you!" he shouted.

But Debby was equally angry. She had put up with a lot from Carl to feed her habit, but this was too much. Without waiting for a further reaction from him, she stormed from the room. However, that wasn't the end of it as far as she was concerned.

She went to the place where he kept his supplies. Careful to leave the heroin intact, she took out the mixing substance together with all of the drugs that Carl had already skimmed, and made straight for the bathroom. In a fit of rage, she threw the lot down the toilet and flushed it repeatedly, until the last of the powder had disappeared.

The noise of the repeated flushes must have alerted Carl because he had followed her to the bathroom. But she had already anticipated his reaction, and had locked the door.

"Open the fuckin' door!" he shouted, banging and cursing.

"No, not till it's all gone."

"I swear to God, Debby, if you don't open this door, you'll be sorry."

When his threats had no effect, he pleaded with her.

"Debs, don't be stupid. We can still use it; I'll just reduce the amount. It was OK before I increased it."

"No way, don't be so stupid!"

His pleading had turned to aggressive shouting and cursing again. Her hands were shaking as she tried to fish the last remnants of powder out of the corners of the polythene bags. As well as banging and shouting, Carl was now ramming against the door, and she could hear the anxious cries of one of the children. She knew what Carl would do when he got hold of her, but for once she was determined to stand up to him.

A Gangster's Grip

Debby had finished with the last of the polythene bags when the door burst open, the lock breaking from its frame, leaving splinters of wood. Within seconds he was upon her, grabbing the polythene bag from her hands and throwing it down in disgust. Her eyes followed his to the toilet basin where the powder had now dissolved and been flushed away.

"You stupid bitch!" he yelled, as he struck her across the head. The force of the blow unbalanced her, and she smacked her head on the cistern, as she fell to the floor. The last thing she saw before she passed out was one of the children in the bathroom doorway, sobbing.

***

Tuesday 28th May 1991 – late evening

Leroy was having a drink with Mad Trevor in a Moss Side shebeen. Mad Trevor had invited him on the pretext of having a get together, but Leroy suspected there was another reason, and he had a good idea what it was. Word about the overdose in Longsight had already reached Leroy, and he deduced that Trevor would be asking questions. He wasn't wrong.

"Heard about that OD in Longsight?" asked Mad Trevor, almost as soon as they had bought their drinks.

"Yeah, bad news wasn't it?"

"Yeah. Sounds like somebody's been skimming."

"I know man, bunch of amateurs if you ask me. Anyone knows you don't mix any crap with H; it's asking for trouble."

"Don't suppose you got any idea who it might be, with you living in Longsight?"

"Me? No, I don't hang out round there much. It's just a base since my old woman moved round there."

"I thought you didn't live with your old woman now."

"No, I moved in with Jenny, but she lives a few streets away from my mam. Still, like I say, it's just a base. I don't hang out round there much. It's not the same as the Moss, is it?"

Leroy sensed that Mad Trevor wasn't convinced, so he decided to ratchet things up.

"I've heard rumours about some new outfit round there but don't know anything more. I tell you what, though, if I do find out who they are, I'll have their balls on a plate. It's tossers like them that give us all a bad name, and frighten the punters off."

"Dead right man. If you ever find 'em, give me a shout. I wouldn't mind having a go at 'em myself."

Leroy hoped that his display of indignation, coupled with the fact that he was regularly seen in Moss Side, would have persuaded Mad Trevor that he wasn't involved. He had a good idea who the culprit was though, and he would personally see to it that he was punished.

But Leroy was no fool. There was no way he was going to share his information with Mad Trevor, or any of the gang. To do so would be suicidal, as it would alert them to the fact that he was obtaining his heroin from another source. From then onwards, it would only be a matter of time until the Buckthorns found out who that source was and, once they knew, it would all be over for Leroy.

***

Wednesday 29th May 1991 – afternoon

"What did your Jenny want?" asked Julie, when Rita had finished her phone call.

"It wasn't Jenny."

"Oh, who was it then?"

"You won't believe this … It was Debby."

"Debby?" asked Julie, astonished.

"Exactly, that's what I thought. After the way things were last time I went to see her, she's the last person I expected to hear from. She wants to see me."

"What for?"

"I don't know, but she says it's important and it won't wait."

"Jesus, that sounds a bit strange. Are you going?"

"Dead right. I want to find out what it's all about."

"What do you think it could be?"

"No idea, but I get the feeling it isn't gonna be good. Either way, I've got to know. After all, Carl works with Leroy, so it could be connected."

"Jesus, Rita, be careful."

"Don't worry, Julie, I'm always careful."

Chapter 25

This time Rita was prepared for the rancid odour that assailed her when she arrived at Debby's. One thing she wasn't prepared for was Debby's appearance, which was worse than last time she had seen her.

A large bruise ran from the side of her forehead, over her eye, and down most of one side of her face. On the other side of her face, there was minor bruising under her eye. Rita could tell that Debby was nervous, and she shunned the offer of a drink, eager to find out what the problem was, although she suspected it might have something to do with Debby's domestic situation.

"Well, what is it?" Rita asked. When Debby stared back blankly, she continued. "What have you brought me here for, Debby? You said it couldn't wait, so you might as well get straight to the point."

Debby toyed with the fringing on the shabby armchair as she spoke, hesitantly at first, while she assessed Rita's reaction.

"Somebody died in Longsight from an overdose. They think his drugs were skimmed."

"Skimmed?"

"Yeah, it's when they're mixed with something else. Some of the dealers do it to make the heroin go further so they make more money. Anyway, I think I might know where he got the drugs from … I think it might be Carl."

After an initial pause, she gabbled the last few words as though she wanted to unburden herself as quickly as possible. Their toxicity stunned Rita, and for a moment she was speechless. But Debby had opened Pandora's Box. There was no going back now, so she continued her outpouring.

"I've seen him mixing the drugs; he does it here. I told him not to, but he wouldn't listen. And now he's got us right in the shit. I'm scared, Rita. I don't know what to do. What if the police find out, or worse, what if Leroy finds out?"

"Shut up!" Rita shouted. "For God's sake, let me think." She stood up, and began her frantic pacing and running her hands through her hair. "Where are the children?" she asked.

"At my mam's."

Rita was relieved that at least they hadn't heard her outburst.

"And what about him? When will he be back?"

"He won't be back till late."

Despite her shock at Debby's revelation, Rita could also feel a mounting anger, and she wanted to make sure no-one else was around to hear what she had to say.

"Right, now you listen to me! You're telling me that somebody's just died because of your fella, and all you can think about is yourself. All you're bothered about is what will happen to Carl if he's found out. I suppose that will make it awkward for you if you can't get hold of your drugs anymore, will it? You make me sick! Have you not stopped to think about the lad that died? What about his family? His parents! His brothers and sisters! Don't they matter?"

"I only said it might be Carl. It might not be."

"You know full well it's him! You wouldn't have brought me here if you didn't think so. Even without the mixing, what he's doing is well out of order. It stinks! It's the lowest of the low. Don't you understand? You're shooting up in a house where two little kiddies live. Doesn't that bother you? Just how the hell did you end up like this Debby? Look at the state of you! What's happened to you?"

Rita glared at Debby who was now snivelling.

"It wasn't always like that," she cried. "It started out as a bit of fun, just me and Carl getting high. Then somehow it got out of control. And now ... now I can't do without."

"How can taking drugs ever be fun, Debby? Don't you listen to any of the warnings? Have you forgotten what happened to a friend of ours a few years ago?"

"Who?"

"Amanda, of course."

"Oh, yeah, you mean Julie's friend."

"OK, she might have been Julie's friend, but let's not pretend that what happened to her didn't affect us. Or maybe that's how you deal with things, Debby, by turning a blind eye. As long as it's someone else's family, it doesn't matter. Is that it?"

"No," Debby countered, her voice breaking.

When Rita had ran out of steam, she sat back down and tried to think logically about how to handle the situation. There was no doubt in her mind that Debby had invited her here so she could share her burden and ease her conscience. Knowing Rita as she did, Debby probably felt she would take decisive action, freeing herself of that responsibility.

But although Rita could be fiery, she was also astute. After a few minutes' thought, she had reached a decision. She ran through her idea with Debby, then said goodbye to her; for the last time, she hoped.

***

Wednesday 29th May 1991 – afternoon

The journey back to Julie's had given Rita plenty of time to think about her predicament, and by the time she saw Julie, she had decided what to do.

"Julie, there's something I need to share with you, but this needs to stay between us. Before I say anything, you need to promise me that you won't go to the police. I can't tell Yansis for that exact reason; he'd go straight to the police. He wouldn't understand the repercussions. It's probably best not to tell Vinny either. The fewer people that know, the better."

"Jesus, Rita, you're scaring me! What the hell's happened?"

"It's that slimy little toad, Carl. He's only been mixing bleedin' drugs, and somebody's died because of it."

A Gangster's Grip

"Oh God, no!"

"Yeah, that's why Debby wanted me round there. She was worried enough to confide in me, but not to do anything about it herself."

Rita knew she could rely on Julie not to report Carl to the police. Unlike Yansis, Julie had grown up in the same area as Rita. She therefore understood the implications of getting the police involved. By contrast, Yansis had had a sheltered upbringing. He would want to do the right thing which, as far as he was concerned, meant going to the police. He didn't have much experience of the kind of people who preferred to mete out their own form of punishment.

Nevertheless, although she could trust Julie, she still decided not to tell her about her plans to help Jenny and Winston escape to Greece. She felt bad about keeping secrets from her best friend; they'd always shared everything. But she was doing it for Julie's own protection.

"What are you going to do?" asked Julie.

"I'm in a no win situation, Julie, and completely out of my depth. My first instinct was to go to the bloody police, and sod the consequences. But I daren't. If I do that, all hell will break loose. Carl would know that the police had somehow found out through Debby, and I wouldn't put it past her to point the finger at me, when questions were asked about who grassed him up.

"I think that's why she told me. She feels bad about what he's done, and in a way she wants something done about it, but she doesn't want it to come back on her. Carl hangs around with a lot of bad people, including Leroy, and I'm frightened of what they might do if they found out I'd gone to the police."

"Debby wouldn't put you in the firing line, would she? I thought she was a friend."

"She was before she got addicted to heroin. Now her biggest concern is where her next fix is coming from. Although she wants to put a stop to what Carl's doing, I think she's more bothered that she won't get any supplies if he's off the scene. You wouldn't believe how she's changed, Julie. Now I wouldn't trust her as far as I can throw her."

"What will you do then?" asked Julie.

"I've already done it. Well, the only thing I could do under the circumstances. I've put the ball back in her court. Her and Carl are more frightened of Leroy than anything. If he finds out Carl's been mixing drugs, he'll go ballistic; apparently it's a complete no no as far as the Buckthorns are concerned.

"So, I've told her to call Carl's bluff. She's to tell him that unless he stops skimming, she'll make sure Leroy finds out. I told her I won't do her dirty work for her but, to make her threat to Carl sound convincing, she can mention my name if she likes. She can tell him that I already know, and that I'll tell Leroy about him mixing drugs if he doesn't stop."

"Do you think she'll do it? I thought you said he might knock her about a bit."

"Oh, he definitely does. You should have seen the state of her face. She told me how he knocked her about for throwing some of the mix down the loo, when she found out about the death."

"So she's not all bad then?"

"No, just bloody stupid, same as she's always been. But I've tried to convince her that if she can stand up to him once, she can do it again. He's a typical coward. I think that once he's threatened with Leroy, he might see sense. And once she's got something over him, he might stop being so handy with his fists too. I've also told her to get herself down to the doctors to see what help she can get with her drug problem. Whether she will, I don't know, but what else can I do?"

"Not a lot. It's like you say, Rita, you're in a no win situation. But what will you do if Carl turns nasty on you."

"I'd like to see him bloody try! It'll take more than that little wimp to frighten me off. I've told you, he's a coward. The only reason he knocks Debby about is because he thinks he can get away with it. She wants to get off the bleedin' drugs, then she'll have no reason to stay with him. See how the little shit copes then, once she pisses him off. I just wish I could stop him dealing in drugs altogether, but I can't. At least if I can stop him mixing, though, it might save a few lives. The little bastard! Honestly, it makes my blood boil."

Julie stayed silent. She knew better than to interrupt Rita when she was riled.

Chapter 26

While Debby had been unburdening herself to Rita, Carl was busy visiting Leroy to carry out some damage limitation. There was nothing he could do about the victim who had already died, but Carl's worry was whether anyone would find out that he was responsible.

He had to make sure Leroy had someone else in his sights who he could blame. Carl knew that he and Winston were the only two people dealing drugs in that part of Longsight, and that it was just a matter of time before the exact location was revealed. He had an advantage over Winston, because Leroy trusted him more, and Carl had decided to play to that advantage.

"Who d'you think sold the dodgy drugs?" he asked Leroy.

"Search me, I ain't got a clue. You any ideas?"

"Yeah, between you and me, I think it's Winston. You said yourself you couldn't trust him to do owt. I've always thought he was a sly bastard. Think about it, Leroy; there's only him it can be, unless there's another crew operating in Longsight. I've had my eyes peeled, though, and I've not spotted anyone; not near where we deal anyway. I never thought he'd stoop to this though."

Carl had kept his own name out of the list of possibilities; it was a calculated move to make Leroy focus on Winston as his primary suspect. He watched Leroy's reaction to his speech, hoping that he had convinced him, but his facial expression gave nothing away. Leroy took a few agonising seconds before responding.

"Maybe … it might be Winston. Leave it with me. I'll have a think about it. If he has been up to summat, then he needs to be taught a lesson."

Carl was careful not to show his relief. Once the precise location where the drugs were sold had been established, Leroy would know that it had to be Carl or Winston who had sold the dodgy drugs. Carl therefore needed to pin the blame on Winston before it came back to him. He felt bad about it, but he reasoned with himself that it couldn't be helped. Either he or Winston had to take the rap, and he wasn't going to run any risks to save Winston's skin.

Having put Winston in the frame, Carl was ready to part company, but Leroy stopped him.

"Hang on. Where you off?"

"Thought I'd go for a few bevvies with my mates, and then go and shift some gear later."

"Are you off your fuckin' head, man?"

"What?"

"The Pigs are crawling all over the place. You gotta stay low for a couple of weeks."

"You're joking! What am I gonna do for cash?" asked Carl, exasperated.

"I don't know, and I don't fuckin' care. Do what you did before."

Carl knew when he'd pushed it too far with Leroy, and he moderated his tone as he asked, "How long will it be for?"

"Shouldn't be long. They have to be seen to be doing summat. But I don't think they're really that interested in some low-life junkie. It should only be a couple of weeks. I'll let you know when it's sweet again."

"Right, OK," Carl replied, attempting to hide the fury building inside him, as he bid goodbye to his nemesis.

***

Thursday 30th May 1991 – late evening

Carl had arrived home late the previous evening, and strutted into the house. The combination of his cockiness at having convinced Leroy of his innocence, and frustration at having to lie low, because of the heavy police presence in the area, made him intolerable. Debby had listened to his bluster, and wondered why she put up with him. Then the reality of her situation hit her; she put up with him because she had no choice. She was a heroin addict who relied on him for her supplies. He had her exactly where he wanted her. That knowledge both sickened and angered her.

It was late in the evening, and she was too tired to argue with him, but when she went to bed she decided that tomorrow she would tackle him. Not only that, but she would readdress the balance of power in their relationship.

By the time Carl got up in the morning, Debby had already tended to the children and had her first fix of the day. She was ready for him.

"So, tell me what Leroy said then. Are you sure he didn't suspect you?"

"Dead right. He doesn't suspect me, and neither does anyone else," he bragged.

"How can you be so sure?"

"Because he thinks Winston did it."

His wicked grin told her all she needed to know.

"You've set Winston up, haven't you?"

"Not really; Leroy thought it was him anyway. There was only me and Winston it could be, and Leroy trusts me," he said.

"And what if Leroy finds out it's you? What will happen then?"

The veiled threat was obvious, even to someone of Carl's limited intellect.

"Are you fuckin' threatening me?"

As he spoke, he grabbed the front of her clothing, ready to strike out if he wasn't happy with Debby's reply, regardless of the children who were playing just a few metres away.

"I wouldn't if I were you," said Debby. "You see, I'm not the only one that knows what you've been up to."

"What the fuck are you on about?"

His words were bold, but Debby could detect the shock and fear that they masked.

A Gangster's Grip

"Let go of me, and I'll tell you."

When he released his hold on her, she stepped back in case he reacted when she revealed what she had done.

"Rita knows. She said she won't say owt, as long as you stop skimming." She delighted in the bemused expression on his face as she continued. "She's not too happy about you knocking me about either, especially in front of the kids. In fact, if you don't stop skimming and knocking me about, she said she won't even bother going to the police; she'll go straight to Leroy."

"How the hell does she know? Did *you* tell her?"

"Yeah, I did. I've had enough, Carl."

His anger was palpable, and she braced herself as he made towards her with his fist drawn back.

"Just you dare! You lay one finger on me, and I'll be straight on the phone to Rita."

Her words jolted him, and he dropped his arm. He still sought an outlet for his anger, though, which he vented through a stream of invective aimed at both Debby and Rita. When he had exhausted his list of derogatory terms, he kicked at the furniture before stomping out of the house in a rage.

As soon as he was gone, the children, who had been afraid to react in his presence, now began to whimper. Debby picked up the youngest, "Shshsh, it's alright," she cajoled. "Daddie's just a bit upset, but he'll be fine when he gets back."

Chapter 27

It was the day of Rita and Yansis's follow up appointment, and they had been hanging around the house for the last half hour. They were both aware that their window of opportunity was closing in. They needed to have intercourse between two and four hours before their hospital appointment, and time was running out. The problem was that Julie was working in her home office, and Yansis felt uncomfortable going upstairs while she was in the house.

"Yansis, we'll have to go upstairs sooner or later," Rita said.

"But what if she hears? The bed might bump and creak. It will be so embarrassing."

Just at that moment, Julie walked into the living room. "What will be embarrassing?" she asked.

"Oh nothing. It's just a situation Yansis has at home," Rita improvised, trying to spare his blushes.

"I just popped in to find out what time your appointment is, and to wish you luck," said Julie.

As soon as she had spoken the words, she realised what was troubling Yansis, and his quick exit from the room confirmed her suspicions.

"Oh shit," she whispered to Rita. "I forgot about you having to do the business. Is that what he's embarrassed about?"

"Yeah, the daft sod. I told him you wouldn't bother, but he feels really embarrassed about us getting it on in broad daylight when you're in the house."

"Sorry, Rita, I didn't think. Listen, if it makes him feel any better, I'll make myself scarce for a bit. I've got to nip out and get some shopping anyway."

"You don't need to do that, Julie."

"It's no trouble, Rita. Like I say, I was going out anyway. Let me switch the computer off and get my coat and shoes, and I'll be out of your hair."

Five minutes later, she was gone and Rita went to find Yansis. She guessed that he was in the bedroom waiting for her. "Hey, lover boy," she shouted up the stairs, giggling, "It's time to make babies."

They'd left themselves little time to spare, so it was more of a quick routine task than a moment of passion. Still, at least the job was done, and they could go to the hospital ready for their next set of tests.

Where Rita hadn't been nervous for her first hospital appointment, on this occasion she was. It hit her in the car on the way there, and the time spent in the hospital waiting room added to her anxiety.

She thought that her apprehension may be because they might find something out today. During their last visit, the doctor had carried out various tests, so they were expecting to hear some results. Rita had also brought along the temperature chart for the doctor to check.

After an interminable wait, their names were called, and Rita stood up and took a deep breath, before following the nurse into the doctor's surgery.

"Hello Mr and Mrs Christos. Please take a seat," said the doctor.

Rita tried to read something into the doctor's speech and body language, but he was giving nothing away. It was a different doctor from last time. This one was older, about mid-fifties, she guessed, and slim with greying hair. She handed him the temperature chart, and she and Yansis watched him analyse it.

"Ah yes, let me see … um … aah … yes."

A couple of minutes later, he passed the chart back to Rita, and wrote something in his notes. She rolled her eyes at Yansis as they waited for the doctor to speak. Once he had finished writing, he put his pen down, but instead of turning to speak to them, he stared at the wall for several seconds. Then the doctor cupped his chin in his hand and tapped on his nose with his forefinger, as though lost in thought.

"Have you had intercourse before your appointment today?" he asked, without making eye contact.

"Yes," Rita and Yansis both answered at once.

"What time was that?"

Rita remembered when it had been, because they had been so preoccupied with getting to the hospital on time, so she answered for both of them.

"I'd like to examine you, Mrs Christos," said the doctor. "Mr Christos, if you would like to return to the waiting room, we will call you shortly to discuss the results of the various tests."

Yansis's face was full of concern as he looked at Rita, before leaving the room, and she couldn't help thinking how this doctor's approach differed from the one they had seen previously. He was far too aloof for her liking. Strangely, that made the examination less difficult to cope with than the first time around. Rita found it easier to detach herself when she was dealing with someone who was so impassive himself.

When the examination was over, the doctor sent her back to the waiting room, and told her she and her husband would be called in together. Thankfully, it wasn't much longer before they were back at his desk. His face was still expressionless as he spoke to them.

"We have the results from all of the tests we have taken," he said. "We'll start with the tests carried out on Mrs Christos. The results indicate that there are no problems. However, in order to be 100% certain, we would have to run further tests. It is usual to do so because, in cases of infertility, it is easier to pinpoint problems with the female. Therefore, even if initial tests indicate that the problem may lie with the male, we would rule out any possible problems with the female first.

"With regard to the tests carried out on Mr Christos," he continued, "the results of the seminalysis indicate a very low sperm count. We have also run a postcoital test to analyse the activity of spermatozoa in the vagina following sexual intercourse. Unfortunately, we could not find any spermatozoa present."

Rita looked at him, puzzled, and was about to speak, when he held up his hand and bowed his head, to silence her.

"The combined results of these two tests suggest possible male infertility. However, this is not necessarily the case. A low sperm count will not necessarily preclude conception. This is why we have to rule out potential problems with the female since ..."

"Hang on a minute," Rita interrupted. "I'm having a job taking all this in. Can you speak to us in English please, instead of quoting a medical encyclopaedia? My husband is Greek, and if I can't understand you, then what chance has he got?"

"Very well, Mrs Christos, but I am simply quoting the correct medical terminology," he said.

"Well, we aren't qualified doctors, so I'd rather you spoke in words we can understand. And, for your information, the 'female' is called Rita, or Mrs Christos if you prefer, and the 'male' is Mr Christos.

"Very well," said the doctor, who tried to retain an air of superiority while he explained the results in laymen's terms. Rita had got the general gist of it, but she could sense Yansis's confusion. She knew that what the doctor had to impart would be a blow for Yansis, and she gripped onto his hand while the doctor explained.

The upshot of it was that the problem most likely lay with Yansis. His low sperm count, added to the fact that the sperm weren't reaching the vagina, indicated that he may well be infertile. That wasn't conclusive, though, but it was difficult to pinpoint what exactly was causing the problems, without carrying out a whole range of tests on Yansis. The doctor explained that those tests could take months, and that while they were carrying them out, they would also run further tests on Rita to make sure that everything was functioning normally.

"So what happens now?" asked Rita.

"I will need to take a complete medical history of Mr Christos, first of all. Although we have already asked several questions, I will need to go more in-depth. I will also need to take a blood sample from Mr Christos, and carry out another seminalysis before you go home. That is the test in which we find out the sperm count. If the results still show a low sperm count, then we will refer Mr Christos for further tests."

Rita looked across at Yansis. Although he had stayed quiet throughout, she could tell he was upset. Without giving him chance to recover from the bad news, the doctor opened his notebook, ready to start asking questions.

He addressed Rita, "Would you like to sit in the waiting room?"

"Do you want me to stay with you?" she asked Yansis.

He only shrugged, so she decided to stay knowing that, if she didn't, the doctor would baffle him with medical terminology. Besides, she wanted to be there to support him.

Rita was glad she had stayed when the doctor showered Yansis with a deluge of questions. Had his testes been slow to descend in childhood? Had he had any venereal diseases? Had he ever fathered a child? The questions seemed to go on relentlessly, and Rita felt sorry for poor Yansis who gave lacklustre, monosyllabic responses. The expression on his face showed a whole gamut of emotions; sadness, disappointment, embarrassment and discomfort.

It was a relief for Rita when the questions were over, but for Yansis there was still the blood test and the seminalysis to go. Once Yansis had given a blood sample, he took the container from the nurse and left the room, with his shoulders hunched and his eyes cast downwards.

Before the doctor could dismiss Rita, she took the opportunity to ask a few questions. She needed to know what the possible outcome would be. Then maybe she would have something to hold onto; something she could tell Yansis that might give them hope during the difficult times that lay ahead.

***

Thursday 6th June 1991 – evening

They had already arranged to go out with Julie and Vinny that evening. Rita was glad, in a way, because Yansis had been difficult to talk to since they had got back from hospital. They had been so busy having tea and getting ready to go out, that they hadn't had chance to discuss matters with Julie and Vinny. The way things stood, Rita preferred to talk to Julie while Yansis was out of earshot. So, when they had returned from the hospital, and Julie had asked whether everything was alright, Rita had replied, "I'll tell you later" before rushing upstairs after Yansis so she could speak to him first.

It hadn't been easy. Within the space of a few hours, Yansis had become sombre and withdrawn, and he met all of her suggestions with negativity. But at least that was an improvement on the trip home, when he hadn't spoken at all. She was trying to be patient, knowing it was a massive blow to his male pride, as well as a big disappointment.

While she was showering and putting on her make-up, she had replayed the scene at the hospital in her head. How different this appointment had been from the first one! It was amazing how the emphasis had switched from her to Yansis. And no matter what the doctor said about things being inconclusive, his focus on Yansis suggested that he believed the fault lay with him. She could have throttled that doctor for his lack of subtlety. Poor Yansis!

Thinking about it, Yansis must have had as big a shock as her. She had always assumed that the problem lay with her and, judging by Yansis's reaction, she now realised that he had made that assumption too. Yansis's way of dealing with the situation was different to hers, though, and things were going to be tricky where his emotions were concerned. She would have to handle him like a day old chick.

The plan was for them to have a few drinks in the local pubs. Yansis and Vinny often enjoyed a game of pool, so Rita anticipated that this would be her chance to chat to Julie. Unfortunately, Julie didn't wait till they were on their own.

"Are you two gonna tell us how you went on at the hospital?" she asked, when they were in the pub.

Noting Yansis's pained expression, Rita quickly answered. "There's no rush. I thought you lads would be having a game of pool. You normally do when we come in here."

Rita spotted the look of relief on Yansis's face, and was thankful for her quick thinking.

"Yeah, Vinny, I bet I win this time," he responded.

"Oh dear! Have I just put my foot in it?" asked Julie, once Yansis and Vinny had gone.

"Oh, don't worry; it's not your fault. But, for future reference, don't mention the hospital in front of Yansis. It's a sore subject."

"Why, what's happened?"

"He's only firing bleedin' blanks. I've tried talking to him, but he's been really moody since we got back."

"I thought he hadn't been himself. I wondered what was wrong."

"Well, apparently he's got a low sperm count. On its own that wouldn't necessarily mean that we can't conceive, but we got the results of that other test too. You know, the one where we had to have sex, and then they look inside me to see what's going on?"

"Oh, yeah?"

"Well, they couldn't find any sperm."

"What d'you mean? What's happened to it? Has it slid back out or summat?"

"No, you daft cow," Rita replied, laughing. "I know what you're talking about. What we call sperm is actually called semen. Sperm is short for spermatozoa, those little tadpole things that wriggle up your tubes and go to find the egg. There should be millions of them every time a man ejaculates, but they couldn't find a one inside me."

"Oh God, does that mean he's infertile then?"

"Well, that's where it gets confusing. Listening to that doctor explain everything was like listening to double Dutch. I'll swear he'd swallowed a bleedin' medical encyclopaedia. Anyway, I got him to explain it properly, and from what he says it's looking that way, but they won't know properly until they carry out loads more tests.

"The problem is that it's really complicated with men. There are loads of different things it could be, and it could take months to find out what's causing the problem. He did say that the problem might be temporary though, and there are things they can do in a lot of cases, depending on what the cause is. Oh, and they'd run a few more tests on me too, just to make sure everything's OK, but from the results they've had up to now, all my bits seem to be in working order."

A Gangster's Grip

"Jesus, I bet Yansis is gobsmacked, isn't he? I believe virility is very important to Mediterranean men."

"He's not very happy, no. He wants to go back to Greece now. He thinks it's a waste of time waiting around for more tests, but I think it's really because he couldn't stand the humiliation of going through it all. The problem is, I don't want to go back to Greece yet; I can't risk leaving our Jenny with the way things are. I want to make sure she's OK."

"I can understand that, Rita, but don't forget to take care of yourselves too. Yansis is hurting now and he needs you. Perhaps once he calms down, you can talk to him again and persuade him to have some more tests."

"Yeah, that's what I'm thinking. He's only just had the bad news, so he needs time to get used to it. Once he's in a better mood, I'll have another word with him, and see if I can persuade him to stay in Manchester for a bit longer. If we can at least hang on until after Jenny's had the baby, I'll feel better. That's if you don't mind us staying with you for a few more weeks."

Rita almost slipped up and told Julie about their plans to help Jenny escape to Greece, but she corrected herself just in time. To leave no doubt in Julie's mind about her intentions, she added, "Maybe once she's had the baby, she might stand up to Leroy and break things off with him. That's what I'm hoping for anyway, but I want to be around in case things turn nasty."

"Whatever you decide, Rita, you know I'll always be there for you. You stay as long as you want. Friends for life," she added and they raised their glasses.

Chapter 28

Leroy had found a phone box in a quieter part of Moss Side, where there would be nobody around to listen in on his call. As soon as the phone was answered, he began his tirade.

"What the fuck's going on? Why hasn't it been done?" After a moment's pause, he continued. "It should have been done over a week ago. What's taking you so long? What d'you think I'm paying you for? Another pause, then, "It better had be!"

He then loosened his grip on the telephone receiver as he listened to his contact, before tensing again, "I don't want it traced back to me. Whatever you do, you gotta cover your tracks. You get me? This is between you and me. Don't tell no-one, and I mean *no-one*!"

The person on the other end of the phone had calmed him down a little, as his voice was more suppressed when he rounded up the call. "Tonight? OK, sweet. Let me know when it's sorted. Usual method of communication, alright?"

Leroy put the receiver down abruptly and sauntered off towards the centre of Moss Side.

***

Friday 7th June 1991 – late evening

It was a day since Rita and Yansis had received their devastating news from the hospital. Rita still hadn't had a proper talk with Yansis, but he seemed to be in a better mood since he had walked in from work with Vinny. As the four of them sat watching TV, she was relieved by his continuous displays of affection. Although it appeared on the surface as though Yansis was back to his usual self, Rita felt that matters remained unresolved.

A Gangster's Grip

Between her concerns about Yansis and her anxiety over Jenny, Rita was feeling on edge by the time she went to bed. Yansis was in a different frame of mind, though, and he soon made it obvious what his show of affection had been leading up to. It couldn't have been further from Rita's mind; despite her empathy for Yansis's situation, she wasn't going to submit to his wanton desires in order to massage his ego. She tried to let him down as gently as she could.

"Not tonight, Yansis, maybe tomorrow. I'm knackered and feeling really stressed."

His reaction took her by surprise, "What is the matter? You think I am not a man now?"

For a moment she stared at him open-mouthed. This was so uncharacteristic of Yansis. "For God's sake, Yansis. You're being ridiculous. As if that would make any difference to how I feel about you."

"What is so ridiculous? It is perfectly normal for a man to desire his wife. Or maybe you think I am not normal now, eh?"

"Yansis, you are being ridiculous," she snapped. "It's got nothing to do with that and you know it! There are more important things in life than your male pride, you know."

As soon as she spoke, she regretted it. Of course, it was important to him. He wanted a baby desperately and, to him, his ability to father a child was everything. She didn't mean to snap but she found his self-pity irritating, and he had no right to suggest that the only reason she didn't want sex with him was because he might be infertile. Her reaction inflamed the situation even more.

"That is the problem, Rita. You think everything is more important than me. Sometimes I wonder why you came back to Manchester. Was it really to have a baby, or did you just want to sort all your family's problems out for them? Why don't you let them sort out their own problems and start caring about us more?"

"Now come on, Yansis, that's not fair," she replied, her voice shaking. "It's not a 'them or you' situation. I didn't know what I was walking into, did I? Don't you think I'd prefer to be back in Greece, rather than having to deal with shit every day of my life? Have you any idea what I'm going through?"

"Yes, I know, Rita because you tell me all the time."

"Well that's just where you're wrong, because I don't bloody tell you! I try to protect you from it half the time. I try to protect you because I don't want you to have to deal with it. I beat myself up because I think that I might be spoiling your cosy little life, with your nice restaurant and your lovely family. And what do I get in return? You putting more pressure on me! You're just a self-centred bastard! Maybe if you started thinking with your brain instead of with your dick, then we might get somewhere."

When she saw the shock on his face, she wished she hadn't gone so far. Her anger consumed her as it had done so many times in her life. Rita couldn't help herself. She could still feel the adrenaline pulsating through her body, her limbs shaking and her heart beating erratically. And as she felt her eyes fill with tears, she turned away, not wanting him to notice.

The adrenaline was driving her to do something, so she stomped to the window and yanked the curtains shut. Then she plonked herself down on the edge of the bed and changed into her nightwear, pulling her clothing off furiously.

Instead of inciting Yansis, her loss of control seemed to quell his rage. He came over to her and spoke more gently. "Rita, I am sorry; I didn't mean to upset you. I know you have a lot of problems to deal with, but it has been difficult for me too."

"I know," she said, on the verge of tears. "I'm sorry too. I shouldn't have lost it, Yansis. I know it can't have been easy for you, especially with what happened yesterday … but we need to talk about it and decide what to do."

She could tell he was trying not to get angry again, as he replied, "Rita, I already told you; there is no point in having more tests, not after what they told me."

"But there might be something they can do, Yansis."

"Yes, and there might be nothing they can do, and we could be having horrible tests for months and months, just to find out what we already know."

"Aw love," she said, hugging him, "Won't you at least try?"

"We can't anyway, Rita. We need to get back to the restaurant. My family and friends have been very good in looking after it for us, but we can't expect them to do it forever. They never expected that we would be away so long. And what about Julie and Vinny?"

"Julie's fine. She won't mind."

"It's still difficult with the restaurant, Rita, and I am missing my family and friends."

"You know there's another reason why I want to stay, don't you?"

"I know, because of your sister."

"Yes, can't we at least stay till she's had the baby? It will only be a few weeks."

"Perhaps, but first I need to know everything, Rita. You said you had been protecting me, but you shouldn't do. I am your husband and whatever happens to you, we have to go through together. I need to know everything that has been happening."

Rita wished that she had kept her mouth shut, but in the heat of the moment she had confessed that she had been keeping things from him. Now she knew that if she stood any chance of persuading him to stay for at least another few weeks, then she had to open up.

She braced herself as she went through the whole of the events, including the nasty way her father had acted towards her, the weapons that Jenny had discovered hidden in her home, the recent death due to skimming and Debby's suspicions that Carl might be responsible.

When she had finished, he said, "Oh, Rita, I am so sorry that you didn't feel you could tell me. I wouldn't have gone to the police. I understand that it is risky because of the gangs. You must tell me everything in future. I know it is bad but it isn't your fault ... OK, we'll stay a few more weeks and we'll have to think what to do about the tests. Maybe we could come back just for appointments in the future but it would be very expensive ... I don't know."

"I know. Let's not worry about that now," she said, clutching his hand. "One thing at a time. We're still young, Yansis; we've got plenty of time to decide what to do. If you don't want to go through loads of tests, there might be other things we can do. It's just too much for me to think about at the moment, love, with everything else that's going on. Once we've made sure that our Jenny's safe then, I promise you, we'll focus on us. Our next hospital appointment won't come through for a few weeks anyway, so it'll give us time to think about what we want to do. OK?"

"OK," replied Yansis, before giving her a reassuring squeeze.

Chapter 29

It was unusual for Leroy to come home for tea on a Saturday evening. Jenny could understand it in a way because he had been lying low since someone had died from drugs bought in Longsight. The police were still swarming all over the place and, from what she could gather, he was spending most of his time either with her or at his mother's house. She knew Leroy was somehow involved in the death. He didn't tell her everything but, as time went on, he was letting more and more things slip.

What she couldn't understand was why he had rung her and suggested they have tea together. That was so out of character for Leroy. He usually just turned up when he felt like it and demanded something to eat, or sent her round to the take-away. In the circumstances, she decided it was best to keep him sweet. So, she would make him something tasty for tea and hope he was in a good mood.

At 35 weeks pregnant, Jenny had reached the stage where she tired easily. After standing at the sink preparing vegetables for several minutes, she was beginning to feel heavy on her feet. She was looking forward to ending the task when Leroy arrived home.

It was while she was still at the sink that he strolled up to her and made his casual announcement. She thought it was strange that he had been so attentive, wrapping his arms around her from behind while resting his chin on her shoulder, and nuzzling her neck. It was during his embrace that he said it.

"Oh, by the way, I got a bit of bad news today ..." He paused, giving her chance to react before delivering the final blow, "Winston's dead."

She spun around, dropping the potato peeler and covering her face with her wet hands. "Oh my God! What happened?"

Leroy stepped back, scrutinising her. "Seems he upset a few people.

You *do* know about Winston, don't you? He was a drug dealer and he liked his women. Well, other people's women. Only, this time he pushed it too far. He played around with the wrong man's woman, another drug dealer. And these drug dealing gangsters don't like that. So he got what was coming to him."

Jenny knew then for certain that he had known about her and Winston. The colour drained from her face and she felt lightheaded, her legs weak beneath her. She grasped the draining board behind her with both hands, and leant back against it to steady herself. Conscious of Leroy analysing her reaction, she fought to control her emotions.

"Cheer up, babe," he said. "I know it's bad. No-one's more gutted than me, but he was nowt to you, was he? After all, it's not like I've been killed. I could understand you being upset then."

She hated this sick game he was playing. Jenny wanted to scream. To howl. To cry! But she couldn't. If she let him see how much she was hurting, she would be openly admitting the truth. That would be more than his pride could take. And it would put her own life at risk. She knew that now. So, instead, she had to play along and force back her tears, when inside she was crumbling.

"H-how did it happen?"

"Shot, last night. He'd just left home."

"When?"

"What the fuck does it matter? Talkin' about it ain't gonna bring him back, is it?"

Jenny had asked too many questions. Shown too much interest. But she had needed to know. She was tormented by the thought of him brutally gunned down in the street. And now she would never see him again. The man she loved! She tried to suppress the thoughts that were threatening to overwhelm her. As a distraction, she carried on preparing the vegetables, peeling and chopping them savagely.

She loathed the cruel way Leroy hung around until they had finished their meal, studying her across the dining table as she struggled to get through the food. It wasn't until he had eaten his last morsel that he announced he was going out, and taking the dog with him. Thankful for this reprieve, she sank to her knees and let the tears flood out. It took a good half hour until she was calm enough to think about her next step.

***

Saturday 8th June 1991 - evening

Rita was becoming accustomed to desperate late night phone calls giving her bad news, but this latest one was the worst yet. Jenny was in a terrible state and she kept screaming, "Winston's dead."

A cold fear gripped Rita on hearing these words.

"No! Shit, no. I don't believe it!"

Despite the shock, Rita tried to think rationally. Jenny needed her. Was she alone? Was Leroy there? Had he done it? Was Jenny in danger? Think, think. What to do. What to say.

"Jenny, Jenny, calm down. I know it's a shock but I need to know what's happened. Was it at your house?"

"No," Jenny whimpered.

"Where then? Did Leroy do it?"

"Outside his house. On the street, last night," she wailed. "I don't know, he might have."

"OK. Is Leroy there now?"

"No."

"Right, hang on, I'm coming round."

Rita knew she wouldn't get much sense out of Jenny over the phone as she was still in a state of shock. Her sisterly instincts told her she needed to be there. Yansis was by her side. He had overheard the phone call and was asking questions.

"Winston's dead," she garbled. "She thinks Leroy might have done it. Come on, we need to get round there."

Yansis stopped her reaching for her jacket, "Wait a minute, Rita; you need to let the police deal with this. If Leroy has killed Winston, then he is a very dangerous man."

"She doesn't know if he's done it. She only thinks so, and he's not there at the moment. It happened last night outside Winston's house. I need to find out more. I need to speak to her. Yansis, please! Jenny could be in danger. I need to be there with her. She's in a right state."

"Rita, why do I let you talk me into these things? It is madness."

Despite his protests, he was already getting ready to take Rita to Jenny's house.

"Should I ring the police?" asked Julie, who had overheard their conversation.

"No, I need to find out what's happened first," Rita shouted, on her way out.

Within fifteen minutes they had arrived. Thankfully Leroy was not yet home, but Jenny was still inconsolable. Rita marched over to Jenny and flung her arms around her. Over Jenny's shoulder Rita watched Yansis's anxious face casting nervous glances at the clock, and knew that she would have to push sentiment aside. She released her grip on Jenny, holding her by the shoulders and staring into her face.

"Jenny, I need you to tell me what's happened before Leroy gets back."

But it was no use. Jenny was so emotional that she had become incoherent. The more she tried to speak, the more worked up she became, her words intermingled with loud, pitiful yelps.

"It's him … I know it is … he wasn't bothered … he wasn't bothered … he was … wasn't … both … er … ed."

Sensing that she was becoming hysterical, and only just able to keep her own emotions in check, Rita gripped her shoulders and started shaking her.

"Jenny, calm down!"

"He … wasn't … both…"

Slap! The sharp smack to the side of Jenny's face brought her to her senses, and she stared back at Rita, astonished.

"Sorry, Jenny, but you were becoming hysterical. I need you to stay calm. I want you to tell me what happened, before Leroy comes home. We need to find out whether he's a danger to you."

Then it occurred to Rita to give Jenny a cup of tea for the shock. In fact, she could do with one herself, and a cigarette to settle her nerves. When Rita had calmed Jenny down, she told them everything that had happened. It was a bit rushed because she kept saying she was frightened of Leroy coming back home, but Rita and Yansis managed to get the story out of her.

Hearing from Jenny how she had reacted to the news of Winston's death, made Rita realise just how different they were. Unlike Jenny, she would have hit out if someone had casually announced that the man she loved was dead. There was no way she wouldn't, no matter what the consequences of her reaction might have been.

And if she believed that the person bringing the news was responsible for the killing, her anger would have consumed her. She recognised that, in this respect, she hadn't changed much. Rita still had her fiery temper; she had just learnt to control it more as she had got older. But if anybody should ever hurt somebody she loved, her rage would know no bounds.

Once they had heard the full tale, Rita tried to persuade Jenny to get out of the house as soon as possible but, to her surprise, Jenny resisted.

"What if he comes back and catches me packing? He'll go mad. He could be back any minute. I think he's only gone to his mam's. He hasn't been staying out much lately, not since, you know … that guy died.

"Anyway, where can I go, Rita? If I go to my mam and dad's, he'll find me. Julie won't want me there. If I go to any of my mates, he'll find me. I can't afford to stay at a hotel or guest house while I'm waiting to have the baby. Anyway, even if I find a guest house, look at me. I'm pregnant! I'll need to go to the hospital. He knows that. He'll be hanging around the hospitals when the baby's due."

"Find a guest house in another bloody city then!"

"What, and have the baby all on my own? I can't do that, Rita. Anyway, even if he killed Winston, he's not going to do anything to me. If he was going to kill me, he'd have done it already. For one thing, he wouldn't want anything to happen to the baby. Believe it or not, it means a lot to him."

Those words hit home. Rita could understand the importance a lot of men placed on fatherhood.

"Not only that," Jenny continued. "He's punishing me in another way. Having to look at his mean face every day, knowing he's probably done it. Not being able to grieve. Having to hide how I feel about the man I love. Having to pretend …"

Rita interrupted, sensing that Jenny was on the verge of hysteria again.

"OK, OK. I understand, Jenny. Now, listen to me. You won't be on your own. I'll be with you when you have the baby, and I'll look after you. Then, as soon as the baby's born, we'll go to Greece like we planned, alright? In the meantime, you need to get out of here. Don't worry about the cost of a guest house; me and Yansis will pay. Your safety is more important. Do you hear me, Jenny? You have to get out!"

Rita was relieved when she finally got through to Jenny. She couldn't persuade her to leave right away though, because Jenny was too worried about Leroy returning and finding her packing her bags. Although Rita had begged her to leave everything and go as she was, Jenny insisted that there were things she needed to take with her; personal items and things she had bought for the baby.

In the end, they compromised and Jenny agreed that she would leave as soon as Leroy was out of the house for a sufficient length of time. She would call Rita once she was ready to leave. In the meantime, Rita was going to make some enquiries and see if she could locate a suitable guest house where Leroy wouldn't find Jenny.

"I'll be alright till then, honest I will, Rita," she said, her voice shaking. "I've put up with him till now. I just have to do it for a bit longer."

"OK, you just hang onto that thought, Jenny, and once we get you away, he can whistle for his bleedin' baby. He's only got himself to blame. A man like him doesn't deserve to be a father!"

Her words were heartfelt, and full of added poignancy in view of her own situation. How could it be right for him to father a child? A man who treated life with such disregard. And yet, a good man like Yansis was denied that privilege.

A Gangster's Grip

Once Jenny's appearance was restored to a state bordering on normality, Rita knew that it was time for them to go. Jenny was becoming increasingly edgy about Leroy coming home and finding them there. It wasn't unusual for Rita to visit her sister but, under the circumstances, the reason for her visit would be obvious.

They left her at the door. When Rita got inside the car, she glanced back at her heavily pregnant sister waving at them from the doorstep. A strange feeling of foreboding seized her, and she hoped she was doing the right thing in not taking Jenny with them straightaway.

Chapter 30

Carl thought it was strange that Leroy had asked to meet him in Alexandra Park, at 10 o'clock at night behind the old lodge. Extending to 60 acres, Alexandra Park is considered to be a place of national importance because of its heritage. Unfortunately, by the 1990s many of its original buildings were in disrepair, and the park was in need of some updating. It was also a place where youths hung out in the evenings, drinking and taking drugs. However, they generally kept to the same areas, with each group of friends having their regular hangouts.

Leroy had told him they were having a secret gang meeting, so Carl assumed this must be an ideal location for clandestine assignations. At least in a place of that size, they could find an area where nobody could overhear their discussions. Now, though, he was apprehensive as he approached the meeting place. The park was eerily quiet at night and, when he arrived at the lodge, he couldn't see any sign of the other gang members. He was relieved when Leroy showed up a few minutes later, with Tyson in tow.

"Alright mate?" said Carl.

"Sure, c'mon it's over there," said Leroy, leading Carl across the fields.

After they had walked for about twenty minutes, they entered a wooded area. The trees were thinly scattered at first but then became thicker. It was difficult to see, and Carl's imagination was on overdrive as the branches of the trees seemed to grasp at him, like the tentacles of an octopus. The nocturnal sounds made him jittery too; strange animal noises, twigs snapping underfoot and echoing laughter becoming fainter as they got deeper into the woods. He tried to hide his nervousness from Leroy. They persevered until they passed through the trees and into a clearing, surrounded on all sides by dense foliage and branches.

"Nice one," said Carl. "All we need now's a few chairs and some cans of beer, and this could be a really cool meeting place."

Leroy didn't reply. Instead, he stopped to tie the dog's lead to a tree then leant back against a large trunk, casually crossing his right leg over his left one. He lit up a spliff without bothering to offer Carl one. Carl picked up on Leroy's lack of generosity, which he suspected was deliberate. The silence was ominous, and Carl was starting to have a bad feeling about Leroy's motives for calling this meeting.

"What time are the others due?" he asked.

"What others?" Leroy took a drag from his spliff then exhaled a long plume of smoke.

"I thought we were having a meeting."

"We are, me and you."

"Oh."

Now the fear was kicking in. Carl couldn't think of one good reason why Leroy would want to meet him alone at night, especially somewhere as deserted as this.

"So, what d'you think about what happened to Winston?" asked Leroy.

Carl thought that Leroy was trying to test his loyalty, so he decided to tough it out. "Bastard got what was coming to him for skimming."

"Oh, so you think that's why he was killed, do you?"

"I thought so, yeah."

"Well that's where you're fuckin' wrong. You see, Carl, you've gotta be doing worse things than skimming to get yourself killed. For skimming, you just get the shit kicked out of you, but messing with someone else's woman ..." Leroy paused and sucked his teeth before adding, "... now that can get you killed."

Carl gulped. "Right, d'you think that's what happened, that he was messin' around?"

"I *know* he was. In any case, he wasn't skimming."

Carl sensed what was coming. He was tempted to run but he

wouldn't get far. The trees would slow him down. Leroy was probably tooled up anyway, so it would be easy to put a bullet through him before he could escape. And if he did, who would come to his help? There was no-one around.

Leroy's last statement had prompted a question, which Carl felt obliged to ask.

"How do you know he wasn't skimming?"

Leroy took another drag of his spliff then tossed it to the ground, and made a great show of grinding it into the earth with his huge feet, before answering. "What you forget, Carl, is that there's not much goes on that I don't find out about. So I've been asking a few questions, and I found out that the guy who died had his mate with him when he bought the H. Guess what his mate said?"

Carl was sweating now. He knew Leroy was tormenting him, dragging it out.

"I don't know."

"He said that the guy they bought the H from was white. So it can't have been Winston then, can it? And there's only two people that sell H in that area; you and Winston. So, who does that leave, Carl?"

As Leroy raised his voice, Tyson began to growl. Carl stared at Leroy, dumbfounded.

"I said who does it fuckin' leave?" Leroy repeated.

Without waiting for a reply, Leroy had covered the ground between them in a fraction of a second. Carl felt the impact of Leroy's knuckles as they connected with his right temple.

"Who does it fuckin' leave?" he asked again.

"Me, I'm sorry, Leroy. I didn't expect anyone to die …"

Slam! Leroy's right fist connected with Carl's face again. He aimed a series of blows about his head, and Carl was powerless to defend himself. When Leroy threw a sharp uppercut, it sent Carl reeling backwards. Losing his footing, he stumbled and fell to the ground. Carl rolled into a ball to protect his face from further blows. Capitalising on the opportunity, Leroy switched from fists to feet, raining kicks on Carl's foetal form. Tyson had witnessed this show of violence and was becoming excited, straining at the leash.

When Leroy began to tire, he paused to regain his strength. Carl took this as a sign that his punishment was over, and tried to stand.

"Stay down!" Leroy shouted, and he aimed another kick at Carl's back to emphasise his point.

The dog was now becoming agitated, wanting to jump to its master's aid but restricted from doing so. Leroy had tied the lead to a narrow trunk in a loose knot. This left a good length of strapping, enabling Tyson to leap around and pull at the leash. His movements were so frenetic that the knot had loosened more.

When Leroy stopped kicking, Carl raised his head slightly, his eyes following the sound of Tyson's frenzied barking. Thankfully, the dog calmed down once Leroy's attack had ceased but, to Carl's dismay, Leroy noticed this too.

"Come on Tyson, seize him, seize him!" he yelled, kicking Carl again to give the dog encouragement.

Carl couldn't recall much of what happened next. He felt trepidation as the dog bounded up to him and gripped his jacket between its teeth, ripping, snarling and biting. He covered his head with his hands when he saw the blood spurt. Then he felt the dog's teeth lock around his arm, and he screamed at the intense pain. The next thing he remembered was Leroy disappearing through the trees with Tyson on its lead.

"Don't leave me!" he shouted. "Leroy, I'm sorry mate. I'll never let you down again. I promise."

But Leroy was already gone, leaving Carl to figure out how he would get his bloody, damaged body out of the park and back to a place of safety.

***

Sunday 9th June 1991 – late evening

Debby had been having a relaxing evening. The kids were in bed,

Carl was out, and she was making the most of it by watching a romcom video. She'd just reached the highlight of the film when she heard a light tap on the front door, and wondered what it could be. She peered around the curtains, checking for safety before opening the door. It looked like Carl but it was difficult to tell in the gloom. The man standing there was slumped forwards as though drunk. Taking no chances, she sidled up to the door, and whispered, "Carl, is that you?"

She heard his voice on the other side; it was faint but it was definitely him, "Yeah, open the door and let me in."

The man outside was hardly recognisable, and she gasped in astonishment when he lifted his head to face her.

"Jesus, Carl! What the hell's happened?"

Carl's clothing was bloodied and torn. The flesh around both of his eyes was red and puffed. One eye was almost closed and she could see the beginnings of a bruise from his temple to beneath his cheekbone. Blood was clustered around his nose and mouth, and his lip was so swollen that he lisped when he spoke.

"Get me in the house, I'll tell you later."

Debby took his arm around her shoulders, and helped him through to the living room, where she settled him onto the sofa.

"My God, look at the state of you, Carl! What's happened? Who did this to you?"

"It's that fuckin' Leroy and his mad dog. Help me get cleaned up. Are the kids all asleep? I don't want 'em seeing me like this."

"Yeah. Don't worry, they went off hours ago."

She rushed to the kitchen, returning with a bowl and flannel. The bowl had a greasy tide mark around the top, and the flannel was used to wash the children's grubby faces, but in a house devoid of cleanliness, it was the best she could do. Carl flinched as she bathed his wounds and tried to remove the mud that stuck to them.

"Where the hell has all this mud come from?" she asked.

"Alex Park. The twat told me we were having a meeting. I knew there was summat wrong when he led me into the woods but then I saw this clearing in the trees. Like an idiot, I thought we were just waiting for the others. It was miles into the park. The crafty bastard took me there so no-one could hear me scream."

Bite marks covered part of his torso and arms, and in other places the skin was bruised and swollen as a result of Leroy's savage kicking. Looking at the condition he was in, Debby was amazed at how he had managed to get back to his car and drive home from Alexandra Park. The worst of the bites was one on his right arm, and when Debby had cleared away the dried up blood, she could see that the bite had punctured deep into his flesh.

"Carl, I think you're gonna have to go to the hospital with this one. You're gonna need stitches."

"No way! As soon as they see the state of me, they'll bring the cops in. I don't want 'em asking questions. If Leroy finds out the cops are involved, I'm a dead man."

"OK, suit yourself," she said, trying to bathe the deep wound as gently as possible. "Why did he do it? Was it the skimming?"

"Yeah."

"I warned you, didn't I?"

"Alright, don't start! How was I to know he'd find out?"

"What about your legs?" she asked, when she had finished bathing his face and arms, and had wiped them with the threadbare towel. "I saw you limping when you came in."

"I don't think they're cut, but he stuck the boot in everywhere. Have a look."

Debby eased his legs onto the sofa, and took down his jeans so she could inspect them. She was horrified to see that they were already covered in a mass of bruises.

"Jesus, they look sore, but there's no cuts there. It's a good job you had jeans on."

"They're killing me! But just you wait; I'll get the bastard back for this. Wait till Mad Trevor finds out what he's been up to. If Leroy thinks he'll be chuffed about him getting his gear from the Cheetham Crew, he's got another think coming."

"You wouldn't?"

"I fuckin' would. The bastard deserves it after what he's done to me."

Debby hoped it was just bluster, spoken in the heat of the moment, because he was suffering the pain and humiliation of a good beating.

When she had finished cleaning and drying his wounds, she looked for something to treat them with. She didn't have any sterile lint or roll of adhesive strip, nor did she have any antiseptic ointment. The only thing she could find was a few small plasters adorned with cartoon characters; the type she used to pacify the kids if they grazed their knees. She placed some on the smaller cuts, but there was nothing with which to cover the larger wounds.

"Help me up to bed," he said.

She struggled upstairs with him. It was too awkward to remove the rest of his clothing, especially with his arm in such a bad way. Debby therefore helped him to get onto the bed where he lay in his tee-shirt, with his arms and legs bare. He stayed there for three days, on sweat stained, bloody sheets until the pain had subsided enough for him to venture downstairs.

During those three days, he only came out of the bedroom when Debby had taken the children out of the house to her mother's. Debby told them that their father had had a little accident, and that they weren't to disturb him until he was feeling a bit better.

***

Sunday 9th June 1991 – late evening

Jenny had been in the bath when Leroy shouted upstairs that he was taking the dog for a walk. That was over two hours ago. It was the first time he had been out that day, and she wished she had taken the chance and fled while she could. She had thought about it but decided that by the time she got out of the bath, dried and dressed, then packed her stuff, he would have returned. After all, he was only taking Tyson for a walk, and that didn't usually take long.

She looked at the clock. It was a quarter to twelve. Surely he wouldn't be coming home now. He had probably bumped into someone and decided to stay out. Maybe he was at his mam's; he might have even been with one of his other women. Having stayed at home for most of the last week or so, he was perhaps growing bored of her company and missing his other diversions.

To hell with it. She'd get out now while she still had a chance; she didn't know when she'd have another opportunity. That was the trouble; you never knew with Leroy. There was no pattern to his comings and goings.

While she was in this determined frame of mind, she went into the bedroom and dug out a large suitcase, which she put on the bed and started filling. She grabbed things at random, starting with the baby equipment as well as a bit of clothing for herself. Items which she'd lovingly collected over several months, she now threw haphazardly into the case; bottles, breast pump, steriliser and bibs.

Jenny was just grabbing a bundle of Babygros when she heard Leroy return home. Tyson's enthusiastic barking let her know that they were in the hallway and making their way to the back of the house. With her heart racing, she slung the Babygros back into the chest of drawers. She didn't have time to put the other things away; Leroy would hear her moving about. Reacting swiftly, she slammed the case shut and stashed it under the bed, hoping to God that he didn't find it.

By the time Leroy heard her moving around, and shouted up the stairs, she was ready.

"Coming," she shouted back.

Two minutes later she was downstairs.

"Hiya love, I was just going to bed when I heard you come in," she announced, walking into the kitchen where she found Leroy cleaning blood from round Tyson's mouth.

"What happened?" she asked.

"He got hold of a rat and wouldn't let go. I had a right job getting it off him." Then, turning to address the dog, he added, "You're a vicious little bastard when you sink your teeth into something, aren't you mate?" As he spoke, he rubbed the top of Tyson's head affectionately.

Noticing the blood stains on the back of Leroy's hand, Jenny said. "He must have had a right go at it, judging by the state of you both."

"Oh, he did," Leroy laughed.

"The poor rat," said Jenny. "Do you need any help cleaning up, or are you alright if I go up to bed?"

"Me and Tyson are fine." He turned to Tyson again, stroking and rubbing the dog's back with one hand while he cleaned around its mouth with the other, "Aren't we Tyson? Good boy, good dog!"

Chapter 31

On the fourth day, Carl made it downstairs. He was still sore, but the bruising wasn't as bad, and the swelling to his lip had now reduced. It was his bites that were causing Debby concern. She'd done her best. First thing Monday, well, as soon as she was up, she'd dashed to the chemists and got him some witch-hazel, antiseptic cream and sterile dressings. But it was too late for the wounds. By that time the bacteria had already set to work, and the bloodstained, malodorous bedding hadn't helped.

The chemist had advised bathing his wounds twice a day in salty water that had been boiled and cooled, then applying the cream and dressings. Debby examined his wounds as she tried to clean them. Most of them had become infected, and were weeping puss, but it was the large bite that worried her. Its entire surface was now a green, festering mess, and she knew that Carl would need medical attention.

"Carl, I'm ringing an ambulance," she said. "You'll have to go to hospital with this. It's turning nasty."

It took her a while to persuade him to go to the hospital but he eventually capitulated. They agreed that he would just say he was attacked by a dog, and that he'd banged the side of his head on the ground when the dog felled him. Since the attack, the bruises had changed shape and colouration, and Debby now felt that they could put forward a convincing argument for the damage to his face having been caused by a blow to the head. As long as he kept his legs covered, she hoped the medical staff would be none the wiser, and if they did ask questions, they would just deny everything.

As soon as Debby had dropped the children off at her mother's house, she called for an ambulance. When they arrived at hospital, the nursing staff were amazed that they hadn't come straightaway. Debby told them Carl was frightened of hospitals, and he had only agreed to come now because of the infection.

The doctor was appalled at the sight of Carl's bites.

"May I ask why you didn't come to the hospital as soon as the dog attacked you?" he asked.

Debby jumped to Carl's defence, and repeated her story about Carl's fear of hospitals. The doctor looked unconvinced, his distrust reflected in the narrowing of his eyes.

"You must never leave a dog bite unattended. It's important to have a tetanus injection as soon as possible," he admonished.

He then instructed a nurse to give Carl the requisite injection, and prescribed a course of antibiotics. Once he had left instructions with the nurse regarding follow up treatment, he moved onto the next patient.

Debby was glad when he left them, but she still couldn't settle, half suspecting that he would phone the police once he had finished his rounds. After three hours at the hospital, she was relieved when they left with Carl patched up. It had been a nerve-wracking time, but at least the doctor hadn't brought the police in. Debby was so thankful there would be no repercussions. Now she just had to carry out the nurse's instructions to help Carl's wounds heal, and everything would be alright.

***

Thursday 13th June 1991 – afternoon

Ever since Leroy had delivered the news about Winston, he had rarely left the house. The only exception had been Sunday when he'd been out for over two hours. Since then Jenny hadn't had any other opportunity when she could have escaped. Fearing that he might discover the half-packed case under the bed, she had even unpacked it, a few items at a time.

Although he had hung around a lot lately, his behaviour had changed following Winston's death. In fact, it was almost as though he was his old self again. Maybe he regretted Winston's death, or perhaps it was because he didn't have a rival for her affections anymore. Whatever his reasons, she was just thankful that he was no longer hostile towards her.

There was also a tiny part of her that was beginning to doubt his involvement with Winston's death. He had been so attentive in the last few days that she somehow couldn't reconcile this with the sort of person who would callously kill someone he had known from being a child.

As long as he carried on this way she could cope until it was time to leave. He was bound to start going out more sooner or later. Then she would seize her chance like she'd promised Rita. Like she'd promised herself. She'd do it; she hadn't changed her mind. No, she was just waiting for the right moment.

***

Friday 14th June 1991 – 7.20pm

It was Debby of all people who had given Rita the tip off, and now Rita and Yansis were on their way to Longsight, with Yansis driving at lightning speed.

Debby had been in a state when she rang to tell Rita that Carl was on his way to see Mad Trevor. He was going to tell him about Leroy buying heroin from the Cheetham Crew. It was Carl's way of getting revenge against Leroy for giving him a beating. As they were sworn enemies of the Buckthorn Crew, Mad Trevor would be furious about Leroy's betrayal.

She would have been grateful to Debby for doing the right thing, if it wasn't for the fact that Carl had been out of the house for twenty minutes before she rang her. As Rita recalled Debby's words, her anger threatened to overwhelm her:

'You need to get to Jenny's as soon as possible to warn her. Carl's gonna show the gang where to find Leroy. He's already been gone about twenty

minutes.'

Twenty bloody minutes! So Debby had obviously deliberated before making the call, perhaps out of misguided loyalty towards Carl. And now Jenny was in serious danger!

Within moments of setting off, Rita realised they had acted rashly, fuelled by impulse. They should have rung Jenny and warned her, maybe rung the police. But what would they tell them? There might not be any crime to report yet. It was too late now; if they doubled back it would waste more valuable time. Besides, what if Debby was wrong? Rita hoped she was.

As they sped along the A6, they established a rough plan of action through their frantic discussions. They would act cautiously when they arrived. If there was any sign of Mad Trevor, or any other gang members at the house, she and Yansis would find the nearest phone box, dial 999 and wait for the police to arrive.

They were making record time. The traffic lights were mostly in their favour, apart from one glitch. It was while they had been approaching a pelican crossing. Rita could see some teenagers messing about. Something told her they were about to press the button just for the hell of it. Sure enough, as they approached the crossing, the lights turned red although no-one wanted to cross.

"Carry on!" shouted Rita, and Yansis shot through on red.

Soon they arrived at the estate.

"Cut through," Rita urged. Taking her advice, Yansis avoided the road that snaked around the estate, saving precious minutes by mounting the curb and spurting across the grass verge. His tyres dug into the heavy mud, carving the grass and tearing away strips of soil, before crossing the pedestrian pathway and hacking across another grass verge.

Then they plunged into a mud pool. Yansis revved the engine, ramming at the accelerator, but the wheels spun round aimlessly, the tyres slashing through the dense matter. Rita got out of the car to push. Despite her will, she wasn't strong enough, and she cursed while the car refused to budge and a group of kids hung around laughing. She stopped and sighed, glaring at the kids until a thought occurred to her.

"A quid each to help me get this car out of the mud."

Within seconds her potential adversaries became allies. Their enthusiasm was heartfelt, and together they soon had the car moving. Rita hurled some money at the kids while Yansis waited for her to get back in the car. She noticed the state of her legs in her short skirt. They were covered in mud. She tried to wipe it off but the thick, earthy mess clung to her. Wet, sticky and congealed in her hands.

Chapter 32

Carl had known exactly where to find Mad Trevor on a Friday evening; the Buckthorn Inn. It was fortunate that he had chosen early evening, before Trevor and the other gang members got wasted.

"Alright? Thought I hadn't seen you for a bit. What happened?" asked Trevor, when he saw Carl's face.

"I got jumped, last weekend. The bastard's robbed me then did a runner."

"Looks like they've given you a good seeing to. Who was it? Any ideas?"

"Dunno. They got me from behind and ran off before I could see them."

"Ugh," was Mad Trevor's response, on realising he could do nothing to exact revenge on Carl's attackers. "Where's Leroy, anyway?"

Carl cursed inwardly at the implication that he had to be accompanied by Leroy, but he answered the question. "At home with his missus. He's been keeping his head down since the OD in Longsight. But that's not all he's been up to."

All eyes were on him, and he felt the pressure of expectation. He had a moment of uncertainty; perhaps he couldn't pull it off. But he was here now. He had to see it through. He disguised the slight quiver in his lips as he spoke.

"I don't like to be the one to tell you this, but there's something I think you should know. It affects all of us." He looked around from member to member, meeting their eyes, engendering trust. "He's been buying H from the Cheetham Crew, and I thought you should know."

"You what?" asked Mad Trevor amongst a rising cacophony from the other gang members, as they made their feelings known.

"How long has this been going on?"

"A few months."

"You're fuckin' joking!"

Carl had sensed Mad Trevor's initial suspicion to what he was telling him, but he then felt a shift in his mood, emphasised by his bulging eyes and the taut veins in his neck. However, Mad Trevor wasn't fully convinced yet.

"Hang on a minute. What the fuck would he be doing with H? I ain't seen him selling no H for the last few months. He's been hanging out in the Moss, selling crack and other stuff."

"He's been getting me and Winston to sell it in Longsight." Noting Trevor's rising temper, he added, "I didn't want to. He made me do it. It's been eating away at me for months, but I've had enough. I can't deal with it no more. Fuck Leroy! You've gotta know. I owe my loyalty to the Buckthorn Crew."

Mad Trevor's rapid rise from his chair told Carl that his emotive words had had an effect.

"Come on guys, finish your drinks. Quick! I ain't standing for this … D'you know where he lives?" he asked Carl.

"Yeah, I can take you there if you like."

Carl was overjoyed. Not only would Leroy get what was coming to him, but he would be there to witness his shame and defeat.

"Leave your car here. You can get in mine and show us the way," ordered Mad Trevor.

Paying no heed to the law, six of them crowded into Mad Trevor's silver Golf GTi, with Carl sitting in the front passenger seat next to Mad Trevor. It took ten minutes to arrive at Jenny's house. The car screeched to a halt as Mad Trevor slammed on the brakes, leaving it parked haphazardly outside Jenny's house. He grabbed his gun from the glove compartment before getting out of the car.

The gang's furious knocking at the door brought a swift response. When Jenny opened the front door, they dragged her inside with them while they went in search of Leroy. One of the men had the foresight to close the door behind them, so their actions couldn't be seen by outsiders.

Mad Trevor stormed into the living room addressing Leroy, who was sitting in his armchair having a beer and a smoke.

"What the fuck's this he's been telling me about you dealing with the Cheetham Crew?" he demanded, hauling his witness in front of Leroy.

His aggressive action caused Tyson to get worked up, and the dog jumped at him barking fiercely.

"Fuckin' shut it!" he shouted, aiming a kick at the dog, which reacted by launching itself at him. Before it could latch its teeth around his leg, there was a loud bang followed by a spatter of blood from the dog as it dropped to the ground.

Jenny ran to Tyson and Leroy stood up, heading towards his precious dog. "That's my fuckin' dog. You just shot it, you bastard!"

"Shut it, sit down!" said Mad Trevor, aiming his gun at Leroy. "You, get over there," he said to Jenny, pointing to where Leroy was sitting. "I don't give a shit about your dog. I wanna know what you been up to. Is it true? You been buying H from the Cheetham Crew, and getting him and Winston to sell it in Longsight?"

Leroy shrugged his shoulders. "You're a fuckin' shithouse, Carl! Have you told him about you buying it too?"

In his haste to punish Leroy, Carl hadn't thought about the possibility of things backfiring on him. "I never," he protested, but his words were wasted. He couldn't back them up.

"You know summat, Leroy, you're right. The guy is a shithouse. I could never figure out why you hung out with him. Anyway, we don't need him no more."

Trevor shifted his aim to Carl and took a quick shot at his chest, which was followed by several shots to his head and torso from a fellow gang member. Carl felt the impact of the first bullet, as though someone had jabbed him really hard in the chest. Then there was nothing.

***

A Gangster's Grip

Once they had made it across the grass verge, the car was back on the pavement. It bounced off the edging, then Yansis swung left into the road, skidding, the tyres screeching. The car ricocheted before regaining its momentum and leaving a trail of muddy imprints on the road. Rita spotted a silver Golf GTi passing them in the opposite direction. It seemed to be in just as much of a rush as they were.

Thankfully, there were no cars other than Leroy's outside Jenny's house when they arrived. Rita took this as a good sign. When Yansis pulled up, Rita ran out. Then several things happened at once. She could feel a restraining hand on her arm. Sense curtains twitching as frightened neighbours remained indoors. Hear Yansis telling her to wait. See blood on the path. Bloody footprints. Heading away from the house. The blood getting thicker towards the front door. The door left ajar.

They'd already been.

"Wait a minute, Rita. I'll go in and have a look."

But she couldn't wait. She had to know. She had to see for herself.

***

As soon as Trevor aimed the gun at Carl, Leroy jumped up from his chair. He grabbed Jenny and dragged her in front of him. Then Trevor quickly switched his aim back to Leroy.

"You're next," he said.

"Shoot a pregnant woman, would you?" asked Leroy.

"Please don't," Jenny begged. "Leroy, let go!"

"Let the fuckin' woman go!"

"No way!" shouted Leroy.

Mad Trevor was out of options. He took one shot at Jenny. Then, when she dropped to the floor, it was open season on Leroy. As soon as

217

Mad Trevor started shooting, the rest of the gang joined in. Once Trevor was certain there was no way Leroy could survive, they hurried from the house.

***

Rita raced through the hall. They were too late. Inside the living room, the bodies of Jenny, Carl, Leroy and Tyson the dog lay in pools of blood. It was everywhere; soaked into the carpets, splashed onto the sofas and dotted around the walls. The stench of human excrement hung in the air.

Her first impulse was to run to Jenny, crying and screaming her name. Meanwhile, Yansis checked the other bodies for a pulse, "They're both dead," he said. "The dog's dead too."

This drew Rita's attention to Leroy. "I don't care about that scum! What about my sister?"

Before Yansis could stop her, she rushed up to Leroy and vented her anger by kicking the body repeatedly, shouting, "It's his fault. The bastard! He killed my sister."

Yansis grabbed Rita, pulling her away from the body while she fought to break free.

"Rita, Rita! You cannot do this. He is dead! It is wrong. Calm down."

After a few moments struggling, and with no other outlet, her overwhelming emotions culminated in a flood of tears. Yansis drew her close, attempting to soothe her pain, but there was something more important he needed to do. Gently releasing her, he approached Jenny's body and checked her for signs of life.

"Rita, Jenny is still alive," he whispered. Before Rita had a chance to react, he added. "Stay calm now. I think she is in a very bad way."

Rita knelt down next to Jenny, taking her hand and speaking to her in as calm a tone as she could while trying to stifle her sobs.

"Jenny, can you hear me?"

A Gangster's Grip

While Rita was kneeling next to Jenny, Yansis phoned the emergency services. Acting on their instructions, he grabbed a clean tea towel from the kitchen and used it to staunch the bleeding from the wound at the top of Jenny's left breast.

"What are you doing?" Rita cried out.

"I have to stop the flow of blood Rita until the ambulance arrives. It is important. You mustn't touch it, not with the mud on your hands."

His words penetrated Rita's fuddled brain. She watched as he tried to hold the wound together, noting how the blood seeped through the tea towel despite Yansis's efforts.

"Rita, I also need to look for an exit wound. Please can you wash your hands and find another tea towel that we can use? It looks as though there is a lot of blood coming from underneath Jenny."

Rita followed his instructions, rushing around the house so she could be back at Jenny's side. She relied on Yansis to keep a clear head, and carry out whatever medical attention was necessary until the emergency services arrived. Meanwhile, she gripped onto Jenny's hand, staring into her face and clinging to every response. When Jenny groaned as Yansis tended her wounds, Rita felt her sister's pain.

She recalled hearing somewhere that it's important to keep someone awake to prevent them dying. She didn't know how true it was, but knowing what a dire state Jenny was in, she was desperate to maintain contact.

"Jenny, it's me, Rita," she sobbed. "Don't you go bloody dying on me. I need you to stay awake. Come on love."

She was rewarded by a weak blink of Jenny's eyes. As Rita heaved a sigh of relief, she tried to think what she could talk about. What would keep Jenny going until they could get an ambulance to her? Then it came to her.

"I know you want to see Gran and Granddad, but they're not ready for you yet. I still need you here. You'll have to wait for Gran's home baking."

Once she had started, she couldn't stop. The tears streamed down her face as she recounted tales from their childhood and the times they had shared with their precious grandparents.

"Do you remember when my granddad used to take us swimming, and then he'd take us to Sivori's afterwards for a cup of Oxo to warm us up? He used to put pepper in his, so our John asked to try it once to see what it was like. No matter how much he told him he wouldn't like it, he insisted on giving it a try. He coughed his bloody head off for ages after, then he had the cheek to blame my granddad for putting it in his drink."

She kept up her reminiscences despite her upset, watching her sister for signs of life. She and Yansis remained kneeling on the floor next to Jenny for several minutes till they were disturbed. Rita sensed another presence in the room, then heard the sound of someone approaching them. She looked up to see her mother, immobile, her hand covering her mouth in shock as she took in her surroundings.

"Oh my God!" she yelled, withdrawing her hand when she caught sight of Jenny.

Rita rushed to her side. "It's OK, Mam, calm down. She's still alive. We've called for an ambulance. They'll be here soon. We need to keep talking to Jenny, keep her awake."

Her mother took tentative steps on trembling legs, and knelt down next to Jenny. "Jenny, love. Are you alright? Can you hear me?"

Rita watched Jenny's lips parting, and knelt by her mother's side. "She's trying to say something. What is it, Jenny?"

Jenny's facial muscles tensed as she uttered the words, "Rita … I want you … to …"

But the effort of speech was proving too much, and Jenny's voice drifted off. Rita and her mother exchanged puzzled looks. Although she was curious, Rita found it distressing watching her sister struggling to speak. "It's OK," she said, stroking Jenny's hair. "Save your energy. You can tell me later, when you're feeling better."

Despite her brave words, Rita wasn't 100% certain whether Jenny would pull through, and she had to walk away for a moment as emotion overwhelmed her. While she was sobbing in the hallway, the ambulance crew arrived. Yansis took Joan gently to one side so the crew could tend to Jenny.

"She's still breathing," Rita heard someone announce, and the three of them ran after the ambulance crew as they took Jenny out on a stretcher. Rita and Joan got into the ambulance with Jenny, not wanting to leave her for a minute, and Yansis followed them in the car.

"How did you know? Rita asked her mother on the way there.

"Julie rang me. She'd been trying to get hold of Jenny but there was no answer, so she rang me."

"What about Dad?"

"He's in the pub, but I've sent Denise from next door round there to tell him."

There wasn't much else to say. All they could do now was speculate and leave it in the hands of the professionals. Rita watched the ambulance man looking after Jenny, and hoped to God that they had got to her in time. She was glad when they reached the Manchester Royal Infirmary.

Chapter 33

It's funny what thoughts pop into your head in moments of crisis. Rita remembered thinking when they arrived at the hospital that it was just like on TV. The ambulance crew wheeled Jenny into the building and fled along the corridors, shouting out details of her vital signs to nursing staff, on the way to a treatment room. As Rita and Joan rushed to keep up with them, Rita was aware of bright lights, people staring and the drone of other voices in the background.

When they reached their destination, they wheeled Jenny straight in for assessment, and asked Rita and her mother to wait outside. One of the nurses led them to a small waiting room and stopped with them to take Jenny's details.

"What's happening in there? What are they going to do to her?" asked Rita.

"We'll know more when the doctor's had a look at her and decided what treatment is needed. Once I've finished taking the details, I'll go and see what I can find out for you," said the nurse.

"OK, thanks."

They had been waiting for the nurse to return from the treatment room, for a few minutes, when Yansis joined them.

"We're waiting for the nurse to come out and tell us what's happening," Rita babbled. "The doctor's got to see Jenny. We won't know anything till then. She's just asked us if there's any other family we want to contact. Jesus, Yansis, it must be bad if she's asked that!"

"It is OK, Rita," he said. "It is natural for her to ask that. Jenny has been shot. We don't know how bad it is yet till the doctor has seen her. Do you want me to ring anyone?"

"My mam's already sent someone to the pub to let Dad know. What about our John, Mam?"

"I'll ring the army base when your dad gets here."

"Would you ring Julie and Vinny for me please, Yansis, and tell them what's happened? I don't want to go anywhere in case the nurse or doctor comes out. Have you got enough change for the phone?"

"Yes, it is OK. Try not to worry. The doctor might take some time."

After a few minutes, the nurse came to see them and sat next to Joan.

"Mrs Steadman. The doctors are with your daughter now. I'm afraid there isn't much we can tell you at the moment. We're doing everything we can, and we'll come back to you if we have any more news."

"What about the baby?" asked Joan. "She's not due for another four weeks."

"We'll do all we can to save the baby too. A 36 week old foetus is fully formed and has a good chance of survival."

The nurse patted Joan on the knee before standing up and leaving the room.

Rita didn't know how to feel; despair that the nurse hadn't given any guarantees, or relief that at least Jenny was still alive. She wasn't thinking about the baby at the moment as she hadn't formed an emotional attachment. All her thoughts were with Jenny.

It turned out to be a long wait, during which time her father arrived. As soon as she saw him Rita felt irritated at his inebriated state. He stormed into the waiting room, complaining because it had taken him a while to find them, and demanding to know what was going on.

"I've just been to our Jenny's. The coppers wouldn't let me near the place. They said she's been taken to hospital. What's happened? Is she havin' the baby early, or summat?"

"The doctor's with her now," said Joan. "She's in a bad way, Ged ..."

Joan's voice was shaking, and Rita could see that her mother was having difficulty carrying on, so she picked up the story.

"She's been shot, Dad, and she's lost a hell of a lot of blood. The nurse came out before, and said they were doing all they could to save her. They're going to let us know as soon as they can tell us anything else."

"Shot? How the hell did that happen? How long will it be till they tell us owt?"

"We don't know. They can't tell us anything else yet."

"Well that's not bleedin' good enough. I want to know what's happening to my daughter!"

Rita grabbed his arm before he could get away, and Yansis stood between Ged and the door.

"Don't, Dad, this isn't helping," she said. "The doctors need to spend their time with Jenny, not with us. It'll take as long as it takes."

Ged turned back, yanked his arm from Rita's grip, muttered some profanity under his breath, then plonked himself on the seat next to Joan who explained to him the details of what had taken place.

"What about our John?" he asked, a few seconds later. "Has anyone rang the army base?"

"No," Joan wept. "I was waiting for you. "Me and Rita didn't want to go anywhere in case the doctor came in. Would you ring them for me, please love?"

"I suppose I'll have to, won't I?"

He returned a few minutes later.

"They couldn't put him on the phone, but they'll get an urgent message to him. I don't know how long it'll take him to get home, though. He'll have to get a flight as soon as he can."

The wait for the doctor seemed interminable. Despite her father's irritating behaviour, Rita was determined to stay in the waiting room. She wanted to be there to hear any news of Jenny's condition. Thankfully, her father seemed to sober up a bit during the time they were waiting, so his behaviour improved a little.

When the doctor stepped into the room, wearing a grave expression, Rita could feel her heart speeding up. And when he asked who the next of kin was, it went into overdrive.

"I'm afraid there's no easy way to tell you this," the doctor began. "We did everything we could but, I'm sorry, we weren't able to save your daughter. She had already lost too much blood by the time she arrived at the hospital, and I'm afraid it was just too late. However, we were able to save the baby."

Nobody spoke, and for a few seconds the doctor stood, awkwardly awaiting their reactions. Rita began to cry, her emotions taking over while her mind was struggling to process the information.

"But she was still conscious when we were with her," she said, between sobs.

"She lost consciousness shortly after arrival. Unfortunately, she never regained consciousness, and we were unable to revive her."

"C-can we see her?" asked Rita.

"Yes, we're just transferring her to another room, but once she's ready, I'll send one of my nurses out to let you know."

"OK, thank you."

Once the doctor had gone, Rita's grief turned to fury. She thought about how she had warned her father about the danger Jenny was in, and how he'd treated her concern with scorn.

"This is all your fault!" she shouted. "I told you what Leroy was like. I told you Jenny was in danger, but you wouldn't listen! You were too busy protecting your own interests, and now look what's happened."

"What could I have done? As if she would have listened to me! Anyway, it wasn't Leroy that shot her."

"Don't split hairs with me, Dad! It was because of Leroy. If he hadn't been involved with drugs gangs, they wouldn't have come to Jenny's looking for him."

Once she had vented her anger, she started sobbing uncontrollably. Yansis took hold of her, trying to calm her down while Joan tried to pacify Ged.

"Come on, Rita," said Yansis. "We need you to be calm so that we can go to see Jenny when the nurse comes for us."

She was thankful that she had Yansis because, as far as she was concerned, her parents had let her down badly. She wept in his arms for a few minutes until the nurse came to fetch them.

Rita attempted to compose herself as they approached Jenny's bedside. Her sister looked so peaceful lying there, as though she were sleeping. Rita and Joan each took a seat at either side of Jenny while Ged and Yansis hovered in the background.

Rita held Jenny's hand, which was still lukewarm; it was hard to believe she was gone. She sat with her for a short while then said her goodbyes and stood up, indicating to her father that he should take the seat. Rita moved to a chair further along. She felt Yansis's comforting hands on her shoulders.

Once Ged was faced with the grim reality, his sorrow, previously hidden behind a cloak of anger, now manifested itself in a torrent of tears. Rita found it difficult to see her parents in such despair. For a few minutes, she sat weeping silently into a tissue. She was so absorbed in grief that she failed to notice the sound of the baby crying until the nurse approached them with the child in her arms.

"I'm sorry to interrupt you," she said to Rita and Yansis, who were nearest. "But the baby wants feeding."

"Eh, do you mind? Our daughter's just died!" snapped Ged. "We want nowt to do with it."

"Hospitals are short staffed, love," said Joan. "It's not her fault." She looked across at Rita. "I think Jenny would want you to do it love. Maybe that's what she was trying to say. She wanted you to look after her baby."

Joan's voice broke as she spoke these last few words. The memory of her daughter just before death exacerbated her sorrow, and she lowered her head, covering her face with her hands.

Rita recalled Jenny's last words, and understood now what they had meant. She was surprised that her mother hadn't wanted to look after the baby, but knew that Joan would respect Jenny's wishes. Besides, her mother would face opposition from Ged who wouldn't want a baby to interfere with his lifestyle. Rita turned to the nurse and said, "It's OK, I'll do it."

The nurse stepped closer to Rita.

"What is it?" Rita asked, as she reached up to take the baby.

"It's a boy."

Rita took the tiny bundle in her arms and looked into his expectant, angelic little face. She could see Jenny's features reflected in the baby's expression, and it tore at her heart. A lifetime's memories came flooding back, and she swore that she would always love and protect this poor child just as she had tried to do with Jenny. The tears gushed from her, bringing with them gut-wrenching sobs, which made her body shudder and added to the baby's distress.

She attempted to put the bottle into his mouth, with shaking hands, but her clumsiness made it difficult, and he screamed in frustration. She so wanted to do this right. But when her distraught state led to failure, she looked up at Yansis, her eyes pleading.

Rita didn't need to ask. He was already waiting, and she awkwardly handed the baby to him. He reached out to steady her and took the child with ease. She could sense a pride in him, which he was trying to mask to spare her feelings. Nevertheless, she needed to reassure him that it was OK.

"Yansis, will you feed him?" she asked. "He needs you."

He smiled back tentatively with tear-filled eyes. God, she loved that man!

While Yansis fed the baby, she sat down and tried to calm herself. Once she had regained some composure, she watched Yansis with the baby, so natural and self-assured. And as she watched them, she knew that as long as she had Yansis by her side, she could cope with whatever the future held for her.

THE END

I hope you enjoyed 'A Gangster's Grip'. If you want to be the first to find out about forthcoming publications, why not subscribe to my mailing list at: http://eepurl.com/CP6YP, and receive a free digital copy of my short story collection? I use my mailing list solely to notify readers about my books and will never share your details with any third parties.

***

Acknowledgements

I would like to thank everybody who has given me help and support during the writing of this book. This includes the community of authors and avid readers who are always on hand to answer questions and point me in the right direction.

During the research stage of this book I utilised a number of handy resources. As well as referring to Internet sites on the topics of drugs, gang warfare, the Greek health services, weather reports and general points of law, I found a number of books helpful, not only with factual matters but also to give me a feel of the gang culture of 90s Manchester. The Internet sites are too numerous to list, but these are the books that I found useful: 'Manchester Blue' by Eddie Shah, 'Gang War' by Peter Walsh, 'Still Breathing: The True Adventures of the Donnelly Brothers – From Organised Crime to Kings of Fashion' by Anthony Donnelly and Christopher Donnelly, and 'The New Fertility' by Graham H Barker.

Thanks to my excellent team of beta readers who have given valuable feedback to help me improve the book. They are the lovely Rose Edmunds, Emma Dellow, Rita Ackerman and Jean Coldwell.

Big thanks also to the very talented Chris Howard for once again designing a top notch book cover. Chris is great to work with. He can translate your initial ideas into wonderful finished products, but is also willing to give input if he has other suggestions. You can contact Chris by email at: blondesign@gmail.com.

I would like to thank my family and friends for all their support, not only with this book but ever since I started my career as a published author. Special thanks go to Barry, Andi, Karen, Diane, Mary, Sarah and Elaine for helping to spread the word. Last but not least, I would like to thank my husband Damien and my two children for all the support they have given me in bringing this book to market. A special thanks also to my son for checking my facts relating to a medical matter that is referred to in the book.

About the Author

Heather Burnside started her writing career 16 years ago when she began to work as a freelance writer while studying towards her writing diploma. During that time she had many articles published in well-known UK magazines. As part of her studies Heather began work on her debut novel, 'Slur', and wrote several short stories. She has since written outlines for a number of other novels.

Despite interest from a couple of literary agents, Heather didn't quite succeed in finding a mainstream publisher for 'Slur'. Disheartened, she eventually put it to one side while she focused on other areas, but was determined to return to it one day.

When not working on her books Heather runs a business offering writing services to various companies and individuals. Through her writing services business, Heather has ghost-written many non-fiction books on behalf of clients covering a broad range of topics.

'A Gangster's Grip' is the second book in 'The Riverhill Trilogy'. The first book of the trilogy, entitled 'Slur' is available from Amazon, and the final part of the trilogy will be published in summer 2016. Heather has also published a collection of short stories which are available for download on Amazon Kindle. You can find all Heather's books on Amazon by checking out her Amazon author page at: http://Author.to/HBurnside. Heather publishes regular updates about writing related topics on her blog at: www.heatherburnside.com.

You can also connect with her on Twitter and Facebook at: @heatherbwriter and www.facebook.com/DMPublisher

Disclaimer

All of the characters in 'A Gangster's Grip' are fictitious. They are products of the author's imagination and are not intended to bear any resemblance whatsoever to real people. Likewise, the character's names have been invented by the author and any similarity to the names of real people is purely coincidental.

***

Slur

If you missed my debut novel Slur, you might enjoy reading an excerpt:

Slur – The Riverhill Trilogy: Book 1

Chapter 1 Excerpt from Slur
Saturday 21st June 1986

It was Saturday morning and Julie lay in bed dreaming of last night; she could feel the throbbing beat of the disco music. As she came to the throbbing intensified and she realised that this was no longer a dream. It was a loud hammering on the front door. The after effects of too much alcohol meant that the noise multiplied tenfold inside her head.

She staggered out of bed and reached for her dressing gown, but somebody had beaten her to the door. The hammering was followed by the sound of raised voices that Julie didn't recognise, and she dashed to the landing to see what the commotion was about.

As she peered down the stairs her father glanced towards her bearing a puzzled but grave expression. There were two strangers in the hallway; a plain, manly-looking woman of about 30, and a tall middle-aged man with rugged features. Julie's mother stared up the stairs, her face a deathly pallor, her voice shaking, as she uttered, 'They're police. They want you love.'

Julie panicked and began to walk downstairs while asking, 'What are you talking about, Mam? What would the police want with me?'

She saw the policeman nod in her direction as he addressed her father, 'is this her?'

'Yes,' Bill muttered, and hung his head in shame.

The policeman then focused his full attention on Julie as he spoke the words that would remain etched on her brain for the rest of her life:

'Julie Quinley, I am Detective Inspector Bowden, this is Detective Sergeant Drummond. I am arresting you on suspicion of the murder of

Amanda Morris. You do not have to say anything unless you wish to do so, but what you say may be given in evidence.'

Julie stared at the police officer in disbelief and confusion as she tried to take it all in. She wanted to ask – What? Why? When? but the shock of this statement rendered her speechless and she couldn't force the words from her mouth.

Inspector Bowden, heedless of Julie's emotional state, was keen to get down to business straightaway. 'Sergeant Drummond – accompany her to her bedroom while she gets dressed and watch her very closely.'

He then turned to Julie's parents. 'As soon as your daughter is dressed she will be taken to the station for questioning while we conduct a thorough search of the house.'

'What do you mean, search? What are you searching for?' asked Bill.

'Drugs Mr Quinley,' the inspector stated.

On hearing the word 'drugs' Bill was unable to contain himself any longer and Julie watched, helpless, as he metamorphosed into a frenzied maniac.

'Drugs? What the bloody hell are you talking about, drugs? My family's never had anything to do with drugs, never!' he fumed.

He shocked Julie by grabbing her shoulder and shaking her violently as he vented his anger. 'What the bloody hell's been going on Julie? What's all this about drugs and … and … people dying. Just what the hell have you been up to?'

Inspector Bowden took control of the situation. 'Mr Quinley, can you please let go of your daughter and let Sergeant Drummond accompany her while she gets dressed?'

Bill mechanically released Julie and stared at the police officer in horror. This was a side of Bill that Julie, at twenty years of age, had never witnessed. Although he had often complained about her lifestyle, she usually shrugged it off, content in the knowledge that he was a kind and caring father who thought the world of her. Seeing him like this, though, she submitted to tears as she struggled to reply. 'I'm sorry, Dad, but I really don't know! I've never done drugs in my life!'

Slur

Then she began to sob in desperation, 'Drugs? I don't know anything about drugs ... Amanda's dead ... Oh, Mam, tell him please?'

Julie's mother, Betty, turned to address her husband, 'Leave her alone Bill. Can't you see she's in a state? You're only making matters worse!'

Inspector Bowden continued, officiously. 'Now, if you will permit me to explain to all concerned - Amanda Morris died of severe intoxication and a possible drugs overdose in the early hours of this morning. As she was in the company of Julie Quinley and one other until approximately twelve thirty this morning, and returned home with them in an extremely drunken state, I have no alternative but to place Julie Quinley under arrest and take her down to the station for questioning. Now, if you will permit me to continue in my duties Mr Quinley, nothing further need be said at this point.'

Julie's father retreated into the living room, mumbling to himself in despair. 'I can't take no more of this, I really can't!'

Led by Sergeant Drummond, Julie mounted the stairs dejectedly. From the corner of her eye she could see her mother standing motionless in the hallway until Inspector Bowden disturbed her. 'Mrs Quinley, could you help me to open the door please?'

When Julie's mother had released the awkward door latch, he stepped forward, shouting, 'in here men, start in that room there, then work your way through to the kitchen.'

Julie's senses were on full alert, the adrenaline coursing around her body, as the police officers charged into the house with her father issuing a barrage of complaints at them. She was aware of her mother's distress emanating from the dismal figure at the foot of the stairs. Apart from that, she could feel her own fear and helplessness, then shame and anger as, turning back, she noticed a group of nosy neighbours shouting and jeering at her mother. When one of them had the audacity to enquire, 'Everything all right Betty love?' her mother shut the front door in response.

Once inside the upstairs bedroom, Julie could sense Detective Sergeant Drummond scrutinising her as she put her clothes on. They didn't speak but Julie tried to dress as covertly as possible while the police officer's eyes roamed up and down her body. She could feel her hands shaking and her heart beating, and could hear people talking downstairs. One of the voices was her father's and he sounded angry.

Julie headed towards the bathroom to wash her face, which still contained traces of make-up from the night before, but she was informed that there was no time to waste and they wanted her down at the station for questioning as soon as possible. 'What about my hair?' Julie asked.

'If you're so concerned about it, you can take a brush and do it in the car.'

Julie grabbed her hairbrush and placed it inside her handbag, which she threw over her shoulder.

'I'll take that if you don't mind!' said the sergeant, indicating Julie's handbag. 'It'll have to be searched.'

Julie, aware of the sergeant's hostile manner, replied, 'That's all right, I've got nothing to hide!'

She passed her handbag to Sergeant Drummond, then cringed with embarrassment as Sergeant Drummond rummaged through it and withdrew a packet of Durex and a small, empty bottle of vodka, which she proceeded to scrutinise. Once Sergeant Drummond had finished her thorough search, she tossed the bag back to Julie.

After several minutes Julie was ready to leave her bedroom without having showered, brushed her hair or even cleaned her teeth.

They began to descend the stairs.

Inspector Bowden materialized in the hallway and instructed Sergeant Drummond to lead Julie out to a waiting police car. He then ordered his men to check the upstairs of the house. As Sergeant Drummond was propelling Julie through the front door, Betty took hold of Julie's arm and wept, 'I hope you'll be all right love.'

The look of anguish on Betty's face brought renewed tears to Julie's eyes, but she was too distressed to utter any words of reassurance to her mother. Her father, who had now calmed down a little, said, 'don't worry love, they can't charge you with anything you haven't done,' and

Slur

he put his arm around Betty's shoulder in a comforting gesture. Julie knew that this was Bill's way of apologising for his earlier accusations.

When Julie stepped outside the front door she was horrified at the sight that met her. The crowd that had gathered on the opposite side of the street had increased to such an extent that people were spilling over into the road. As Julie stepped onto the pavement with Sergeant Drummond gripping her arm, the excited mutterings of the crowd subsided and there was a series of nudges and whispers.

Julie was now the focus of everybody's attention and she became painfully aware of her unkempt appearance, her untidy hair and unwashed face with mascara now streaked across her cheeks because of crying. The few steps from her house to the police car seemed to last longer than any other steps she had taken in her life. Although she knew she was innocent, she felt embarrassed in front of the crowd and ashamed that she had brought this on her parents.

She knew that they would be subjected to malicious gossip for weeks to come. For anybody who had ever held a grudge, or felt envious of the Quinleys, it was now payback time.

The sight of the over inquisitive mob soon refuelled Bill's anger and Julie heard him, first arguing with the police officers, and then shouting abuse at the intrusive audience. 'Have you nothing else better to do? Get back in your houses and mind your own bleedin' business! Our Julie's innocent and she's better than the bleedin' lot of you put together. Now go on, piss off!'

His shouts were interspersed by Betty's uncontrolled sobbing.

Not one of the crowd flinched. Julie had no doubt that her father's spectacle had added to their entertainment. It occurred to her that she had never before seen her father so out of control, never seen her mother so upset, and her neighbours had never before seen Julie looking anything less than immaculate. For her it marked the beginning of a prolonged descent.

Suddenly, Julie caught sight of her younger sister, Clare, heading towards her. She could hear her astonished voice repeating to her friends, 'It's our Julie!' As she became nearer, she shouted, 'Julie, what's happened, where are they taking you?'

A policeman rushed in front of Clare, preventing her from making any contact with her sister, and Julie was bundled into the police car. As she repositioned herself on the rear seat, Julie could hear her younger sister's frantic screams and, while the officers tried to restrain Clare, she shouted, 'Get off me, leave me alone, that's my sister, you can't take my sister!' It was all too much for an eight year old to take in.

The police car began to drive away. Julie heard her father shouting at the crowd again. 'I hope you've enjoyed your morning's entertainment. Now bugger off home the lot of you!'

She turned to see her mother trying to comfort Clare as the Quinley family stepped back inside their defiled home.

Inside the police car Julie tried to put aside her feelings of sorrow and despair in an attempt to pull herself together. She needed to remain calm in order to tackle this situation. But despite knowing she was innocent, she felt degraded and helpless.

She eased open her handbag, aware of Sergeant Drummond's observation. Julie took out a mirror and held it in front of her face. Her reflection echoed the way she was feeling about herself. She removed a tissue and used her own saliva to dampen it so that she could wipe away the remains of stale make-up. Having achieved that, she set about brushing her hair.

Sergeant Drummond turned towards the officer driving the police car and quipped, 'Look at that, her friend's just snuffed it after a night out with her, and all she can think about is what she looks like!'

Julie tried to ignore the caustic comment. She needed to remain as composed as possible under the circumstances. For Julie, looking good meant feeling good, and she knew that it would help to give her the strength to get through this ordeal. In complete defiance of Sergeant Drummond's remark, Julie continued to work on her appearance, adding a little blusher and lip-gloss.

She then attempted to think about her situation logically. "Yes, they had spiked Amanda's drink with shorts. There was no point in denying that. Chances were the police would find out anyway and that would only make matters worse. But what about the drugs?"

She thought about whether there had been any time when somebody could have given drugs to Amanda, but decided that it was impossible to account for everybody's whereabouts throughout the entire evening. She had been too drunk herself for one thing.

As thoughts of Amanda flashed through her mind, she could feel her eyes well up with tears again, but she fought to maintain control. *"I mustn't let them get the better of me,"* she kept repeating to herself. Then she remembered the inspector's words when he had said, *'possible drugs overdose.' "So, there's a chance that no drugs were involved anyway,"* she thought, on a positive note. Then her spirit was further dampened by the realisation that, if there were no drugs found there was no possibility that anybody else was involved. That could mean only one thing; that Amanda's death was purely down to her and Rita having spiked Amanda's drinks with various shorts throughout the evening.

Julie's thoughts turned to Rita, and she wondered whether the police had taken her in for questioning too, as she must have been the 'one other' to whom the Inspector had referred. She thought about the surly inspector, convinced that he was going to give her one hell of a grilling once they got inside the station. *"But I can't have killed Amanda,"* she reasoned to herself. *"She was starting to come round a bit when we left her."*

As she pictured her friend's face the last time she had seen her, Julie fought once again to contain her tears, as she went through the events of last night in her mind.

***

'Slur' is available from Amazon in either a Kindle or print version at: http://viewbook.at/Slur.

***

Printed in Great Britain
by Amazon